ISBN: 979-8-9994700-4-1

I0635802

Printed in the United States of America

Table of Contents

For permissions, contact:

Crown Cipher Publishing

crowncipherpublishing.com

ISBN (Paperback): 979-8-9994700-4-1

ISBN (Ebook): 979-8-9994700-3-4

First Edition: 2025

Cover design by Crown Cipher Publishing

Interior design by Crown Cipher Publishing

A Crown Cipher Publishing Release

We protect this F**king House

THE MONSTER BESIDE
THE SILENCE

THE WOLF GOSPEL SERIES · BOOK 1

ALONZO J. CRIPPEN

The Monster Beside the Silence

© 2025 Alonzo J. Crippen

Publisher: Crown Cipher Publishing

www.crowncipherpublishing.com

Prologue

The Silence Ain't Empty

Boom. Boom. Boom.

I already knew what it was before the third knock hit.

Didn't flinch. Didn't run. I just stood there — gun in my hand, blood on the wall, and a body at my feet.

Boom. Police stormed in—boots heavy, guns drawn — but none of them fired.

They weren't looking at a criminal. They were staring at a ghost with a pulse.

C.J. That's what they call me.

The quiet one. The closer. The architect.

Before the clean hands and boardrooms. Before the kingdom.

Before the name James King made the suits shake and the women whisper…

There was a blueprint.

And I was the motherfucker who drew it in blood.

Not just muscle—but mind.

Not just presence—but pressure.

The howling wolf inked on my ribcage ain't for show. It's for me.

To remind myself the wolf don't howl because he sees the moon.

He howls because the hunger never left—even when his belly is full.

That blood on the wall told the story better than I ever could. Brain matter sprayed like art.

His body laid open like a confession. Still twitching, but dead.

I didn't say a word. I let the silence speak for me. Always have.

You've heard of the circle. C Shine. Big Abe. Cal. Money Mack Jim Crews.

Kelly—the only female in the clique, but harder than most men on her worst day.

Fly. Mani. Logan.

And the golden boy himself—James King.

Grim? He was my brother. Blood. Not business.

We moved like myths. Each one with a role.

Me? I was the silence between the gun cock and the trigger pull. The whisper that made killers blink. The shadow that saw all.

I played every position—cornerboy, cleaner, strategist. And when needed? I became the lone wolf.

Sharp. Unforgiving. Surgical.

The game wasn't about chains and rented Bentleys. It was about survival. Mastery. Power.

Not the kind that flashes with canal street jewlery — the kind that folds a room with one look.

The kind that makes a man disappear without a witness or a whisper.

You ever find yourself at Fourth and Monmouth with darkness at your back and a low growl in your ear — there's no prayer that'll save you.

Back when Hip-Hop was still street-funded, and names like Big Meech and Rich Porter weren't punchlines but scripture, I was 15 with a plan.

Not to get there when I was grown, but to get in the room now.

To take my seat before the table even knew I existed.

And while today's clowns rename themselves after gangsters who wouldn't even let them mop the floor,

I remember what the real ones know: There ain't shit glamorous about this life.

Running these blocks don't make you a boss. It gives you scars. Trauma. And if you're lucky? Silence after the storm.

But here's the part they never say out loud: That silence? That made-it-out peace of mind you pry for? It hits like PTSD.

Just like a war vet who survived the trenches — you never stop hearing the gunshots or the silent pain of betrayal. You just stop flinching.

Not celebration.

Just breath. Just darkness. Just survival.

This ain't no fairy tale. This is strategy. This is consequence. This is war.

And I'm still standing. Because I never needed to be the King. I just built the kingdom.

Call me myth. Call me ghost. Call me what they whisper when the streets get too quiet.

But don't ever forget — I'm the monster beside the silence.

And this? This ain't the end of the story. This is where the world learns: The silence you prayed for? I'm what it sounds like when it answers.

"You got the right to remain silent," one of them said.

I smirked. "Then you already know who the fuck I am."

Chapter 1

I wasn't raised in the trenches. My mother worked. My stepfather worked harder. My Pops? He stayed present. Always checked in. Always made time. No broken home. No sad story.

But that don't mean I ain't come from struggle. We lived in a small loop called Country Circle, where the grass grew patchy and the pride grew thick.

Not rich. Not starving. Just that middle stretch—where folks wore uniforms, packed lunch, and prayed they had enough left at the end of the month for a six-pack and Sunday barbecue.

I had an older brother named Grim, and we kept each other sharp.

I was all legs and muscle by twelve—already built like a sixteen-year-old.

Never needed to talk much. The ball court said it all. If you couldn't hoop, you got laughed at. If you couldn't fight, you got washed. I could do both.

That's how I met James King (aka Jay). We were both playing pickup games at the courts behind the old elementary school. He had quick feet and a quicker mouth. I shut both down with a crossover and a stare. After the game, he came up and said, "You play like you own the court." I said, "I do." From that moment, we were cool. Two young wolves, finding the same hunger in each other. We became friends in Country Circle—a bond built through bikes, battles, and a silent respect neither one of us had to say out loud.

Back then, we rode through town like we were casing a city that owed us something. On the way to pick up candy for our hustle, we saw the blueprint of the life we wanted. Hustlers on the corners draped in gold. Big rings flashing. 98 Oldsmobiles and Cadillacs with the rag tops down, bass lines making the concrete pulse. Rakim's "Follow the Leader" was the soundtrack of that era, and it bled out of every system like scripture.

I kept one ear turned west, toward Kennedy Blvd. People said it split into two small camps that held just enough gravity to matter: Divine's people and the Lynn brothers, both quiet about what made them solid. You learned names before you learned faces in this life. That was the point—respect the rumor long enough to survive meeting the man.

A lot of kids in school started calling themselves gods. Becoming 5 Percenters overnight. Trying to find knowledge of self from books they barely understood. Me and James? We didn't knock it. We respected the courage—the way some of them stood up to the fog of Christianity with chest out and head high. But we also saw the other side: the ones hiding behind bean pies and righteous robes, not because they believed—but because they were scared to walk alone. Scared to bleed without a banner. James called them "cowards with a cause." I didn't say much. Just watched.

Girls started noticing us around that time too. I'd be leaning on my bike outside the store, arms crossed, and they'd giggle behind corners or say my name like it was a secret. But I hardly cared to notice. Who needs a girlfriend when you got your brother, your bike, and your homeboy? I knew early: girls brought drama. Dudes fighting in the lunchroom over some hallway look or two-dollar note folded in a locker. Never seemed worth it to me.

James? He saw girls like puzzles—interesting but not urgent. He'd make up a girlfriend every now and then. Said she lived outta town. Had a pretty name and an excuse for never being around. I didn't press. We both had our distractions. Mine just happened to be the hustle.

We didn't want handouts. We wanted opportunity. But when you twelve, nobody's hiring. Especially not two Black kids with ambition and nothing on their resume but potential. So we made our own lane.

There was this spot called The Snack Shop, way on the other side of town. Candy for a dollar a bag—100 pieces for 1 buck.

We started buying bags and selling piece by piece—five cents, ten cents. Kids who'd never make it to that store were lining up before homeroom. Within a week, we weren't just selling—we were taking orders.

Jay had the idea: "Nothing less than a quarter. No more pennies. Fuck nickels," he said. "Let's make the entry price a dollar. They buy in bulk or they don't buy at all." I smirked. "Bet."

That Monday, we sold out before first period. Went from ten dollars a week to fifty. James was hyped—counting his stash, proud he stacked $61 in a month.

I pulled out $227. Didn't blink. I never touched my cut. Just reinvested.

Jay shook his head. "You really don't spend shit, huh?"

"No point in buying gum if I gotta beg for more next week."

We were regulars now. But the Snack Shop clerk? Lazy, rude. Hated counting out our orders.

Two months in, they started pre-bagging candy just for us. Efficiency, whether they liked it or not.

One day, Jay hit him with the play: "How much if we take all 75 bags right now?"

"Seventy-five dollars," the clerk said, without thinking.

Jay didn't flinch. "We'll give you 50. You get rid of 'em all. It costs you half that anyway."

The clerk went red. "Get the fuck out my store. Don't come back."

Jay snapped—kicked over the chip rack. Cursing, loud.

I said nothing. Just smiled. That soft, polite grin that made people nervous. The one that says: "You'll feel me later."

Outside, I told Jay, "He's nobody. Let's find the boss."

He shook his head, still pissed. "You think we can?"

I just looked at him. "He told us no 'cause he has to. I'm looking for someone who can say yes."

We went dark for a week. Jay figured we were done. Then he came to my spot and saw it: 100 candy bags, boxed and ready.

He damn near choked. "How the hell—?"

I shrugged. "Doesn't matter. We're back."

What he didn't know was I'd gone back every day. Bought a soda. Played games in the back. Watched. Waited. Listened.

Eventually I found out who the boss was—old man with silver hair and slow eyes. I walked up, made my pitch clean: "I'll buy 100 bags a week. Seventy dollars. Pre-bagged. Here's four weeks up front."

He looked me over like I was a riddle. Then smiled. Shook my hand. And just like that, we were back.

I told Jay it'd be $35 each, like nothing had changed. He never asked how, and I never offered.

But good things never last. Sales slowed. Kids stopped buying. Next pickup, the deal turned sideways.

The old man didn't just cancel—he got disrespectful. Told me never come back. No refund. Called it my "tax for being greedy."

I smiled. Thanked him. Walked out.

Two weeks passed. Then the howl came. The next morning, every car in the employee lot? Vandalized. Smashed. Destroyed.

Jay and I rode by. The owner ran straight to me, grabbed my handlebars. "You did this!"

We got off our bikes slow. And that same polite grin crept across my face. "Maybe we should start a cleaning service," I said. "Help clean this shit up."

He backed off.

We got back on our bikes and rode.

Jay asked, "You know anything about that?"

I said, "Business is closed. Back to job hunting."

Jay said, "I got over five hundred saved."

I said, "I'm pushing close to a stack."

We agreed: We'd find a new connect. A new lane. Because we weren't built to fold. And we weren't done.

At 13, the hunger was still manageable. But the growl was coming. And soon, the whole city would hear it.

The Congress Apartments weren't far from the Snack Shop—not towering like NYC projects, but just as dangerous if you looked beneath the concrete. We didn't think much of it. Every now and then you'd hear about someone getting robbed or shot at, but rarely shot. Real hustlers knew: violence killed business. You don't pull triggers on your own money.

Occasionally a store window would get smashed or a car would catch a rock to the windshield. Strange how that kept happening to places with bad customer service.

We recognized faces around there. School kids. Cousins. People who lived two zones over but spoke our language. Me and Jay could move wherever we wanted. No one saw two kids on bikes as a threat. That part was about to change.

"You want to roll through Congress and see what's going on?" Jay asked.

"Why not? We're already over here," I said.

There was a path that led from Fourth straight into Congress. Not paved—dirt, glass, trash. We got off the bikes and walked it. Jay stopped suddenly.

"You see that?" he pointed.

It looked like a sandwich bag, half-buried in leaves. I didn't think much of it. Jay had a way of finding loose change like angels dropped it just for him. But this time, it wasn't heaven working. It was the streets.

That plastic bag was filled with crack vials. Clear tops, stacked tight. James picked it up fast.

We ditched the Congress drop-in and pedaled home. His mom worked swing shifts, so her house was always open during the day. Perfect.

We dumped the bag on the kitchen table. 150 vials. Neatly bundled in tens. We'd never held crack before. Seen it from afar. Heard about it. But this? This was inventory.

"Shit," James said. "My mom's going to kill me."

"She's not home," I said. "Unless you tell her, how would she know?"

He nodded, but his face stayed tight.

I said, "Maybe we find someone who wants to buy it off us."

James hesitated. "Sell drugs? No way, man. We don't sell drugs."

"We do when they sitting right here. You want to go put it back?"

"Hell no… but maybe we just sell to someone who already does."

We knew the kids who ran for hustlers. Some were lookouts. Some made deliveries. This wasn't TV. Our town wasn't carved into territories. It was open market. If you had the guts, you could get a spot. No wars. Just numbers.

Congress had a name for being dangerous, but to us? It was just the other side of town. Same kids. Same noise. Just more gold chains and weed smoke.

I kept the bag at his house.

Next day at school, we spotted a few kids we knew were tied to the street. Jay had a friend named Richard, from a short-lived rap group. Yeah, James King used to rap.

We approached him in the hallway. Jay did the talking.

"Yo, we came up on some crack," he said, pulling one vial from his pocket.

Richard blinked. "That's a 20. You can get twenty for each one, but fiends always ask for deals."

"Like what?" Jay asked.

"Two for thirty. Seventeen dollars and some food stamps. Shit like that. My boss, Money, he takes whatever as long as it ain't under fifteen."

Richard grinned. "I got some head from a grown woman for one. Another showed me her tits for a hit. My pay got docked, but I ain't care."

I finally spoke. "What's your cut?"

"Two vials for every bundle I sell. Either sell 'em or trick with 'em."

"Trick?"

"Yeah. You give 'em a hit and they do whatever you want."

James almost passed out. "You saw real live titties for one of these?"

"Fuck yeah. Even sucked 'em."

James looked at me with a face like Christmas morning. I looked back and said, "Fuck no. Don't even think about it."

Truth? I wanted to see some titties too. But my mind said: play this right, you won't have to pay. Girls would flash just to say they did. I wasn't wrong.

Jay said, "Show us where to sell. We'll cut you in."

"Easy," Rich said. "I'll even introduce you to some fiends. If you want to feel what it's like to get sucked off in an alley, I got you."

"Community cooties," I said. "I'll pass."

The final bell couldn't come fast enough.

Instead of catching the bus, we walked with Rich to Fourth and Monmouth. Right near the Snack Shop. One of the workers saw us. Just looked. Jay stared back and threw up two middle fingers.

I never trusted Rich. He had that worn look. Tall, dark, bags under his eyes. One of the fiends who came up that day was his mother.

We only knew it was her 'cause she asked for a discount and called him "baby."

Jay nodded. Gave it to her for less.

I stared at him. Didn't say shit. But he knew from the look: that's coming out your end.

We sold out in two hours. Rich handled the deals. We just stood there like ghosts in training. Almost $3,000 made.

We gave Rich $200. Thanked him. Said we were out.

He nodded. "If you want more, Money sending me to the city next week. You can come."

"We good," Jay said.

I nodded too. But deep down, I wanted more.

Back at my place, Jay gave me the stack to hide. My mom found everything. She'd summon Jesus and burn the house down if she saw that cash.

I had a metal shed in the back. A perfect spot. My mom didn't snoop. My stepfather? Nothing got past him. So I was surgical. Almost $2,500 to my name.

I had just turned thirteen. This wasn't a bar mitzvah, but I was now a fucking man.

We moved quiet, but every step got louder.

Rich took us into the city one Saturday like it was nothing. 133rd and St. Nicholas. The air tasted different there—oil smoke, bus fumes, something burning down the block that nobody flinched at. It smelled like hustle. Like danger.

He introduced us to a Jamaican cat named Tom-Tom. Tall, slim, gold tooth glinting every time he laughed—and that laugh came too easily for someone in his line of work. He had hands that looked like they'd broken a few jaws, but he shook ours like we were cousins.

Rich did the buying first. We watched.

"One hundred a bundle," Tom-Tom said. "But for every one you buy? I give you eleven. One extra. That's your blessing."

Rich nodded, played it cool. Bought 50. We watched him peel off the eleventh from each and stuff them into his coat like taxes. Silent theft in plain sight.

Jay leaned in. "Thought we was only getting ten?"

"Yeah," I said. "Thought so too."

But we didn't walk away with ten. We walked away with thirty.

That day, we weren't kids anymore. We were players.

We didn't need a corner crew or someone else's name behind us. We were a two-man team, independent and dangerous because of it. No one to report to. No one to cut in. Just me and James—and a silence between us that said everything.

And when we stepped out? We made noise.

Our first move was the skating rink. Local spot. Ultra Magnetic was headlining. Everybody was going. Cars packed the lot. Kids from three towns over pulling up just to say they were there.

We didn't even own a car.

But James? He had a spark in his eye that night. "Let's get a limo," he said, like it was normal.

Next thing I know, we're down on Canal Street, buying jewelry. I grabbed a four-finger ring that wrapped across my knuckles like armor. Hollow gold chain—but it gleamed like truth.

James went wild. Gold frames. Rope chains. A Kangol hat tilted like a crown. When he stepped out that night, he looked like he just walked off a Slick Rick video set. Heads turned.

We didn't arrive. We appeared. When that limo door opened, people stopped mid-sentence. Flashbulb moments before phones had flash.

At first, they thought we were the performers. Then they recognized us. The "kids from Country Circle." The ones who used to ride bikes around selling candy.

But the second their mouths opened? It didn't matter. Perception was power. And we owned the moment.

Inside the rink, Ultra Magnetic was tearing the roof off. That sound—raw, sharp, futuristic—it didn't even belong to the decade. Ced Gee on the mic, Kool Keith wild with the delivery. We weren't front row, but we didn't need to be. Their sound carried like prophecy. James was in the mix, dancing hard, feeling every beat. I don't dance. Never did. I stood nearby, leaned up against the wall with my arms crossed, watching him work the floor like he was made for it.

He laughed, glided over to me, still high off the energy. Reached in and grabbed my pockets like I was holding too much. "You saving it for later or what?" he joked.

It wasn't him, not usually. But I loved seeing him like that—even for just a bit. No weight. No worry. Just joy.

That's when they came. Two girls. One whispered in my ear, voice like velvet and heat. The other grabbed James's hand like they'd been a couple for years. Truth? We just met them.

They were the flyest ones there. Everyone saw it. Everyone saw us.

We didn't grin. We didn't pose. We just stood in it—like we were born for this shit.

The night blurred into a memory. The limo ride back was a slow-motion dream. The girls rode with us, leaned on us like we'd known them forever. We didn't know it yet, but danger was watching. Jealousy sat in someone's passenger seat, staring out the window, memorizing our faces.

But even then… our instincts kicked in. That street sense. The gut feeling that told you when eyes lingered too long or laughter had envy under it.

Still, we soaked in the night.

We were kings. And the city was taking notice.

We weren't just part of the scene. We were the scene.

We made the city runs like clockwork after that. Me, James, and Rich. Bus tickets paid in rolled-up twenties. Backpacks zipped with bundles so tight, you'd think they were schoolbooks. Only subject we studied was survival.

By 14, we counted our first $20,000.

Cash. Stacked in shoeboxes under the floorboards. Smelled like power. Looked like proof.

That's when the wolves started sniffing.

There was a stick-up kid named Nygee. Slim frame, dark hoodie, Nike gloves like a uniform. The name alone made corners get quiet. Dealers ducked. Hustlers paused mid-count. If Nygee was coming, you either cleared out or got cleared out.

But not us.

One night, we're outside Fourth and Monmouth. James had just finished a sale and was mid-joke when I saw Nygee cross the street. Everything in me went cold.

He walked slow. Purposeful. Hood up. One hand in his pocket. James saw him, too. I felt him freeze beside me.

And then—James pulled a .38 outta nowhere.

His hand shook, eyes wide, but the trigger clicked like it had been waiting.

Boom.

Boom.

Boom.

Streetlight flickered. A sign shattered. Air cracked with heat.

Nygee broke left and disappeared. James kept clicking. Empty.

He fumbled for more rounds, but the moment had passed. The corner was silent. We were breathing like we just outran death.

I didn't say a word. Just stared at him, still catching his breath. "I wasn't going to let him take shit from us."

And I believed him. It was the first time I saw James scared. And the first time I saw him ready.

After that, we moved smarter. Bigger. James got serious about plug protection. I watched the shadows even harder.

Around then, James met a girl in the city. Pretty, fast, tough. Said she got kicked outta her crib. Started staying with us in cheap motels—Days Inn on Route 9. She was family now. Three against the world.

We fed ourselves. Paid for rooms. Took care of laundry at a 24-hour spot where fiends would trade socks for loose change.

Grew up fast. Laughed hard when we could. We didn't have parents. We had each other. And that was enough.

Until it wasn't.

We got picked up by police. Wrong place, wrong time. Nothing on us. But they locked us in a local juvie hold. A week of metal cots and cold food.

Before we went in, we left our stash with the Marlon brothers— neighborhood dudes we thought we could trust. When we got out? They had new chains. New coats. New kicks. Our stash? Gone.

No apology. Just shrugs and a story that didn't add up.

That betrayal? It didn't break us. It sharpened us.

We got back on our feet quick. Even stronger. By fifteen, people twice our age were avoiding eye contact.

We left the bundle game. Entered the lab game.

Called up Money-Makin' Cee-lo. Childhood friend turned chemical magician. He cooked with precision. Cut it clean but made the comeback better than the first hit.

He taught us the art of the re-rock. And we sold it with honor. Never cheated the fiends. That's why they came back.

James patched holes in the hustle like he'd been born with a blueprint.

Me? I enforced. I watched. I remembered everything.

And together, we rose. No shooters. No killers. But if the moment came? Neither of us would hesitate.

We weren't chasing fame. We were building fear. And fear paid better.

It started with a whisper. Richard said he had a new connect. A real one this time. Said he was getting coke for $14 a gram—clean, straight, uncut.

"Pure as heaven," he said. "Like the old days."

We should've known better.

But James did the math. I did the gut check. And together, we took the risk.

We pooled everything. Seventy grand in ninety days—gone in one move. This was our leap. Our kingdom-expanding buy.

For weeks, it worked. James tightened every corner. We wholesaled to street pups and still hit the blocks ourselves. Our product moved before the sun came up. Fiends lined up like it was church, waiting on communion.

We didn't chase clients. They waited on us.

James had patched every crack in the empire. We had motels rotating weekly, stash spots nobody knew, cash in rotation, and silence where it mattered. But ghosts get hunted too.

One trip back from the city, we're riding the bus. Richard says he's getting off a few stops early.

Didn't think nothing of it.

But as the bus pulled away, we saw it—cops swarming from alleys, cruisers from nowhere. They tackled him like he was Osama.

James grabbed my arm. "We leave the work. Let the shit go."

I shook my head. "We built this."

We stayed on. Got off two stops later. Made our way to the Days Inn on Route 9, room 214.

The plan was simple: bag it up, flood the block, move like nothing happened. But fate had other plans.

Knock at the door. Police. They came in fists first. Beat us like we'd killed somebody. Nothing found at first—just our faces bleeding on the carpet.

James's girl had the stash on her. Tucked in tight. But when the female officer arrived, she cracked. Pulled it out. Game over.

They raided the room. Found James's.45 under the mattress. Saw the scale, the bags, the life we'd built brick by brick. And that's when the real betrayal dropped.

Detective Silverfox leaned in, smirking. "You know… we didn't even know about you two. Not until your boy Richard started singing."

I didn't blink.

"Yeah," he chuckled. "Said—and I quote—'CJ and James got more dope than I do.'"

I should've known. Always felt something sideways about him. That laugh. That slick talk. That fake loyalty. He was right, though. We did have more than him.

And now? They had us. The cuffs clicked tight. Not just betrayal. War.

They dragged us down that motel hallway like animals. Faces swollen, wrists burning, eyes locked on the dirty carpet beneath our feet. James looked over at me once—just once—and I knew. No panic. No fear. Just clarity. This was the cost.

In the back of the cruiser, I sat in silence while James pressed his forehead to the glass. Red and blue lights bounced off the rearview mirror. They were talking shit in the front seat. Laughing. Like we were trophies.

But they didn't know. They didn't know this wasn't the end.

This was the beginning of something different. Something colder.

In that moment, I stopped thinking like a kid. I became exactly what the streets needed me to be. We were no longer building an empire. We were surviving one.

And from here on out, every move we made would be with that lesson branded in blood.

Chapter 2

They hit us with possession with intent to distribute and possession of a firearm. That .45? That was James's. But I held the weight.

The work? That was on his girl. She was barely eighteen. They tried to make it all hers.

Said if we pointed the finger, they'd let us walk. Called it a favor.

James didn't even blink. "It's mine," he said.

They still gave her something light, but he took the bulk. No hesitation.

Me? I took the gun. That was the line.

There were charges that were his I wore. And ones that were mine he carried. We didn't negotiate that. It just was.

Whatever they had on me? Stayed on me. And I damn sure wasn't about to say it was his.

Then came Dirty H and Silverfox—two plainclothes punk-ass detectives who thought they were slick because they didn't wear uniforms. Dirty H talked too much. Silverfox was quieter, like the type that hit you in the dark then handed you a towel after.

They pulled me in a room and tried to play mind games. Said James was flipping. Said he'd already given me up.

I looked at them and said: "James who?" I wanted to follow it with something else. Didn't get the chance.

Next thing I knew, my face hit the floor so hard the lights went out. When I came to, my mouth was full of blood, my ears were ringing, and my arms felt like wet rope.

I was 15 years old. 110 pounds. And I had just learned what silence costs.

They beat me like I was grown. But I never cried. Never said a word they could use.

After that, I made peace with pain. There wouldn't be a single ass-whooping I'd ever fear again.

The first thing you learn in county juvie is that respect moves faster than fear. And everybody's watching.

It was county—not some scared-straight program. Real charges. Real consequences. They didn't send us to no rehab camp or private hall. They sent us where we'd recognize faces. Heads from the block. Rival schools. A few wide-eyed kids from the soft towns nearby who thought they were hard… until the door slammed behind them and they learned otherwise.

Me and James? We got there like we always did—together.

Everybody knew what it was. Didn't matter what pod we landed in. Staff knew. Kids knew. Even the guards. If James had a problem, it was mine. If I moved, he moved. That wasn't loyalty. That was law.

Intake? That was the first punch in the gut.

Strip down. Stand still.

Cold-ass tile floor under my bare feet, the bleach smell crawling up my nose. The walls were this dull-ass pale tan—like they wanted to be calming but couldn't hide the trauma baked into the paint. The lights above buzzed like flies in a jar.

"Lift your sack." I still hear that voice. No venom in it. Just routine. Like checking my dignity was part of the job.

They gave me the standard-issue blues—cheap, scratchy, loose in the wrong places, tight in the wrong ones. One shirt. One pair of pants. One drawstring bag to carry whatever pieces of yourself they let you keep. Only thing that stayed from the outside were my sneakers. That was it. Everything else? Gone.

Inside, it was like the city compressed into a box—Black, White, Puerto Rican, Dominican… every flavor of the hustle. But nobody mixed unless they had to. Separate lanes, mutual respect. Not 'cause we were friends. 'Cause we were all just trying to make it to tomorrow.

That's where I saw Big Jax.

The name said it all. Jax was massive. Seventeen, but looked grown. Not fat solid. Thick. Shoulders like steel beams and a stare that dared you to make it a problem. He didn't talk unless he had to. And when he did? You listened.

Then there was King Born. Born was different. Flashy. Smooth. Had that smile that made girls stop breathing—but his hands could stop your heartbeat if you tested him. He was a knockout artist, but you'd never know it by the way he carried himself—cool, calm, deliberate.

I remember seeing him on Canal Street once, getting fitted for his gold grills. I told the guy he wanted them to say God—he was deep into that 5 Percenter knowledge, always quoting supreme mathematics like scripture. But the Chinese cat doing the work must've misheard him or just didn't give a fuck what he said. When Born got the grills back, they said Dog.

He wore 'em anyway. Didn't flinch. Didn't explain. That's how confident King Born was. He made the mistake look like design.

Only Born and Big Jax could throw up over two hundred pounds during rec. Used to go back and forth with it—no ego, no beef. Just iron and reps. Never settled the score on who was stronger. Didn't matter. They weren't competition. They were pillars.

But if you weren't from our town? And you crossed either one of them? You didn't want that kind of problem.

Life inside moved like clockwork—cold trays with runny eggs, mystery meat with no name, and the occasional fruit cocktail that had kids trading socks and favors just to get an extra cup. That syrup was like gold in a place with no sweetness.

I didn't smile in there. Just watched. Same way I always did.

I stayed close to James, and nobody touched him.

Because they knew — you touch him, you touch us.

Some still had lessons to learn. And lucky for them … my teacher hat stayed on.

There were small freedoms in that place. Saturday afternoons? Nobody fucked with Yo! MTV Raps. That was sacred. Every kid in that joint would crowd around the rec room like it was church. Fights were on pause. Guards didn't say shit unless they wanted smoke. It was understood—you don't interrupt Special Ed, Slick Rick, or the moment Public Enemy dropped Fight the Power. That one? We couldn't see it enough. It made you believe rebellion had a beat. That it meant something.

Special Ed's "I Got It Made"? Everybody wanted scooters and cliques after that. We imagined ourselves riding clean, fast, loud through the block—hood royalty in motion. Even behind bars, that shit got us high.

Fridays we had our own version of Red Alert's Mastermix. Everyone would post up at their cell doors, trading bars and trying to recreate whatever song they half-remembered from the radio. Most mumbled through the verses, making up words like we were born freestyling. The down-to-earth guards let it slide. Laughed sometimes. The others? They'd yell for silence, threaten to take our hour of rec, or worse.

Me? I took a few beatings for noise I didn't even make. Didn't matter. I wasn't breaking for nobody.

I was 15. Thin, quiet, watching everything.

And I had no clue I was rooming with future murderers, stick up kids, arsonists, and predators who hadn't yet bloomed into the monsters they'd eventually become.

They laughed like kids. Bragged about girls. Had dreams. You wouldn't believe who they were.

And some of the female guards? They didn't just see me as a kid. They watched me—like they knew I was built different. I could feel their eyes through the glass when I was in the shower. And if I was in the right mood, I'd let 'em watch.

Not long after we got there, that's when Felix showed up. No way he was 17. That man had to be pushing 25 at least. But no papers meant no proof. And until someone could prove otherwise, he was one of us. And he moved like he ran the place.

Felix didn't talk loud. He talked real. He spoke about Santo Domingo like it was destiny—drugs, money, women, and oceans so blue it hurt to imagine. He said he had people waiting. Said he had a plan.

James was sold immediately.

Me? I listened. I didn't believe much in dreams, but I understood momentum.

The plan was tight. Six others ready to ride. Count schedule memorized. Guard rotations spotted. Two doors between us and freedom. A getaway car on the street, parked and ready.

Felix said all we had to do was move after breakfast—when the shift changed and eyes were lazy.

The morning of the plan felt like every other. Breakfast. Trays. Line-up.

We lined up just like always to head back to our cells. Felix was third in line.

James and I were ninth and tenth. It didn't matter where you were —when Felix moved, everybody was supposed to move behind him.

As we made our way back down the corridor, Felix suddenly jumped out of line and took off forward like a shot.

Three others broke rank and followed.

James instinctively went to go after him—but I caught him. Grabbed his arm. Locked eyes. Something felt wrong.

Felix reached the first door and kicked it open. It gave too easily.

Nobody moved. The guards didn't flinch. Didn't bark. Didn't even react.

It smelled like a setup.

We kept walking, slow and steady, blending into the background as if nothing was happening.

Then came the second door. Felix and his boys charged it, kicked it open — And were met with a wall of guards. Shields. Batons. Boots. Rage.

They beat Felix and the others so bad the hallway looked like a crime scene. Blood painted the floor. Bones cracked. Screams that didn't sound human echoed against the walls.

Me and James? We were ghosts. Present, but invisible. Nobody ever heard us say a word. Nobody could prove a thing.

Felix's connect? Arrested before the escape even started. Somebody snitched. One of those six was a fucking rat.

The others? They got sent to the hospital—beaten nearly to death. Us? cUnscathed.

Then came sentencing. Cold courtroom. Heavy words.

They gave me two years for each charge. Twelve in total. James got two years for each of his eight.

And when the judge read it out, I stood still. Didn't blink.

But James? He dropped like a sack of bricks. Thought we were doing every charge back to back.

I thought I just got hit with 24 years. Thought he got 16. Didn't understand what concurrent meant. Didn't know it just meant we'd do two years total—the highest charge, not the total sum.

He woke up on the floor. I never let him live it down.

"You passed out like a White woman on Dynasty when JR got shot." That line followed him for life.

Then came the bus. We were leaving county. Not just the building, but the illusion.

Because county juvenile wasn't like state. Yeah, we were locked up. Yeah, it was rough. But it wasn't razor wire and towers. Wasn't rows of cages or yards built for war.

That was coming. We were about to enter the real world. The place where monsters stopped pretending to be kids. Where the system stopped whispering and started roaring.

Our little world was over. The real time was about to begin. We both turned 16 inside the belly of a state juvenile facility. They called it a youth center. It looked like a damn college campus.

Except nobody came here to graduate. I'd be lying if I said a part of me didn't still hold out hope.

Hope that maybe Felix was right. Maybe one day I'd wake up in Santo Domingo, sun in my eyes, gun on my waist, empire in my hands. But that dream died when Felix's ribs cracked under boots and nightsticks.

So did my last thread of hope. Fuck it. I'm here now.

I thought state would just be a bigger version of county. I was wrong. This place was massive. Like a factory that built broken boys in bulk.

They put us in tan uniforms—itchy-ass things that smelled like sweat and defeat.

You worked outside in the heat, pushing wheelbarrows, pulling weeds, cleaning shit that didn't need cleaning.

And the White guards? Some didn't miss the chance to remind us we were property. "Ain't nobody took your freedom," one of them told me. "You gave it to us. You just too stupid to not get caught."

I hated how right he sounded.

Everybody in there swore they were smarter than the next man. Swore they had it figured out.

I listened. I watched. And silently thought—you dumb motherfuckers belong right here.

Because no matter how careful you were, there was always a snitch. Always somebody playing both sides to survive. Always a Judas in juvenile khakis.

The only one I trusted was James. And even that bond got stretched thin.

There were maybe 2,000 kids inside that place. Only four ran the whole damn joint. They weren't just big, they were sculpted.

K-Rock looked like a teenage Mike Tyson in the face of God's rage.

My boy Ty hated me on sight. Didn't know me. Didn't care. Just didn't like how I carried myself.

They were from a town full of hitters, and the kids from that town treated them like kings.

If you weren't from their zip code, you weren't shit. We were from county—the little zone. But we held ours. There were times we had to fight four, five, six at once.

Didn't faze us.

After you've been stomped out by 12 to 15 kids doing the latest stomp-down remix, five-on-two feels like a warmup set.

Me and James? We got so good, we stopped worrying about sleep. Posted up like back-to-back statues in our dorm like cottages.

You go to sleep in here? You wake up with a sock full of soap crashing against your skull. Or worse—a piss-filled pillow smothering your face while fists rain like hail.

Some nights I didn't sleep at all. Bags under my eyes like a trucker on a triple shift. But I didn't care.

Any time my eyes were open, I was ready.

We never ran. They started trying to split us up. Waited until James was in class or I was in rec. But it never worked. Because whoever they sent? They better land that first punch. Because when we came back, we came back swinging until our knuckles cracked and our shirts soaked through with blood and spit that wasn't always ours.

We didn't win every fight. But we never backed down.

And even in loss, we earned something no swing could buy: Reputation.

The cafeteria was a battlefield of its own. Big room. Long tables. Eyes everywhere. They mixed us in sometimes with the girls' units —mostly during classes or education hours.

Some of those girls were popular. And for whatever reason, a few were drawn to me. Maybe it was the silence. Maybe it was the stare. Maybe it was the fact I never tried too hard.

But I already knew better. "Some of the worst rage in here came over a girl." I wanted no part of that.

Guards were no better. Some of the women COs wore their pants tight and their smirks tighter. They'd flirt, tease, give long looks.

And kids? Kids acted like fools. If a female guard sat down, it was a race to smell the seat she left behind. Like they thought the scent was currency. Like there was a prize waiting at the end of that inhale.

The boys told war stories during chow. Wild tales about girls they smashed. Streets they ruled. Cars they drove.

Then the TV would come on. Didn't matter what show—if a pretty woman showed up? You'd hear someone breathing too heavy.

Or worse—you'd look up and realize the kid next to you was jerking off like you weren't even there. The less fortunate? They got hit in the face with cum rags — socks soaked in shame.

Disgust was survival. You learned fast how to live without television. They had Walkmans. Some boys walked around bumping music in their heads.

Not me. I refuse to put anything on my ears that makes me miss a sound. Sound was survival. Every cough, every footstep, every cry. That was my soundtrack. The rhythm of a place where silence could kill you.

Some of the older "model inmates" were lifers—good prisoners now, turned mentors. They'd talk to me. Try to give game. Say things like, "you got leadership in you, youngblood." I let them talk.

By sentence three, I was looking right through them, already planning the storm I'd unleash when I got out. Parole was the closest thing we had to hope.

If you had your GED, your chances skyrocketed. Near the end of the month, the GED classes were packed. Kids studying like it was salvation.

I asked James if he was going to do it. He said yeah—but he wasn't going to no stupid-ass class. He took the test cold. Scored one of the highest marks they'd seen.

I studied my ass off. Took it. Passed. Said fuck it—up for parole. They gave me a release date. Said I'd be on juvenile parole for 3–4 months. I could breathe again.

James refused to go to his parole hearing. Said it was a trap. That they'd let you out just to bait you into coming back and doing real time. He wasn't wrong.

But I couldn't stay in that hell another day longer than I had to.

He didn't flinch. Didn't argue. Just stood firm in his paranoia.

And once I knew his mind was made up? I let him be. I was leaving.

Letters came from my aunt in Virginia like warm fronts. She wrote that my cousin Logan still fixed bikes for half the block and never took full price from anybody's mother. I didn't need more than that right then—steady hands, calm voice, a man who could keep a room from breaking before it knew it was bending. Some people brag; some people repair.

But I wasn't the same kid they brought in. I came in 110 pounds of lean silence. I was walking out 160 pounds of bruised calculation.

Back then, I didn't know what to call it. But looking back? That was the moment the monster opened his eyes.

When I got my parole date, I didn't know to keep my mouth shut. Nobody ever told me the first rule of freedom: "Shut the fuck up about it." Because the minute you tell someone you're getting out, that's when the snakes start slithering.

I didn't talk to many people. Kept my circle tighter than my fists. But I still had a few folks I was cool with—kids from the same town, same block, same bloodlines of pain.

I let it slip. Didn't shout it. Just mentioned it. And that was enough.

King Born came over later that night. Quiet. Calm. Looked me dead in my eyes and said: "Don't tell nobody you leavin', motherfucker. Or you might not be leavin'."

I nodded. Didn't argue. Didn't really understand. Until I did.

A few days later, here comes this nobody — a bottom-feeder I barely acknowledged. Mouth loud, chest puffed, like he had something to prove. Starts barking. Trying to bait me. I told him plain: "Say one more word and I'll make sure you never speak again."

He kept barking—but not too loud. Because his crew was weak. And all three of them knew, if it came to it, King Born would mop the fucking floor with them just for fun.

Born had tight high-top fades, clean like he stepped out of a Fresh Prince episode. It was always sharp. Always on point. So of course, that's what they went after.

A few days later, we're walking to the cafeteria. Bullshit talk. Nothing serious.

I catch a glance to my side — Ty is posted up and stepping forward. That look in his eyes says it all. He throws a beautiful two-piece — textbook technique. Would've slept me. But I was faster. Slipped it smooth, never broke stride.

Kept walking. He called after me: "You know I'm fuckin' you up before you get outta here, right?" I believed him. But it wasn't going to be as easy as he thought.

Later that night, we're back in the cottage. That's what they called the dorms—rows of cots, 20 to 40 heads packed in tight. Some sleeping. Some watching the small TV near the front. Some plotting.

I'm away from the action. King Born is posted up by the TV. I hear it before I see it — the shuffle of sneakers. Low grunts. Quick breath.

Then it jumps off. 10–12 kids rush Born. No warning. No pause. Straight ambush.

Before I can blink, me and James are in the mix. Charging in like we've lost our damn minds.

Then another eight or nine pile in. It's a sea of fists, knees, elbows. Bodies moving in violent rhythm. It's not a fight—it's a riot.

We held our own. Didn't win—but we didn't die either.

King Born never dropped. Busted open. Shirt torn. But standing. Still ready to rock.

The guards came in after the damage. And beat us three like we started it. Figures.

That was the last time I ever saw King Born inside. He made parole too. But unlike me, he kept it quiet. Smart move.

I was one week from walking out. Trying to stay clear. Keep my head low.

Then it happened.

I'm outside. Basketball court. Weight benches nearby. I'm watching someone rep the bench —

kid from another town. Nothing major.

Then boom. Another kid sneaks up with a 10-pound plate, swings it overhead, and brings it crashing down on his skull. His head splits. The bar crashes on his chest.

And then comes the rush — a full-on pack of kids stomping him like they're auditioning for hell. The kid's probably dying, and they keep going.

In that chaos, I see eyes. Not any eyes — Ty and K-Rock. Coming straight for me. 200 pounds each, pure muscle, pure hate.

And it's just me. I had sharpened two toothbrushes for this moment. Been filing them down since the last setup. Both wrapped in cloth. Points clean. One for the throat. One for whoever came second. I was done being prey.

They got about six steps away — When one of the old heads, one of those "model inmate" lifers, stepped in. He saw it unfolding. Read my eyes. Shoved both of them back. Took the weapons from my hands, and stuffed them in his pants like he'd done this before.

He said nothing. But he saved me from murder that day, and maybe saved me from myself.

Next morning, they told me to pack up. No warning. No James. No goodbye. Just "You're out."

Don't know who pulled strings. Don't care.

I walked out alone. But I left a warzone behind me. I didn't know when James would get out. But I knew one thing — He'd have a place waiting when he did.

Chapter 3

They picked me up the day I got out. My mother. My sisters. My older brother Grim. They hugged me. I hugged back. But it wasn't the same.

I still smiled—but it never made it to my eyes. They used to call me kind. Sweet, even. That was a long time ago.

I could feel Grim watching me during the ride. Not judging. Just … clocking the shift. He didn't say much.

That was one thing about Grim—he didn't need to. Loyal as fuck, even if we ran in different circles. He always knew how to move when it mattered.

We didn't talk heavy. But we felt everything.

On the inside, I stopped eating pork. For a while I stopped eating meat altogether. Not outta principle—but because I had no clue what the hell they were feeding us. Some of it didn't even smell like food. It smelled like punishment.

For months, I planned my first meal out like it was a homecoming. But when it came time to eat? I barely touched the plate.

So much had changed. The game changed. The players changed. Even the price of coke was up.

You didn't need to hit the city anymore—wholesalers were right there in town now. No more risky rides, no more traps on bridges. Everybody thought they were king.

My father had moved to 8th Street—just four blocks from 4th and Monmouth.

That might not seem far. But in this world, four blocks was a different country.

Instead of returning to the corner I helped build, I started eyeing the block like a blueprint.

I didn't want to reclaim anything. I wanted to build something new.

I kept a map in my head that never needed paper. Laurel was loyalty first, small and sharp; MLK was a jungle with one way in and one way out if you weren't born there; KP moved like a separate country that still spent our money. I didn't draw lines to own them. I traced routes to leave fast.

No beef. No jealousy. No rivalries.

I had four months of parole left, and I was never going back.

I didn't ask for favors. Didn't need to. I was smart with my money before I left.

And if I was lucky, that metal shed I buried it under? Still standing.

My mother helped me land a job. Some warehouse. Some nobody yelling orders like he had power. I lasted five days.

On day six, I told him: "I don't take orders from men who ain't survived what I have." And I never clocked back in.

First thing I did when I got home? Wrote James. Told him I had him the second he touched down. Let him know that Santo Domingo was still on the table. Not a dream. A contingency. Because monsters need options too.

The streets weren't the same. Stores I used to know were shuttered. People who used to be kings were crackheads now.

An old girlfriend I used to love like breath tried to slide back in like she never left. Never wrote. Never called. The old me might've melted. The new me? I looked at her once. Said nothing. And walked away like she never existed.

Then came the mission: the stash. The spot was still there. But a Hispanic family had moved in.

Pitbulls in the backyard. Chains tight. The shed? Still standing. My cash? My future? Buried beneath it. How do you get to it without landing right back inside?

That's when nostalgia hit. I boarded the same city bus me and James used to ride. Same route we used to run bricks down and bring cash back. We moved weight like we were grown. If we were adults, we'd have been facing life.

But this ride? This wasn't about the game. It was about the terrain. Seeing who was still playing. Seeing who remembered us. Seeing what moves were left on the board.

I didn't go to cop. I didn't go to flex. I went to feel.

Because before I made any moves …I needed to remember what the streets felt like in my bones.

They say you can't go home again. That ain't true. You can go back—but you won't come back the same.

When I hit Country Circle, it wasn't to reminisce. But it happened anyway.

Same cracked sidewalks we used to play touch football on. Streetlight still flickering near Ms. Brown's old spot. Fights happened right in the middle of the street back then. That's where reputations were made—not behind screens, but fists and scars. I watched legends get born right outside my mama's window.

But no one hustled in Country Circle. That was home. Sacred ground. You didn't mix business with the place that raised you. We never did.

Now I had three or four months to rebuild what we lost. James was still inside, and when he stepped out, I wanted him to have what we always dreamed about—money, a car, and women ready to drop just to say they were part of our story.

But I also knew none of it would matter if I ended up back in chains before he even got out.

Some of the old crew was still moving. I could've taken shortcuts. But I turned down the offers—not outta pride, but strategy. I learned something inside:

Good intentions will get you locked up or killed almost as fast as trust.

When the noise got bigger than the block, I watched the places the old men kept for themselves—rooms with smoke that hung like rules. I wasn't old enough to be invited, but I noticed who came out different than they went in. You can learn a lot from a threshold.

The only one I trusted out here? My older brother, Grim.

I never chased the street game. I didn't need to. But he was loyal to the marrow. Back when I was just learning how to break rules, he taught me how to break in without leaving a trace. Sliding glass doors. Backyard entries. Ghost-level movement. I had the heart of a thief, but the discipline of a monk.

When I told him I needed to get something I left behind at our old house, he didn't even blink.

"We masking up and walking in? Or doing it like back in the day?" That was Grim—always ready.

There were two targets. One was cash I had stashed in the backyard under the old metal shed. The other was half a brick I left in a floorboard cutout in my bedroom closet. That second one? More risk. It could wait.

So we cased the house. Daylight. Nighttime. Hispanic family had moved in. Deep. Kids. Adults. Someone always home. Two pitbulls in the backyard, barking like they had something to prove.

I knocked on the door one day, pretending to look for someone. Dogs damn near shattered the sliding glass trying to get to me. Porch light didn't even flicker on. They must do this every day, I thought.

To handle the dogs, I reached out to MMC—Money Making Cee-lo, the crack-making magician. Brought it back better than anyone. Always wore gloves. Mask. Surgical with everything he touched. Even handed me the knockout dose like it was nitroglycerin. Didn't ask what it was for. With us, if no one offered details, you knew better than to ask.

I took it home, heated some food I barely touched, and poured the powder into a small plastic bag. Then I saw the letter. From James. Thick. Heavy.

I stared at it a long time. I couldn't read that shit right now. Not before the mission. I placed it on the dresser, lay down in the bed I shared with Grim, and closed my eyes. For the first time in what felt like two years, I slept like I was free.

The night was still. Not quiet—still. Like even the air was waiting. I moved through the field behind the old house. Dogs already barking before I hit the back fence. Perfect.

No lights turned on. Nobody peeked outside. I dumped the entire bag of powder over the fence, right near where the dogs had worn a trail into the dirt.

The barking slowed. Turned to soft whines. Then nothing. I hopped the fence. Made my way to the shed.

Same old rust. Same crooked lean. I started digging. Slow. Focused. Shovel met resistance more than once. Roots, stones, clay—this ground didn't want to give up my past.

30 minutes in, my back was on fire, 40 in, I heard it. Thud. Plastic.

I dropped the shovel and started digging with my hands. Fingernails tore. Dirt filled every line in my palms. My whole body was shaking.

And then I saw it. The bag. Still thick. Still sealed. I let a smile crack through. Still got it.

I hopped back over the fence, bag in hand. And for once—just once—I did something I never do. I didn't check my surroundings.

I was floating. Caught in the high of it. That was my mistake.

Click.

Cold steel touched my left shoulder. "Give me the fucking bag." Voice was high. Nervous. I didn't move. Didn't speak. Just listened.

He was close. Too close. Amateur.

"You pull a gun that close, you'd better use it or be ready to get your bluff called", I smirked.

Snapped my head back. Felt nose bone shatter. Twisted out of range. He stumbled.

Didn't even see the freight train coming. Grim hit him like lightning with fists.

We didn't speak. We just unleashed. It wasn't a fight. It was years of rage. Pain. Revenge. A symphony of fists, elbows, knees.

I blacked out. Saw red. Saw County, state, Felix, Born, my mother's face — Everything.

When I came to, the body was convulsing. Grim stood over him, smiling. "Ain't so little anymore, huh?"

We picked up the bag. Grabbed the pistol. Started to walk away. Then I turned. Pulled the mask off.

Fucking Charlie. Silk-shirt smooth talker turned stick-up kid. Laid out in the dirt like a broken promise.

Grim looked down. "Charlie?"

I didn't flinch. I spit in his face. Shoved the gun in his mouth. Voice low. "CJ is home, motherfucker. And next time you so much as cross a T on a piece of paper with my name on it… your grandmother dies first, you punk bitch."

We made it home. Quiet.

Rinsed off outside with the hose. Water cold. Dirt swirling down the driveway like we were washing off sins.

I stared up at the house. Mama's light still on.

Grim didn't say much. He didn't need to. What comes next? That was the question I asked myself. Bag in hand. Blood on my boots.

I had enough cash to move. To rebuild. But trust? That was off the table. Unless it was James or Grim—and even with them … I love them enough not to trust them.

Trust is for emergencies. Break-glass shit. Because when you don't trust anyone, you never get crossed. And if you do get hit? You already know who it wasn't.

I saw that shit firsthand in juvie. Felix trusted. James was ready. But to this day, I still don't know who the rat was.

What I do know? If they didn't know shit, they couldn't say shit. Now I was back in. Silently.

I watched my mother work hard. Step-pop too. Good man. Roof over our heads. But bills came faster than paychecks.

First thing I did? Grabbed every envelope in the "pay later" pile and paid them all. Not a word. Not a hint. Just silence—maybe blamed on a billing error.

But my step-pop wasn't stupid. A man's man. Didn't do handouts. Every time I walked in the house, I got that side-eye. That tension. But pride? You can't cash that shit at any bank.

I laid down that night. Fat stack under me. More cash than most would see in a year.

Grim blasting music like always. I missed the noise.

I had a plan. And I had to move.

The price of coke was up. Not outrageous, but enough. 121st and Morningside? Still moving.

C Shine had put me on to that spot before I went down. Moved with the same code of silence I did.

And behind him was Big Abe—his enforcer. The gentle giant you never wanted to see angry.

We weren't just family in the struggle—we were blood cousins.

C Shine had a harder time staying away from the shine, but not with dumb shit like jewelry. $500 shirts with no logo—just expensive enough to feel rich if you ever got close enough to touch. Only person I ever knew who ordered cars off the boat and told the dealership:

"Don't open the crate until I get there. And don't you dare put your little dealership logo on the back unless you're paying me for the advertisement." He had class.

Big Abe had a heart as big as his right hook—and an appetite to match.

Together, they were a silent force that ran the rooming houses a few blocks away. They moved right. Quiet. Deadly.

Amsterdam had a few backups in case one place got greedy.

I took the bus in. Train back. Watched the city like a wolf in church clothes.

Movies like New Jack City always made me laugh. Nino Brown? G-Money? Dead in a week out here.

Nobody needed to be kidnapped to buy crack. Ice-T would've been found slumped in a Buick on day three.

I smiled. Thought about all the killers I knew. The ones I won't ever name. Because see, murder got no statute of limitations.

If someone knows about it? They got a get-out-of-jail-free card. All they gotta do is drop that body on the table, and their own sentence disappears.

I spent half the cash. It was enough. I was back. Quiet.

Stayed off Fourth and Monmouth. Still hot. Still clown city.

Kept it simple. Forman Mills for the basics. Cheap but neat.

But sneakers? That was different. Dropped $500 on a pair just to make a silent statement.

Money right. No job. Product in hand. Two months before James comes home.

I wrote him seven times. He wrote me back every time. I didn't open them. Just made sure he had money on his books.

Made sure if anyone in juvie mentioned his name, they knew he was my people. Was he good? He wasn't.

My Pops—my biological father—always met me with wisdom and open arms. He never judged me. Never tried to change what couldn't be changed. I knew his son wasn't built to sit still, wither away, or take shit from anyone for long.

But one thing we both understood without ever saying it: No work at home. That went for my mother's place and my Pops' house. Those were sanctuaries.

But Pops' spot? That's where I set up shop.

Two small hood complexes within walking distance. And if you were coming from the north side to make your way down to Fourth and Monmouth, you had to pass 8th Street to get there.

So I made 8th and Clifton my world. Two blocks from Monmouth. Four from Fourth. Far enough to avoid heat, close enough to intercept the flow.

Payphones sat on the corner like they were waiting for a cameo in The Wire, but this wasn't no TV show.

I didn't talk on phones. I didn't let others talk on them. Phones were for bitches and pussy.

If I had something to say, I said it face-to-face. Always quiet. Always close. Whispers only. That was the code.

I got my first car. An Acura. Clean. Smooth.

Every time I heard Kool G Rap spit: "And I Ack in my Acura…" It felt like confirmation.

And when LL Cool J dropped Walking With a Panther? That one track, "This is how I'm coming" — hit so hard I had it airbrushed under the damn car. Just in case you forgot whose lane this was.

Didn't have no license. No insurance. But I drove like I had both. Drove clean. Drove confident.

Traffic court? That was a joke. I never moved dirty enough for it to matter. And I knew the streets better than any cop could pretend to.

But that night… I decided to finally open the letters. James. I lined them up. Read them in order.

Each one hit a little different. Not because the time was hard—but because he was changing.

The boy who used to dream big? Who used to sketch out entire blueprints for criminal empires on the back of composition notebooks? He was writing about working. School. Stability. Shit we never talked twice about.

Jobs were for motherfuckers named Stanley or Herbert. Not for us. And reading those letters? That shit hit me hard. I felt him unraveling. Not breaking—conforming.

He used to say he'd be the next biggest rap star out. Said he'd fund his rise with the hustle, and once we got there, we'd get out of the game clean.

He rapped with passion so strong, it made you believe—even if you weren't a dreamer. And every one of his verses? I was in it. He rhymed our pain into purpose. Gave our grime some glow.

So I wrote him back.

This time? Different. I addressed everything he said. All of it. Told him I was still moving blind, but I begged him—don't give up on our dreams.

IOAO. Independently Owned And Operated.

No bosses. No ceilings. Our world. I didn't say much more. I knew he'd feel it.

The next letter came. Thin. Simple. "See you in 10 days."

That was all. But that was everything. James King was coming home. And I was rebuilding our kingdom.

Just shy of six figures in cash. Airtight click. Some old blood. Some new.

But nobody trusted beyond eyesight. Nobody touched the circle unless I said so.

10 days came and went like nothing. But when that tenth day hit? I had it all laid out.

James didn't step off no bus. His mother picked him up. He came back into this world the way kings are supposed to—surrounded by blood, history, and love.

The throne was ready. And the only person I needed to complete this chessboard was on his way home.

Shit wasn't just about to get real. It was already real.

I was getting back the one thing I needed most: The best strategist I ever knew. The only person whose mind could match mine. The King.

Chapter 4

I pulled up slow to James's mom's house in the Acura, idling low, Kool G Rap humming under the tension like the whole car was narrating. I didn't cut the engine. Just let it rumble, steady and confident, like me.

James came out alone. No bag, no bounce in his step. He was dressed neat—old sweats, fresh tee, but they didn't wear the same way. He used to dress like every outfit was a movement. Now? It was like he just threw something on to be decent.

We dapped. Hugged. Hard. Shoulders clapped, but our chests never met. That told me more than any word could. There was distance between us now. Not beef. Just life.

He looked at the Acura and circled it slow.

"You got a license?" he asked, smirking.

I chuckled. "Hell no. But I will soon."

He nodded, and for the first time I saw that flicker of pride. "This ride is clean, C. Real clean."

He got in the passenger side—and winced. Tried to play it off, but I caught it. His body still remembered juvie in ways he wasn't ready to say out loud. He moved slower now. Healed, but not whole. Scar on his forehead still visible if the light hit right. Quiet pain in every shift of his weight.

"Where we going?" he asked.

"Nowhere special," I said. "Everywhere important."

I pulled off. Windows cracked. Just the city humming. We rode like ghosts, quiet but full of memory. Country Circle came first.

Our old block. Touch football in the street. Where kids learned to fight and lose and laugh and still be kings. I watched James look out the window and drift.

"You ever think about how many fights started right there?" he said, nodding at a corner.

"Fights and legends," I said. "That spot made men."

"I remember this one time," he said, grinning. "You had them white Pumas on, tryna juke Do Dirty, and he hit you so hard, your shoe came off and landed on Miss Beverly's porch."

We both laughed. "She never gave it back, either," I said. "Claimed it was a sign from the Lord."

Then Fourth and Monmouth. Still loud. Still clown central. Still flashing money they didn't have, calling attention they couldn't afford.

"Same old shit," James muttered.

"Nah," I said. "Worse now. They ain't even got rules."

We dipped over to 8th and Clifton. My new spot. Quiet. Clean. Nothing flashy. Just surgical moves in shadows. He clocked the corners, the posted lookouts, the low-key motion.

"You really got this up and running already?"

"Soon as I got back."

He nodded again, slower this time. Like he respected it. But also like he was visiting a past life he had no plans of revisiting.

"You hungry?" I asked.

His eyes lit up. "Hell yeah. You already know."

We pulled into the McDonald's. He didn't even need to look at the menu. "Big Mac. Large fries. Coke. Extra ketchup." Classic

James. I watched him inhale it like it was his first meal out. It wasn't, but it was the first one that felt real.

He leaned back, wiped his mouth, smiled. "Ain't shit changed with this. Still hit."

"You used to eat that same order every Saturday before we took the bus to the city," I said.

He nodded. "Back when we thought we were invisible."

"New routes now," I added. "Too much heat on the main arteries. If I'm bringing anything in bulk, I got it staged at 133rd through back-end delivery—same product, less shine. But it moves clean. And I move cleaner."

He raised his eyebrows. "You really thought all this through."

"I've had time. Ain't just about selling anymore. It's about position." I paused.

"Remember when we used to map out which trains ran fastest to which blocks? Penn Station to Times Square, cut up Amsterdam to 145th, loop around to Sugar Hill like we were playing chess while everybody else was still counting checkers."

He chuckled. "And we were carrying enough weight back then that if they caught us, we'd be doing life as adults."

I nodded. "But we didn't get caught."

We let the silence sit there. Comfortable. Familiar. Then I told him about the money.

"Remember that stash I buried before I went in?"

He laughed. "Under that busted-ass metal shed?"

"That's the one. Still there. Had to deal with pitbulls, a backyard full of strangers, and guess who tried to rob me?"

I looked at him sideways. "Nah… not who I'm thinking."

"Charlie".

He laughed so hard he dropped a fry. "That slick-talkin' fake pretty boy? Nahhh."

"Yup. Grim and I put him down easy. Sent him off with a reminder."

"Let me guess. You said some slick shit too."

I smirked. "Told him CJ was home. Then spit in his bloody face."

James just shook his head, smiling. "You never did do soft."

I looked over at him. "Probably still got a half a brick under the closet floorboards in my old room."

He wiped his hands and leaned back. "You wild, C. Always been."

We rode some more. Windows down. Nostalgia thick in the air. Every corner had a story. Every block was a chapter we'd already lived. Same bus stops. Same bodegas. Just newer ghosts.

"I ever tell you that Miss Janine still lives in that duplex by the park?" James said. "She asked about you last time I came by. Still keeps her lawn perfect. Still got that little Chihuahua that hates everybody."

"I used to hop her fence and steal peaches off her tree."

"You did it in broad daylight, too."

"Of course I did. I'm CJ."

He laughed. Then we turned toward the spot. Dead-end street. Quiet. Sacred. The kind of place where old dreams used to feel like blueprints.

I parked. That's when he got quiet. That's when the next part started.

We sat there in the quiet for a long time. Just the tick of the engine cooling and the soft tap of kids playing ball somewhere down the block. James didn't say a word at first. He just stared out the windshield like he was watching a world that no longer belonged to him.

"I'm out," he said finally.

I turned to look at him.

"I got accepted everywhere. Rutgers. Temple. Howard. I'm going."

Silence stretched.

"I'm happy for you," I said.

He nodded slowly. "Going for this new thing. Local Area Networks. Computers. Sounds like it's going to change the world."

"You know anything about computers?"

"Not really," he admitted. "But I'm learning. Fast."

That part hit me harder than the announcement. James had never been the 'learning fast' type. He was the visionary. The spark. But now he was talking like a student, not a king.

"So that's it?" I asked.

He shrugged. "Not turning my back on you. Never could. You call me for anything legal—anything clean—I'm there. You hit that break-glass moment? I'll burn it all down for you." He meant that.

"But the game? I can't chase it anymore, C. Not after that place. That place broke something in me."

He didn't cry. Didn't even blink hard. But the air between us cracked wide open.

"I ain't mad," I said. "I just… thought we'd finish what we started." I looked at him.

"I did too. Before it started eating me," he said.

I nodded. And that was the real goodbye.

"You ever think we could've done it?" he asked. "Like really made it?"

"With you? Hell yeah," I said. "You had the dream. The vision. You made that shit sound possible. You had people quoting bars from a notebook you never let anyone touch."

He smiled, remembering. "You were always in those verses. Every single one."

"I know," I said. "And I believed them. Even when I didn't believe in much else."

I sat back. Looked out the window. "Sometimes I wonder what would've happened if we stayed free just a little longer."

I didn't answer. We both knew that wasn't how the world worked for kids like us.

"We going to be good though," he said. "You're already good."

"I'm surviving," I said. "But good? That depends."

He looked over. "On what?"

"On whether this life kills me before I finish building it."

He didn't laugh. Didn't smile. Just nodded like he knew that truth too well.

He asked how Grim was. I told him he's still the same—quiet, loyal, ready for anything. Told him about how Grim didn't even flinch when I asked him to help me hit that old stash.

"Of course not," James said. "Grim's one of one."

"You'd think we all were," I said. "But I'm starting to see we're not."

I turned the key and let the engine hum again.

"Remember Kool DJ Red Alert?" he said. "Saturday night mixes?"

"Still got one. Cassette label faded but it hits."

"I miss that. Shit was pure."

"You were pure," I said.

He turned back to the window. "Not anymore."

"You still in there somewhere."

"You don't come out of places like that the same. And if you do, then you wasn't in there the right way."

"You ever write anymore?"

"Only numbers and drops."

He shook his head, disappointed. "You had bars, C. The way you put shit together... it was different."

"Different don't feed the block," I said. "Position does."

"But purpose?" he said, "That's something else." That part hit harder than it should've. Because he was right.

"Sometimes I feel like I lost my pen in that place," I admitted. "Like every story I was supposed to write stayed in there. Behind that damn fence."

I looked at him again. "Then write with your life now. Do it your way. But never forget what we were."

"I won't."

We sat in silence again, but it wasn't empty. It was heavy. Like a funeral with no bodies, just memory.

James King was walking away.

And I—the real CJ—was stepping into something bigger than the game, deeper than the hustle.

I wasn't rebuilding anymore. I was reborn. There's a moment when the silence inside you becomes louder than the noise outside. That's what that ride felt like.

After James told me he was out, something shifted. Not just between us—but inside me. It was like the last thread tying me to the dream we'd built together had snapped. He wasn't wrong for walking away. But that kind of peace he was chasing? I'd never felt it, and I sure as hell didn't trust it.

See, the thing about dreams when you grow up how we did? They come with expiration dates. And if you don't chase them hard enough, fast enough—they rot. James tried to preserve his. I chose to weaponize mine.

Everything we'd been through was a forge. County. State. The fights. The failures. The betrayals. Even the silence—it all hammered me into something sharper. Something colder. Something that could carve out a future without needing permission or protection.

I wasn't angry. Not at James. Not even at the game. I was just awake.

People talk about getting woke like it's some spiritual thing. But in my world? Waking up meant seeing every angle, every motive, every weakness in the people around you. It meant watching how long someone looked you in the eyes when they swore loyalty. It meant tracking who repeated stories and who just nodded. It meant living like every step might be your last—and walking like you were good with that.

So when James walked off that night, it wasn't betrayal. It was graduation. He stepped into his world. And I stepped fully into mine.

I wasn't rebuilding anymore. I was the blueprint now.

James didn't ask to be dropped anywhere in particular. He just rode along like he was trying to memorize the city with new eyes —eyes that had seen too much, and still weren't ready to close.

We passed the corner where that kid with the BMX used to do bar spins just to impress the older girls from Jefferson High. James pointed it out, chuckled, then fell quiet again. Like every memory cost him something to say aloud.

He tapped the window once. "You remember that summer we hit every barbershop and record store all over town trying to sell them homemade mixtapes?"

"Yeah. You almost cried when your mom taped over the master copy with a talk radio show."

He laughed, genuine this time. "Man, she said she thought it was a blank. You called her 'The Eraser' for a whole year."

That was the thing about James. His memory was vivid. Colorful. Almost too alive. That's why juvie hit him different. It didn't just take his freedom—it made his memories feel like ghosts he couldn't hold onto.

I pulled over by the park—the old one with the busted slide and the swing set that never sat level. We got out. Just sat on the hood of the car, side by side. The streetlights hummed. The sky was bruised but calm.

He looked up and said, "You ever think about just leaving? Not running, just… leaving it all?"

"I used to," I said. "Back when we thought you could outwalk your shadow."

"And now?"

"Now I know the only way out is through."

We sat like that for a while.

He finally stood, dusted off his pants like he was shaking off the past. "I gotta go back. My mom's waiting. She's cooking tonight. Mac and cheese and sweet potatoes. Trying to make it feel like normal."

"You want me to take you?"

"Nah. Let me walk. I need to feel the pavement under my feet again."

He paused before stepping off. "C?"

"Yeah?"

"I meant it. All of it. I'll always be your brother. I just… can't do this part no more."

"I know."

Before he walked off, we made a pact. We'd still hang out, but with rules. No dirt on our time. I leave the work on the block, and he leaves the lectures at home. Brothers forever—and co-defendants if the world ever called for it.

And with that, he walked off. Not fast. Not slow. Just steady.

That's when the air shifted.

I got back in the car, sat there for a minute, and let the moment burn itself into memory. Then I drove. Not to go somewhere—just to feel control again.

By the time I made it back to my father's place on 8th, the street was asleep but the hustle wasn't. Grim was on the porch, sitting like a statue, hoodie up, one headphone in. He didn't ask anything. Just handed me the newspaper and pointed to the back page.

Another overdose. Young. Local. Not someone I knew, but someone who knew me. Everyone did now.

I sat on the porch next to him. "You good?" he asked.

I nodded. "Yeah. But it's just me now."

I didn't say anything. Just bumped my shoulder with his. We both knew what that meant.

That night, I took inventory. Cash—near six figures. Product—unstepped and primed. Vehicles—clean titles, tags not hot. Crew—tight, hungry, tested.

But something else was there now. A calm. A cold kind of clarity.

I wrote James later that night. Told him I respected his choice. Told him I'd keep sending money just in case he needed books or food or whatever college kids spent on. I told him I wasn't mad. But I never told him I was hurt.

Because I was. Because the wolf pack was dead. And in its ashes, a lone wolf rose.

I changed how I moved. Tighter circles. Fewer names. Less talking. More walking.

I cut through the mall to buy time I couldn't find outside. She was standing near a storefront window with her hands in her coat, looking at a pair of shoes like she wasn't deciding about the shoes at all. The crowd pressed and parted around her, and somehow she stayed exactly where she meant to be. I noticed her posture first—

balanced, unbothered. Some people treat the world like traffic; she treated it like air. I didn't slow down. I just knew I'd see her again.

I became what the system tried to erase—a man too calculating to break, too quiet to predict, and too deep in to ever pull out without pulling blood first. I was CJ. And the world would know what that meant soon enough.

And I knew one thing with crystal clarity: This wasn't about proving anything to the world anymore. It was about protecting the few I still gave a damn about—my mother, my sisters, Grim. And even James, from afar.

There'd be no fake stories. No flashy cars on the block. No fake handshakes with smiling snakes.

I was building something different. I didn't want the crown to shine. I wanted it to fit. Heavy. Unmistakable. Mine.

Every dollar I stacked was a brick in my new foundation. Every silence I kept was a weapon sharpened by patience. Because when the time came, and I stepped fully into what I was meant to be, they wouldn't just respect my name. They'd fear the silence that came with it.

Chapter 5

The last time I heard James's voice on the phone, he asked me if I was good. Not "safe." Not "rich." Just… good.

I told him yeah. And that was the last lie I let cross my lips that year.

We used to have this rule. Once a week, no matter what—we'd link up. No corners, no Cee-lo. Just us. Brothers. Maybe hit a cheap diner, maybe just sit in the car with the windows cracked and music playing low. That was our way of staying grounded. Of remembering we weren't just built by the block—we were built for each other.

But time got funny. His weekends became crowded. Classes, study groups, this girl—no name needed. She talked about opportunity like it was a bus stop he couldn't miss. And he listened.

My weekends? That's when the Circle came alive. Where most saw death after midnight, I saw dividends. James had dreams. I had deadlines.

So the meet-ups turned into phone calls. Then one day, I stopped answering altogether.

Not because I didn't love my brother. But because I couldn't carry the sound of that hope in his voice anymore. I was still dreaming. I was still building. Those two don't mix.

That's when I made peace with it. I took the future. I kept the now.

But if I was going to stay in this now and dominate it, I needed more than corner boys and hype men. I needed thinkers. Movers. Enforcers who didn't blink and lieutenants who didn't fold. I needed architects for a street kingdom—not soldiers for a turf war.

First, I called Cal. My cousin out in Virginia. They called him that 'cause he swore up and down he was moving to California someday. He never did—but the name stuck like a street tattoo.

Cal was measured. Calm. Didn't jump for dollars. He calculated. That made him dangerous.

He didn't want to be James. Didn't even ask about him. He just said: "You building for real this time, or we just flexing?"

I told him: "Real as a casket."

He said: "Then I'm on my way."

Next was Barry. I didn't even have to call him. He found me. Barry lived a block over from 8th. He was the kind of man you didn't put on the front line—you sent him in when the front line failed. Naturally strong. Amateur boxer. Professional street fighter.

He didn't just swing. He aimed. And he didn't miss. Tall, dark as midnight, and slower to speak than most men are to breathe. He had a voice like the South—but not lazy, not country. Just deliberate. Like every word was the last time he'd say it. And that hook? It had ended more arguments than peace treaties ever did.

Nobody in the Circle ever claimed Barry. He wasn't in no crew. He was a local legend, unaffiliated. But the second I nodded at him and said, "I'm starting something real," he looked back and just said: "I know."

That was it. No handshake. No speech. Just I know. Because he did.

Then came Ock B. From Brooklyn, by way of everywhere.

I never liked pretty boys. But Ock wasn't soft—he was sharp. Had that good hair the women loved and that jawline that made them forgive damn near anything. He stayed fly, always smelled like success, and could talk his way into heaven or hell, depending on the day.

But don't let the smile fool you. Ock earned his name the hard way. He didn't wait for respect—he took it. And when he took it, he made it look easy. His block was quiet because no one dared raise their voice without permission. Not to him. Not near him.

He was the only man I ever watched calm a crew down with just a look—and then turn around and put somebody in the dirt without raising his voice.

Ock and I weren't friends. But we respected each other's kingdoms. And in this game? That's rare.

That was my trinity: Cal, Barry, and Ock. Mind. Muscle. Movement.

But I wasn't done.

The next pieces weren't just soldiers. They were gods in their own lanes. I didn't need to give orders—I needed to make alliances.

Enter C Shine and Big Abe—my blood cousins from across the bridge.

You didn't see Shine much. You just felt him. He moved like smoke—quiet, invisible, and always in the right place at the wrong time for somebody else. He owned most of the rooming houses from 2nd Street to Main. That meant he owned access—and you can't raid what you need permission to enter.

Word was, C Shine had a man on the inside. Maybe more than one. But nobody could prove it. At only 21, he moved like a man with a 20-year head start. You never saw him twice in the same ride, and if you did, it was a trap.

Big Abe was the shield. Shine was the sword.

They operated as one. No noise. No mess. And if they had beef? You never heard about it. That's power. The kind even cops whisper about behind the desk. That was the foundation.

I had the mind in Cal. The hammer in Barry. The flame in Ock. The shadow in Shine. And the enforcer in Abe. But every kingdom needs a magician. A miracle worker. Somebody who doesn't just move weight—but resurrects it.

That was MMC. The cook. The chemist. The legend.

Every king needs his court. But mine didn't sit in chairs. They stood. They watched. They waited.

And when the word came, they moved like silence with knives.

Cal handled the ops. Barry made things disappear. Men who hit that clean don't always notice when their ears start ringing. Ock kept the streets honest. C Shine and Big Abe moved like investors in war.

Cal didn't want shine. He took the late calls, the quiet errands, the errands that matter more than gun talk. If I said meet me two towns over with nothing in the trunk and nothing in your eyes, he was already parked, engine off, hands warm. People confuse silence with softness. Cal knew the difference.

But none of it moved without the right product. And the right product needed the right hands.

That's where MMC came in.

I met MMC before the game even touched us. He lived two blocks over from Country Circle, in a house that always smelled like gasoline and burnt plastic. His uncle fixed mufflers. His cousin ran dice. MMC? He watched. Learned. Broke things down and built 'em better.

He gave me my first stolen car ride. I was thirteen. Didn't ask where we were going—just slid into the passenger seat and held on while he whipped it through the alley like a damn video game. Laughing the whole time. That boy laughed like he ain't never lost a thing.

But when he cooked? That's when you saw the real magic.

Some cats lose weight every time they touch it. MMC brought it back. He cooked coke like it owed him an apology. Fish scale, stepped-on, it didn't matter—he'd make it sparkle.

People called him a chef, but he wasn't no street cook. He was surgical.

Crews used to come to him like church. Confessing sins in plastic baggies, praying he could save it. Most times, he did. That's why they called him Black Jesus. He brought trash back from the dead.

But there were rules. My rules. You could be brilliant. You could be strong. You could be feared. Didn't mean I trusted you.

The closer you were to me, the more I studied your habits. Because habits are liabilities. And liabilities get people killed.

I never smoked. Never drank. Didn't chase skirts. Didn't pop pills. I didn't even trust coffee. Anybody that needed something before they could function? Already compromised.

And if you were compromised? I moved you further away. Quietly. Gently. But permanently.

Phones? I stopped using them the moment James and I started drifting. Not because I was paranoid. Because I was focused.

You can't build a throne and answer distractions at the same time.

So my rules were simple:

- No one sits in the room while I talk business.

- Your shoulders? Your people? They stay outside.

- No habits. No phones. No weakness.

- You don't ask who's #1. If you wondering, it ain't you.

I don't share power. I enforce it.

That's why I didn't have lieutenants. I had assets.

Valuable? Yes. Trusted? Not quite. Because the only person I ever gave my full trust to was gone. And when the dreamer left, the dream did too.

Grim was still around. Always was. Not part of the operation. Not part of the crew. But he was mine. Blood in, blood deep. He was the storm I kept chained. The one man I'd never try to control.

His fuse was too short for this new world. Loud mouths. Loose cannons. Flashy fools who mistook attention for power. Grim would've had a murder case in a week. Not because he looked for trouble—but because he never walked away from it.

And wherever it started? That's where he finished it.

Some nights, I'd just sit in the car outside of Country Circle. Engine running low. Barry on the block nearby. Cal across town with the books. MMC somewhere laughing while he worked. And Ock? Probably climbing into somebody's bed with a smile and a switchblade under the pillow.

The empire was taking shape. But the seat still felt cold.

You see... this game ain't about glory. That's what the rappers sell. They talk like they been kings, but most were never even pawns.

Take Biggie, for example. Legend? Sure. Lyricist? Undeniable. But ask anyone who really ran the blocks he claimed—Big was a corner boy at best. Never copped more than an ounce. Never pulled a trigger. Never ran a crew. He reported what the kings did. Turned it into art. A translator for pain he didn't own.

And Puff? A college man. Brilliant. But without the sharks from Bed-Stuy behind him, he'd be pushing promo packs for R&B acts.

There's no soundtrack to real life. Just sirens. And whispers. And the sound of doors getting kicked in at 3AM. That's why I never let the streets seduce me.

I was the exception. The darkroom behind the photo. I wasn't in the picture, but I developed everything.

Now with the team in place, the streets shifting, and the silence growing louder … there was only one thing that made my blood boil. Rich. He went by "Universal" now. Like some righteous rebirth.

Moved to town over, trying to sell the world some 5-Percenter philosophy like he didn't beg for protection in juvie. Rich wasn't built for the inside. So he flipped. Found religion in fear. Preached about peace after selling names for favors.

I didn't hate him. But I never forgot him. See, I got a code. And I might forgive a thief. I might even forgive a coward. But I never forgive a snitch. And Rich? He was on the menu.

Grim was the only one who ever saw me bleed. Not from bullets or blades—but from moments. Moments I never let anyone else witness.

When James drifted away and the dream faded with him, I didn't cry. But Grim saw it. Not in my face—but in the way I went silent. He never said shit. Just sat across the room, arms crossed, jaw set like stone.

That's what made him dangerous. He felt everything, said nothing, and reacted without warning.

People feared Barry. Respected Cal. Resented Ock. But Grim? They avoided him. Entirely. He wasn't in the clique. Not officially. That wasn't his lane. He didn't play the game. He didn't like the rules.

He was born into it but not bound by it. My brother from birth. He never asked for a seat at the table, but the table always made room.

Earlier that week, I'd pulled up to Manito Park projects. Ock B was outside, standing like he owned air rights.

We spoke. Brief. Eyes always scanning. No wasted words, just presence. Respect earned and exchanged.

Then I made my way to MMC's spot. Kitchen smelled like fire and chemicals—familiar and sacred. MMC was laughing about a crew that dropped off garbage weight. "I brought it back though," he said, smirking.

"Shit was flatter than a preacher's daughter. Now it's glistening." I chuckled. Sat down. Watched him do what he did best.

That's when I heard the knock. Not the door. The hood. Steel. Rhythm. Intent. Only Grim knocked like that.

I stepped outside. I was leaning on the car, headband crooked like always. Without saying a word, Grim opened the glove compartment, pulled out two old headbands. Tossed one in my lap. Put his on like it still meant something. I slid mine on too. It felt like armor.

He leaned back. "Rich just left some chick's spot. Walking down Lexington. No lights. Heading toward the Towers." We sat for a moment. Quiet.

Until I said, "You still think you could beat me in a headspin?"

He laughed. "You never even stuck the baby freeze."

We both cracked up. The kind of laugh that sat deep in the stomach. Like back in the day, before betrayal had names.

"You remember when James used to come over Pops' crib just to borrow them old porn tapes?"

Grim chuckled. "Acted like he was coming for a plate. Slick ass."

That moment held us for a beat. Then the sidewalk cleared. And there he was. Rich. Alone. Head down. Moving like he didn't owe anybody pain. Like he wasn't the reason we bled.

I smiled when he saw me. Walked right up like it was love. Hand out.

Grim muttered, "This fucking guy…" and looked away.

Before Rich could speak, I pulled him in. Close. Shoulder to shoulder. He started rambling. Fast. Like words might save him.

I hushed him. "Shhhh…"

Then leaned in and said: "Just tell me why the fuck you told on us… for no good fucking reason. And we call it even."

His face shifted—somewhere between relief and regret.

Then he opened his mouth. And I pulled the trigger. One to the gut. Close range. Held him as he sank.

"I really don't care why," I said. My voice cracked. Tears slipped down my cheek.

"You took everything from me," I whispered. "Including my best fucking friend." I let him drop.

Grim didn't hesitate. He stepped forward and stomped Rich's face until nobody would recognize him.

I didn't stop him. I'd never been the one to get my hands dirty. But this time was different. This was personal. The only personal thing

I ever allowed to compromise my vision.

And as we drove off, headbands still damp with sweat and memory, I stared out the window and said nothing. The streets were colder now. Quieter. Angrier.

That night didn't just mark the end of a snitch. It was the first time I dropped a body over something that mattered to me. And I felt it. In my bones. In my blood.

This game wasn't just war anymore. It was personal.

And now? I was too.

Chapter 6

Months slid by after Rich bled out under a silence he never earned. Out here, the noise died fast, but I kept moving. I turned quiet into motion. What started on 8th grew teeth—ran from 8th to 14th, two blocks west, one north. A rectangle you could feel. The drop times stayed strict. The bags weighed right. No corner grandstanding, no theatrics. If something was sloppy, it didn't survive. Order paid me better than fear.

I wasn't flashing. Not really. Sometimes the leather was imported, sometimes the steel was new, sometimes a woman left a mark on my chest they could read from across a room. That was for me, not them. The streets got the silence. The money got counted. The rules did the rest.

Then I did something stupid on a Thursday.

No work in the car. Paperwork clean. Tags matching. I still punched the gas when the cruiser made a lazy U behind me. I wasn't hiding anything—except the truth I didn't have a license. I wasn't spending a night in a holding cell so some rookie could make his sergeant grin over a traffic stop.

I cut right off King Boulevard, banged a left down Gregory Lane, slid behind the old bakery lot, hopped a fence, and let my legs do what they always did. They weren't catching me in dress shoes or cleats. I made it out. Two days later the car got impounded under a name that wasn't mine.

On day three, a letter landed. No return address. No fluff. One line in all caps:

TAKE YOUR BIRTH CERTIFICATE TO MOTOR VEHICLE AND GET YOUR FUCKING LICENSE. DON'T WORRY

ABOUT ANYTHING. JUST DO IT.

No signature needed. James.

I brought two IDs, said I lost my license. Twenty minutes later a camera flashed and a woman with tired eyes told me to smile. I didn't. Forty minutes later a legit license warmed my pocket. I walked out with a grin I hadn't felt in months.

I see you, Jay.

I pulled the car from impound the same day. Clerk slid me the keys, smirked, said, "You got friends in quiet places, huh?" I just nodded.

Later, C Shine and Big Abe pulled me into a back room behind a pool hall off Banks. Three chairs. One steel table. The kind of silence that wears a crown.

When I needed a room that spoke before anyone did, I slid through the Elks. Old heads in pressed hats, pool chalk on their fingers, secrets kept in the curve of a corner pocket. The VFW was quieter than church and louder than a whisper; if a man wanted to apologize without saying sorry, he bought two drinks and left one full. I learned to hear danger in those rooms—how laughter bends when money is light, how a cue ball carries news before the mouth does.

"A king without counsel don't last long," Shine said.

Abe nodded. He always nodded. One man's whole sermon in a chin dip.

They walked me through protections I wasn't using yet. Shells. Payroll. Paperwork that didn't spend money, just carried weight. "Keep your best hitter on payroll as 'security,'" Shine said. "Pay your girl's cousin for 'marketing analysis.' You don't need them to do a damn thing—you just need the check stubs."

"Get a lawyer," Abe added, voice quiet as a drawer closing. "Not later. Now." I already had one in mind. I put him on retainer that night.

Then Shine said it like he was swatting a fly. "Heard some whispering. MLK. KPs. 'Who the fuck he think he is' type of poetry."

"From who?" I asked.

"Pudge," Shine said. "If he says he heard it, he heard it."

I respected Pudge. He wasn't a gossip line. He was an early-warning system. But I wasn't feeding my paranoia. "Let 'em whisper," I said. "Barking dogs don't deserve bullets."

"Until they bite," Abe said.

"When they bite," I answered.

We didn't toast to anything. We didn't seal it with a handshake. We just left that room tighter than we entered it. On the drive out, I laughed to myself. New Jack City always made me laugh—movie logic holding hands with suicide. They'd have been dead in a week on my side of the map. Carlito's Way felt closer—regret, loyalty, rules that don't save you. That one told the truth by accident.

That night I drove down Bangs and parked outside a lounge I liked for the way it didn't try hard. Red walls. Dark wood. Spanish guitar tangled with jazz until it forgot its own name. I took my corner and a Pepsi—no ice. Second one of the night.

She slid into the booth like the seat had been waiting.

"That seat taken?" she asked, already sitting.

"Not unless you plan on talking too much."

"So I'll talk just enough."

I smirked. The kind of smile I forget I have.

"You always drink soda like it's bourbon?" she asked, nodding at the glass.

"Only thing I want burning tonight is the silence."

She leaned in, elbows on the table, eyes the color of trouble done right. "You ever get tired of acting like you don't need anyone?"

"You ever get tired of pretending that scares me?"

"Touché," she said, and smiled like she knew the shape of my next ten years.

Her name was Maribel. She didn't play pretty, but pretty followed her anyway. Hoop earrings, hair pinned high, grace built from something heavier than luck. She asked small questions that measured large things.

"You always sit with your back to the wall?"

"I like to see what's coming."

"Ever think about letting your guard down?"

"That's how you end up a story someone else tells."

I finished my drink and left her with the last word. No rush, no angle. Numbers swapped, not promises. Outside, Bangs Ave breathed that mix of perfume and spilled beer, and I let the air cool what the room had tried to speed up. If I was going to see her again, it wouldn't be because the night was loud enough to dare me—it would be because the morning agreed.

I kept moving. You can't build a throne and answer distractions at the same time. The rectangle stayed humming. My crew kept the cuts exact. People followed rules because nobody wanted to be the lesson. And I counted the cash in rooms that didn't echo.

Then the street tried to test my patience with theater.

The small storm already passed: the letter, the license, the smirk at impound, the back room with Shine and Abe, and the quiet math I loved more than any applause. I added one more rule to a list I kept taped to the inside of my skull:

Later, after two more days of clean movement and quiet money, a rookie tried to chase heat that wasn't there, and I remembered the DMV lady telling me to smile. James had handled that without a word. That was his magic: not showing up in the room and making the room move anyway.

On nights like that, I let the music talk. KRS, "My Philosophy," windows cracked, highway lights sliding by like veins under skin. I thought about how movie gangsters always monologued into death. Out here, you keep your voice low and your footsteps sure.

I didn't need applause. I needed the silence to stay loud. And for the moment, it did.

Maribel texted, "You eat?"

"Not yet."

"Don't fix that alone."

We met at a small spot on Lake that smells like cumin and Sunday —the kind of place with a chalkboard menu and a bell that's too proud of its job. She chose the corner where the light stayed soft. No speech about what this was. Just two people who understood time and the value of not naming it too early.

"You always sit where you can see the door?" she asked.

"I sit where exits don't surprise me."

"Good," she said. "I like men who plan for the future."

We ate slow. Pernil that knew patience. Rice that didn't pretend to be fancy. She talked with her hands and her eyes stayed still—the kind of still that reads a person without picking them apart. Nights on her feet serving plates and patience. Days for errands and recovery. She liked the work because it taught her tempo—how to hear the room and not get drunk on it.

"You do the same thing," she said. "Different room."

"You don't know what I do," I said.

"I know you read before you speak," she answered, and let it end there.

She told me her cousin kept two calendars—one for shifts and one for hopes; her aunt called them "work" and "why." Maribel learned early to keep a little why in her day or the work ate it. She didn't talk about wanting to be saved from anything. She talked about choosing—her hours, her boundaries, her kitchen knives. There are people who lure you with fantasy; she offered the truth and watched what I did with it.

When the bill came, I reached. She blocked my hand with two fingers and slid her card in first. "If this is a date, it's a date," she said. "I'm not here to audition for your support."

"Noted," I said.

Outside, Lake carried the smell of rain that hadn't started yet. We walked to the waterfront without deciding to. The black water at the bulkhead shivered like a lie telling on itself. She didn't fill quiet to prove she was interesting. She let the sound of our shoes do that work. A gull circled once, twice, like a lazy thought that refuses to leave.

"You bring people home?" she asked.

"No."

"Me neither," she said. "But I'll make an exception if the room is respectful."

"My rooms are."

She looked at me, measuring truth. "Then show me."

I didn't dress the moment with speeches. Respect doesn't need a speech; it needs proof. I unlocked the door and let the apartment breathe. She stepped in and did what competent people do—turned the deadbolt, slipped her shoes off, set her purse where it wouldn't argue with the room. She opened the window an inch to give steam a place to go and rested her back against my counter like she already knew how much weight it could take.

"You always this careful?" she asked.

"Careful is how I pay my bills," I said.

She came close enough for my breath to notice. Her hand found my jaw, the back of the fingers first, as if she were testing the temperature of a thought. We stood inside a kind of quiet that doesn't happen by accident.

"Come here," she said.

We didn't rush. She kissed like she knew the difference between heat and hurry—slow mouth, sure mouth, a press that asked me to show up with both hands and all my attention. She tasted like citrus and a long day finally agreeing with itself. I answered with my own patience. When she leaned back, I leaned with her so the space didn't feel like a retreat. We traded breath until the room chose a rhythm for us.

I followed the line of her cheek with my mouth and learned the soft of her jaw, the place where perfume becomes skin. She tasted like salt-sweet work and something clean underneath it. I mapped my way to her collarbone and stayed there, letting the edge of my teeth suggest and then surrender. She answered by tracing the seam of my shoulder with her mouth and then my wrist, then the back of my hand, like she was teaching me my own pulse. When I came back to her mouth, she kissed me deeper and the taste of her met the taste of me and the math added up to something I hadn't let myself want in a long time.

"Hold," she said at my hairline, guiding my hand to the pins. Not a dare. A rule. I gathered the weight without yanking, and the line of her neck learned my name in a whisper. There is a way to be taught by a body without turning it into a lesson plan. She adjusted my pace with a palm on my hip, a breath against my ear, the smallest tilt that said here and not there, now and not yet. Belonging has a grammar. She spoke it and I answered.

"Don't be careful with me," she said, voice low.

"I won't," I said, and didn't.

I set her palms against the counter and watched her breathe. When I leaned in, she leaned back, not to retreat, but to receive. The city dimmed to a hum. I tasted the inside of her elbow, the flat of her stomach where laugh and hunger meet, and the place at her waist where softness turns to strength. She pulled me by the wrist and I let her, and when I took my time she let me know the time was mine to take. There are nights that borrow from songs and nights that write their own; we were writing.

She turned and pressed her hands to the wall, then reached back and placed my palm in her hair. "Here," she said, and lifted her chin. Not in anger. In belonging we both signed. I tightened just enough to hear the sound she made when weight and will met in the middle. "Eyes on me," she said when she faced me again, and held mine. If I drifted, she called me back with a look. If I hurried, she slowed me with a hand that said we have all night and a standard to keep.

"Look," she said later, lying back, opening, framing herself with both hands as if reminding me what the word beauty owes to presence. "Appreciate." She didn't perform; she participated—guided, received, returned. I did what she asked and what I wanted and let appreciation do the rest. When I moved into her, we both gasped, and in that shared breath it felt like we traded something heavier than air. With each stroke she kept my eyes where they belonged. I carried more of my weight when she asked and less when she pressed my chest to remind me she was part of the decision. I wasn't new to bodies. I was new to this kind of permission.

When I got close she slowed me down, fingers firm at my hip, the smallest shake of her head that said not yet. "We have time," she said. "Own it." So I did—owned the pace, the pressure, the way the room narrowed to two names and one rhythm. She commanded without cruelty, and what I brought met what she offered in the middle of the bed like a treaty written in heat. When it was time she took my face in both hands and didn't let me look away. The room stayed honest for it.

After, we didn't rush to define anything. She stayed on my chest and let our breathing settle into the same paragraph. The window carried a small draft through the curtains. Somewhere, a siren made a decision and then changed its mind. We lay there and believed the night would not betray us with noise.

"Are we good?" she asked into my shoulder.

"We are."

She tied her hair with a satin band and left it on the nightstand as if it knew where it lived now. Before sleep, she touched my jaw again—present, not soft, not hard. I slept with the calm of a man who had been measured and not found lacking.

Dawn took its time arriving. When it did, she moved through the kitchen with the competence of someone who respects walls—cupboards quiet, faucet just enough, a towel folded where it wanted to be. She set a pot on low and warmed leftovers like an offering to the day. We didn't pretend breakfast made meaning; it made fuel. She kissed the corner of my mouth like a signature and stepped into the shower. Water hit tile in a steady percussion, and I stood in the doorway and watched steam outline what I already knew.

"You staring?" she called through the glass.

"Learning," I said.

"Good," she answered. "I like a man who studies."

We ate on the counter, standing. She used the good fork without asking because she intended to wash it. I stacked the bowls because I intended to dry them. Domestic is a loud word people use to make quiet work sound simple. What we did was simpler than that and heavier: we respected the room.

"Tonight?" she asked, rinsing the pot.

"I have to ride the rectangle."

"You'll call?"

"Before I turn the last corner."

She nodded once, no pout, no performative sigh. "I prefer verbs to promises," she said, and left her satin band where it had slept.

When the door closed, the apartment kept her shape for a while—air that remembered her heat, a chair that leaned like it had learned posture, the mirror with a fingerprint where she steadied herself. I walked the rooms and let the evidence teach me something I don't allow often: want without weakness.

By noon, silence put its hand on my shoulder the way it does when it wants to be named. I didn't. I put on work instead. I wrote on a yellow legal pad until my handwriting turned into a metronome. I listed what order costs and what chaos charges. I drew the rectangle twice—8th to 14th to Congress to Monmouth—and wrote notes along the edges: who never late, who always short, who smiles when they lie and who blinks when they tell the truth. The map on the paper is never the map under your shoes. But the paper is how your shoes remember the day before.

I called Cal and said only, "Two." He said, "Copy."

Before I left, I opened the bedroom window one more inch and set her band on the knob like a flag small enough for only two people to recognize. I don't stack memories; I stack signals.

On the ride, I kept my speed one mile an hour under polite. The city thinks it knows how to test a man the day after he lets himself be known to someone. It sends him a siren, a short temper at a light, a fool who wants to sell him a shortcut to tomorrow. I let all three pass me like weather. I don't bargain with weather.

At 8th a corner boy tried to perform hunger with his voice. I adjusted my mirror to the angle that tells the truth and waited him out. Patience is not a saint in this line of work; it's a ledger. If I spend it on show, I'm broke when the real bill comes due.

At 10th a mother opened her second-floor window and shook a rug like she was erasing last year. Men paused beneath out of reflex. I watched who looked up first and who looked down and who used the moment to hand off something small. The map took another note.

At 12th, two new faces laughed like they were owed. One wore a chain too bright for a Tuesday; the other kept his hands hidden like he wanted attention but not accountability. I let the car idle. If a man's rhythm offends the block, the block will fix it for you eventually. You just need to know when to let it.

By the time I reached Monmouth, the rectangle had reminded me of what I already knew—there are nights you take, and nights you steward. Last night I took. Today I stewarded. Both are work.

My phone buzzed once. Not a ring. A pulse. Maribel: "Breathe."

I smiled without letting it reach my mouth. I breathed.

I cut the loop and drove back to the building. Inside, the satin band watched from the knob like a small witness. I showered, shaved the edges, dressed the part of a man who expects doors to open because he chooses which ones to knock on. The afternoon served me the kind of quiet I use to sharpen knives that aren't metal.

When the sun moved far enough west to make the room look like a photograph of itself, I sat at the table and wrote a second list that had nothing to do with streets: what a woman teaches you if you let her; what you owe the room when she's in it; what to do with the weight you wake up with when it isn't only yours anymore. I titled it nothing. I don't title what I'm still learning.

Twilight painted the window frame a color I don't have a word for. It looked like the part of a bruise that means healing. I stood and stretched and felt the night I'd slept back into my shoulders—the night we made smaller by agreeing not to be careful. You don't get many like that and keep your pace. But when you do, you move cleaner after, not slower.

She texted again: "You turned the last corner yet?"

"Not yet."

"Then keep both hands on the wheel," she wrote, and added nothing else. I like a woman who can tell a joke without laughing at it first.

When the sky finally committed to dark, I stepped out. The hall was the same. The elevator said the same lie about coming right away. The street wore its regular face. But I moved through it different—not soft, not distracted. Just measured.

By morning I gave the quiet back to myself—no visitors, no detours, just the map and the math.

I kept moving. You can't build a throne and answer distractions at the same time. The rectangle stayed humming. My crew kept the cuts exact. People followed rules because nobody wanted to be the lesson. And I counted the cash in rooms that didn't echo.

Then the street tried to test my patience with theater.

The small storm already passed: the letter, the license, the smirk at impound, the back room with Shine and Abe, and the quiet math I loved more than any applause. I added one more rule to a list I kept taped to the inside of my skull:

On nights like that, I let the music talk. KRS, "My Philosophy," windows cracked, highway lights sliding by like veins under skin. I thought about how movie gangsters always monologued into death. Out here, you keep your voice low and your footsteps sure.

I didn't need applause. I needed the silence to stay loud.

And for the moment, it did.

Chapter 7

By midmorning I walked into Double G's barbershop. Antiseptic and cocoa butter in the air, clippers humming, laughter bouncing off the mirrors. The kind of place men go to talk loud and tell the truth accidentally.

"CJ in the building!" G-Money yelled from the corner chair. "You here for the trim or the gospel?"

"A little of both," I said, sliding into a waiting seat.

Tone pointed at the TV. "Yo, the Knicks been cursed since they traded Patrick. Irish and Catholic at the same time. You don't trade saints!"

The whole shop cracked up. I let the laugh hit me; I needed it to. For a minute I forgot why the room felt too bright.

"Let me ask you a real one, C," G-Money called. "Woman comes to your crib at two in the morning—you cuddling or you—"

"Cuddling," I said, deadpan.

Groans all around. "Man, if you don't get your soft-ass, slow-jam-loving, cocoa-butter-using—"

I smirked. "A real one can still cuddle."

Mouse claimed he got topped by two girls last night. Twan told him his story was shaped like a toothpick. The kind of nonsense you only hear where men feel safe enough to be stupid. For a minute it helped.

My barber waved me up, set the clippers to the exact number I don't say out loud. "I heard about your boy's brother," he murmured just under the buzz. "That's fucked up."

"What you hear?" My eyes didn't leave the mirror.

"Reckless hit. Wrong place, wrong time. Kid trying to earn stripes."

I gave one slow nod. I finished the cut. When I moved to pay, he waved it off. "Your money don't work in here." We dapped and hugged once, and somebody yelled "DEEZ NUTS!" as I hit the door. I let the smile lift one corner of my mouth and walked out.

Mr. Earl was parked crooked by the hydrant, white towel around his neck like a flag of truce. He doesn't speak unless the city gives him permission. Today it did.

"You walk like you paying for something you already own," he said, eyes on the street and not on me.

"I don't like surprises."

"Surprises ain't the problem. Loud courage is." He adjusted the towel. "It makes men reach for an audience before they reach for an answer."

I didn't argue. The block argued for me: horns, sneakers, a stroller wheel squeaking like it needed a prayer.

"You keep your name on a leash," he added. "Let the dog bark; don't let it run."

I nodded once. Some lessons arrive already memorized. I tipped his chin at the shop. "Gonna pay for that little kid's cut next time you see him. My mother pretending not to count coins."

"I saw it."

"I know." He slid into the driver's seat and pulled off like the street had waved him through. I stood there a beat longer, listening for the part the noise wasn't saying.

Days blurred after that. Grief doesn't keep time, it just drips into everything. I rode my rectangle at dawn—8th to 14th and back—breathing the city like it might answer a question I hadn't asked yet.

Daylight requires a different kind of silence. I cut through the mall to buy time I couldn't buy outside. She was there again—hands in her coat, studying a window like it had more to say than shoes.

"You always stand that still?" I asked.

"Only when I'm moving," she said, eyes on the glass, not me.

Most people treat the world like traffic. She treated it like air.

"I don't sell anything you want," she added, finally turning.

"I don't buy anything I can't carry."

"That why you travel light?"

"It's how I leave fast."

She didn't flinch at truth without decoration. "Good answer," she said, and the corner of her mouth conceded a smile that wasn't for effect.

We didn't trade names. We traded balance. When I left, the crowd pressed and parted around her the same way it had the first time. Some people choose where they stand; the world makes room.

Me and Cal cruised one night, windows down, Pepsi sweating in the cup holders. We didn't talk much, just watched our stretch for the kind of wrong that reads as right until it's too late.

"You feel that?" I asked.

"Feel what?"

"Pressure. Not tension. Pressure. Like the block's holding its breath."

He nodded. We hit four spots in under two hours. Looking fine on paper. Off in the body language. Listen long enough and you can hear a corner lie.

We parked in a quiet lot and I reshuffled the re-up rotation on a scrap of paper. Cal watched me work like he always did—silent, learning.

"Tension snaps," I said. "Pressure sinks."

Cal waited.

"Tension makes a man throw a punch to hear it stop. Pressure makes him shake your hand and hate you on credit."

He looked out across the dark lot. A porch light blinked three times, not a code, just a bulb dying the slow way.

"See that?" I said. "KP does bulbs like that on purpose. You walk in thinking you got eyes, then you don't. We change our approach on KP. No linger, no lean. Hit, check, out."

Cal folded the paper once, then again. "Noted."

"Also—Laurel's pretending to be smaller than it is. That means somebody's trying to hide growth under manners. Put ears there that don't smile."

"Copy."

He didn't praise the plan. He never did. He put it where it belonged: in tomorrow.

By the time we pulled back to the safe house, Barry was outside, arms folded against the brick.

Logan stepped off a bus that didn't belong to our story and made it listen anyway. No speeches. He set his bag down and fixed the back-door latch that stuck every third pull—one twist, one shim, done. "Can't have a man announcing himself to a door," he said, and the room chuckled before it realized it had relaxed.

I walked the floor, eyes counting pallets, corners, men's tells. "Your dolly's wobbling," he added, tapping the wheel I'd been ignoring. In an hour he had the staging tighter, the exits cleaner, the tempers lower. I didn't need to say lieutenant. The crew said it for me by listening before he finished a sentence.

"Take Ridge and Fifth," I told him. "Windows strict. No phones. If it bends, you call it."

He nodded once, still as a level. Some people brag. Logan repairs.

"All good?" I asked.

"As good as it can look," he said, rolling the words slow. "But something's coming."

"Gut?"

"Muscle memory."

He wasn't wrong.

C Shine and Big Abe pulled me to the back where the paint still smelled new and the chairs looked at each other like witnesses. Abe closed the door with two fingers.

"You running the board clean," Shine said, "but cleaning ain't the whole job."

"I know."

"A king needs counsel," he added, soft as if the wall might repeat him. "Not agreement. Counsel."

Abe set a knuckle on the table the way a mason sets a cornerstone. "We ain't here to like your choices. We here to keep you choosing."

I let that sit. Lot of men ask for support when what they want is flattery dressed up as loyalty. I don't buy costumes.

"Pressure's rising," I said.

Shine nodded. "Then lower the room. Not the ceiling. The room."

We were done. You can tell you're done when the air goes back to being air.

I got a call from a blocked number a few days later. Just "Two-thirty." Click. The kind of call that's more map than message. I told Cal to hold the line while I made the run.

I met the connect at a warehouse up north. Same faces, same silence. Things were shifting. "No more deliveries," the man said. "Only pickups. Limited crews. You're one of them."

"I'll bring one," I said. "Sean."

They packed the car in front of us—bricks wrapped and foamed, panels rebuilt like surgery. The craft was beautiful if you're the type that sees beauty in precision.

I watched the lie get dressed: adhesive that respects heat, foam cut on a bias so it swallows rattle, screw heads brushed with dust to match age. Even the panel clips clicked back in with the same tired confidence they were born with. That's the part civilians miss—sloppy lies invite curiosity; clean lies pass as maintenance. The distance between inspection and discovery is life expectancy.

I counted what could fail if a man got lazy—panel flex, foam memory, a shine where there should be dull, a headliner that forgets its crease. Men who love applause cut corners to hurry the clap. Men who love staying outside make the work quiet.

I watched the lie get dressed: adhesive that respects heat, foam cut on a bias so it swallows rattle, screw heads brushed with dust to match age. Even the panel clips clicked back in with the same tired confidence they were born with. That's the part civilians miss—sloppy lies invite curiosity; clean lies pass as maintenance. The distance between inspection and discovery is life expectancy.

I counted what could fail if a man got lazy—panel flex, foam memory, a shine where there should be dull, a headliner that forgets its crease. Men who love applause cut corners to hurry the clap. Men who love staying outside make the work quiet.

On the way back, three black Suburbans boxed us at a light. Sirens, guns, task force. I kept my hands where they wanted them and let the scene play out. Nothing in the car. Nothing in my pockets. I stay clean for exactly these reasons.

I put my hands where they practice looking first—high, slow, empty. You don't narrate moments like this; you breathe them. I watched four wrists and two muzzles, the angle of each shoulder telling me who'd been here before and who was new to the feeling of power. Rotor heat breathed through the wheel well and turned the air metallic.

"Driver, don't move," a voice said that belonged to the watch, not the badge. There's always a watch on scenes like this—the man who times panic to see if it spreads. Sean's breath got loud. I tapped the door with one fingertip—once. Stillness as instruction.

They split us clean: searchers, watchers, writer. The writer stands back and shapes the memory he'll put on paper later. I kept my eyes where they wanted them and answered only the parts of the law that have numbers. They were professional, but professionals get bored, and boredom reaches for theater. Theater is where men get hurt. I stayed out of their story and let them find the ending they brought with them.

Then they found the pills and bundles in Sean's backpack. Not my lane. My side hustle. It was enough to click cuffs and write headlines.

At the barracks, the COs tried to make conversation. I don't barter with chatter. "Lawyer," was the only word I gave them that hour.

Silence does the paperwork faster than talk. They searched for a temperature to set me at and found none. I counted the bolts on the bench, the scuffed spot under the camera bubble, the rhythm of the copier when the shift changed. You keep your breathing even so no one hears a story that isn't there.

They tossed us into a holding cell with two other men. I leaned in and whispered to Sean, "You didn't take that freebie, right?"

I hesitated. I knew before he said it.

"I just figured—"

"Flush it. Now."

I stood, walked too slow, and two ounces hit the floor right as the door opened. The other two were released. Me and Sean were processed. My lawyer had me out in hours. Sean took longer. When he came out, he was shaking.

Back at the spot, I said it plain: "It was Sean. Took the freebie and kept it quiet."

Barry cracked his knuckles. "Want me to handle it?"

"I already spoke on this once," I said. "Don't ask me again."

There's a kind of mercy that rots the floor under a house. You feel kinder in the moment and poorer by morning. I don't hand out that kind. I keep the rules heavy enough to hold the roof, light enough to carry.

A fiend is a fiend. I don't put babies in candy stores and expect them to keep their hands in their pockets.

We moved on. MMC cooked the new line back to something worth bagging. I pulled the table close and kept my voice where men listen.

"No side hustles inside our house. Free gifts get treated like fentanyl—no samples, no favors, no friends of friends. If your pockets feel lighter, you speak before it costs the room. If you take a thing, you name it. If you hide a thing, you're naming yourself."

Cal scanned faces; Barry folded his arms; MMC wiped his hands on a towel like he was washing a thought off.

"This isn't punishment," I said. "It's maintenance. We keep the floor strong enough to hold weight. Mercy that rots wood is still rot."

"Copy," Cal said.

MMC nodded once. "Feed first, then talk."

"Exactly. Our people eat. Allies eat. Everyone else pays the tax and waits their turn."

I let the quiet sit until it stopped being silence and started being agreement. Then I opened the map and we put tomorrow where it belonged. I fed our people first, then our allies—C Shine and Ock B. Everyone else paid the fifteen-percent reminder tax. Logan stood in the doorway while MMC salted like music. "Timer," Logan said, not a question.

MMC grinned. "I cook by feel."

"Feel's fine," Logan said. "Standard's better." He pointed once. "Three minutes off heat before you touch the tray. Seven before bagging. If steam chooses you, you didn't choose the work."

MMC laughed the way he always does when the room's good. "Man wants a regimen."

"I want tomorrow to look like today," Logan said.

The next batch moved like it had learned a language. Talent loves freedom; operations loves repetition. The trick is making repetition feel like proof. Even the whisperers at MLK and KP ate, because a full mouth tells more truth than a hungry one, and gratitude loosens lips. I put ears on both places anyway. I don't confuse charity with trust.

I sat with Cal at the table and tapped the map. "Find out who gave MMC the plug. Pay 'em to shut the fuck up."

"You want exclusivity?"

"Not full. Too greedy. Just enough to limit access. Let the rest get it stepped on and late."

I gave the quiet back to myself—no visitors, no detours, just the map and the math.

When the phone buzzed again, I let it go the first time and answered the second. My name has a way of traveling, even when I make it sit still.

Later, when I finally went home, I found myself up before sunrise. I ran the rectangle again, the same streets, the same turns. The city felt different but looked the same. That's how grief works—it leaves everything in place and removes what you can't name.

The next week I stepped into county. Not state. County. Short stint. Wrong place at the wrong time. Lawyer told me how many hours to expect and what not to say. I said less than that. Word traveled faster than I did. Ock B's name did most of the walking. I ate my tray alone, sat where I could see the door and the mirror. If anybody wanted it, they could test themselves. No one did.

Word did the walking I didn't. Ock B's name opened a space around me that smelled like bleach and old rules. A trustee tried to trade cigarettes for a future and I shook my head once—no sermon. A CO with a church tie asked if I knew a man he swore was his cousin. "No," I said, and let the conversation end where it was born.

County runs on boredom and rumor. Boredom makes men invent enemies; rumor gives them uniforms. I pressed my back to cinderblock and watched the two parade past each other until they forgot why they started marching. When the door finally buzzed, I stood like I'd just been sitting.

Bail came quick. I walked out with my silence intact. Cal pulled up, Maribel waited in her own car and didn't move until I was inside my building. She knew the new lock code without asking. I didn't remember giving it to her.

She'd been idling two blocks back, lights off, letting the street blink first. When I cracked the door, she held up a small brown bag like an answer. "Kitchen," she said. No parade, no pity.

Inside, she moved the way a person moves who respects walls— blinds set to slats, shoes by the door, jacket folded instead of thrown. She washed my hands without making it tender, scrubbed the cuffs where powder hides, and fed my shirt to the washer on sanitize with two taps, like a code I already knew.

"I'm here to make the noise smaller," she said, opening the bag. Sofrito and thyme hit the pan and turned the air into a room. "Eat first. Shower while it cools. If a phone rings, it isn't mine."

I watched the pattern: counters wiped in lanes, faucet run long enough to drown a story, windows cracked to let steam carry what it needed to carry. She didn't perform loyalty; she practiced it.

We ate at the counter. No speeches. She tasted the pot with the back of a spoon and handed me the same spoon like we'd known each other longer than we had. After the plates, she walked past me without asking permission she didn't need. In the bedroom, she undid the day with both hands—steady, certain—the kind of touch that keeps score in breathing, not words.

We found a rhythm that made quiet sound like proof. She didn't treat me like glass. She treated me like a man who could take being seen. When it was done, she stayed on me a beat longer, cheek to chest, listening the way a lookout listens to a block.

"If something knocks that isn't yours, you don't answer," she said into the dark. "I do."

"Why?"

"Because I asked to be here," she said. "That comes with a job."

I didn't sleep that night. I watched the ceiling and let time do what it does.

When time finished, I took back the hour it stole. Shoes on. Keys quiet. I walked one block like a question. Intercoms clicked for nobody, a stairwell light hummed itself tired, and the bodega cat watched the door for a ghost that wouldn't come.

The city looked the same and felt different, which is how you know you're still paying attention. I counted exits I already knew and listened for the sound that doesn't belong when morning thinks it's alone. A bike chain dragged once, a laugh cut off mid-breath, a window shade snapped back slow.

You don't claim a street. You confirm it still listens. When it did, I went home.

In the morning I called Do Dirty. In the evening I called nobody. When you've been hit enough times, you learn which calls heal and which ones bruise.

Third night, same car, same time. I caught her across the street under a bad bulb, hands in her coat, watching the room that happens outside. She didn't wave. The block waved around her.

"Room's quiet," she said when she came close enough for the sidewalk to catch it. "Keep it that way."

She left the air cleaner than she found it. Not a favor. A perimeter.

By the end of the month, the operation was cleaner than it had been. Hydration stabilized the block, gratitude kept the whispers soft, and my circle tightened one more notch. I moved a little quieter. Talked even less.

Maribel fit herself to the edges instead of the center. Groceries showed up when I pretended I didn't need them. A roll of quarters appeared the day the downstairs machines ate dollars. She swapped a burner out without ceremony when the battery gave up the ghost and slid the dead one into a bag with coffee grounds like she'd been doing it all her life.

When I came in late, the lights were already set to live-in, not watched. She left no wrappers, no receipts, no stories for the trash to tell. If I said I was tired, she said, "Shower first," and laid a towel across the back of a chair like an order disguised as care.

She didn't ask where I'd been. She asked what time I needed to be ready tomorrow.

I lay awake after she fell asleep. I stared at the ceiling and felt something I don't let myself feel often: the weight of being loved right.

I let it rest on me without letting it own me.

And in the morning, I was back to work.

Chapter 8

The drought wasn't coming. It was here.

Coke had vanished like ghosts in church. What was left on the streets was stepped-on powder that clung to bags like old perfume.

Crews were panicking. Reups were short. Arguments were erupting between lieutenants who used to finish each other's sentences.

I had seen dry spells before. This wasn't that. This was famine.

MMC slid through early afternoon.

I wore that usual smile, but this time it didn't match my eyes.

Cal was already at the spot—leaning against the counter, arms folded, listening like a statue that moved when necessary.

MMC didn't waste time. "Look... I heard something. Might be bullshit, might be a move."

I looked up. "Talk."

"Cousin of a cousin, out past Montclair. His peoples movin' weight in from Miami. Not bricks—but bulk. Quiet. No flashy movement. But it's moving. Supposed to be decent."

Cal raised an eyebrow. Ain't no one movin' right now."

MMC nodded. "Exactly. Which is why I think it's worth the look."

I stayed quiet. I had rules about chasing whispers. But when the city's starving, even echoes start sounding like answers.

"What's the setup?" I asked.

MMC shrugged. "Says just pull up. Let the product speak. I know how the drought got folks nervous."

I rubbed my jaw. "I'm going. Need a tester."

"You trust Marlon?" Cal asked.

"He's a user, yeah. Sniffs and smokes. But I ain't steered me wrong. I knows what he's tasting."

We hit the road that same day. I drove.

Cal stayed back to monitor things on the home front. Just me and Marlon now. He sat still, eyes shaded behind frames, hoodie low.

We didn't speak much, just scanned the road like every passing car was a question I already knew the answer to.

The building we pulled up to looked like somewhere stories went to die. Three floors, red brick stained with time, chain-link gate hanging loose like a busted seatbelt.

Outside, the muscle was real. No junkies. No loudmouths. Just tall men in silence—hoods up, hands in sleeves, watching everything like they'd memorized my plates an hour ago.

They walked up slow. No one nodded. That was the respect—they let you walk.

A man cracked the door before they could knock.

I stepped inside first. Marlon followed. The air inside was cold, still, and chemical-clean. No furniture but a couch, folding table, and a scale that looked like it hadn't rested in days.

Curtains drawn. Lights low. This wasn't a trap house—it was a transaction zone. Clean. Surgical.

A dude in his 30s leaned against the wall. Braids tight. Chain tucked. Eyes cold. He nodded to Marlon.

I said nothing.

Marlon got to work. Pulled out a blade, made a clean slice. Rubbed it. Checked the texture. One quick sniff. Then another. Sat back.

"Not garbage," he said. "Definitely stepped, but not sloppy. Got some legs on it. No headache."

I looked at the man. No emotion. "We'll talk numbers. But I don't do introductions twice. You short me, I ghost you."

The man smirked. "Respect." He held out a sealed zip—two ounces, bagged and ready. "On the house. Customary."

I raised a brow. "Keep it. Freebies are dangerous. Especially when you gotta make the ride."

Marlon said nothing. But when we turned to go, he slipped the sample in my hoodie pocket. Nobody noticed.

On the ride back, I was calm. Too calm. We'd scored. Not the best product in the world, but it was plentiful. Stable. Moveable. Enough to stabilize 8th to 14th and every block in the rectangle.

We stopped at a dusty shop off the highway. Bought a box of empty baggies—official-looking, zip-tops, no label. No one questioned it.

I didn't ride dirty. Never had. I prided myself on that. No gun. No coke. Just empty bags and clear conscience.

As we got back on the highway, my mind started working ahead. "I might hit up C Shine and Ock B. Let 'em know what I found. Move on it if they feel it. But only if they feel it. I'm not stamping nobody else's weight." I leaned back in the seat.

The road was open. I hit 110 mph, slicing between lanes like the car was reading my thoughts.

That's when it happened. A flatbed truck up ahead lost two stacks of sheetrock.

Boards came tumbling, slamming the ground, splitting—BOOM—white dust exploded into the air like flour bombs.

I swerved. Marlon shouted. I steadied the car.

Didn't think much of it—until the red and blues hit behind them.

Pulled over clean. I was respectful, but clipped. Let them search. Nothing in the car. Still, they weren't done.

"We'd like to take you down to the state barracks," the trooper said. "Just procedure. With that much powder flying, we need to be thorough." I nodded once.

At the barracks, we got placed in a holding cell. Two other dudes in there—drunks or unlucky traffic stops.

I sat down, leaned close to Marlon. "You ain't take that two, right?"

Marlon hesitated. "I just figured—just a little something. We ain't have nothing in the car."

I stared at him. "You brought it?"

Marlon slowly nodded. "Flush it. Now."

Marlon got up, walking fast to the toilet. Pulled the zip. Just as he got there—the door opened.

"Alright, gentlemen. If y'all want to go home, quick strip search and we're done."

The other two started undressing. I stood. Marlon froze. Then moved too slow.

When his pants dropped…two ounces hit the floor. The cell went silent.

The other two were released. Me and Marlon? We were headed to jail.

The booking process was short. But my silence was long. His lawyer had it handled in two hours.

I walked out untouched. Marlon followed later, quiet, pale, and shaking. I climbed into the passenger seat of my car like I was entering a courtroom.

Before the door even clicked shut, I spoke—cold, controlled: "You were supposed to test. Not think. Not touch. Not decide."

Marlon tried to explain. "I didn't mean—"

"Shut the fuck up."

A few beats passed. Marlon opened his mouth again.

I turned and gave me a look—just a look. And that was it. The rest of the ride was dead silent.

Back at the safe house, Cal and Barry were waiting. I entered, hoodie up, face blank.

"It was Marlon," I said simply. "Took the freebie. Didn't say shit until we were already inside."

Barry shifted his weight and cracked his knuckles. "You want me to handle it?"

I peeled off my hoodie and sat down. "Let him be."

Barry raised an eyebrow. "You sure?"

"A fiend is a fiend. Can't bring a baby to a candy store and expect them to keep their hands in their pockets."

I leaned back. "Lesson learned. We got a connect. We move on."

Barry nodded once, then walked out. Cal stayed behind, leaning against the wall. "So what's next?"

I exhaled slowly. "We hydrate our people. That starts tomorrow."

"With MMC?"

"Yeah," I said, nodding. "He's going to bring this shit back better than ever."

I walked over to the wall where a basic street map was thumbtacked—routes marked in red string, names scribbled beside intersections.

"Once we're good, we feed our allies. C Shine, Ock B—they eat first. They pay what we pay. No premium. Just parity."

"And everybody else?" Cal asked.

"15% tax," I said. "Still cheaper and better than anything else out here. And it reminds them—when the city ran dry, who fed them."

Cal nodded, but then asked cautiously:

"What about MLK and KP crews? Ain't they the same ones whisperin'?"

My stare cut over. "Exactly. That's why we feed them. You ever seen a man talk shit with a full plate in his lap?"

"I mean… some would," Cal said.

I shrugged. "Then I'll hear 'em better that way. Gratitude makes mouths loose."

He tapped the corner of the table, then pointed at the burner. "I want you to find out who gave MMC the drop on that connect. Quietly. Pay them to keep it shut."

"Think they'll talk?"

"Not if we respect the favor. But if this play leaks, it's useless. We lose the edge."

"You want exclusivity?"

"Not fully. That's expensive and greedy. I'll pay a little extra just to keep supply limited. Let the rest get it secondhand, stepped on, and late. The streets respect whoever eats first—especially if it tastes better."

Cal paused, then said: "You sure it's the right move to let all these people in?"

I didn't even turn my head. "You ever try to hold a starving dog outside the fence while you barbeque?"

"Nah."

"It barks until someone lets it in. Or it bites someone."

I turned, fully facing him now. "I'd rather let 'em chew than wait till they bite."

Cal didn't argue. My word was final—but it was more than that. I was watching a man think ten steps ahead while never moving my feet.

I sat down, leaned back, stared at the ceiling. I had it all mapped in my mind now.

Where the drought could shift weight. Where loyalty would snap like weak rope. Where opportunity meant control, not chaos.

This wasn't about getting back. This was about building forward.

But even with the plan in motion, something inside me stayed rigid. Proud. But cautious.

Inviting wolves to your table meant they might eat with you tonight…and try to eat you tomorrow. I thought about hyenas— starving, desperate ones.

Didn't matter how big the lion was.

Even a rhino could get rushed if the pack was hungry enough.

I would need more eyes. More ears. I'd feed them, but never sleep easy.

Then the burner lit up on the table.

A familiar number.

James.

The burner lit up, and I didn't even hesitate.

"There's the tech genius," CJ said, voice lighting up.

James didn't skip a beat. "Remember what hallway we slept in most?"

I closed my eyes remembering everything I hoped to forget. "Yeah."

"I'm there. See you soon."

Click.

I grabbed my keys and walked straight out—no words to anyone. Lincoln Arms was only a few blocks away. A low-rise apartment building, tucked just outside my rectangle of control. It used to be nothing. Now, it meant something.

I pulled up, parked, and walked the hallway slowly. James was already leaning against the wall when he got there.

We didn't say a word.

We hugged like brothers do when too much time's passed and too much shit's gone wrong. Firm. Long. Honest.

James spoke first. "Last time I saw you was Elliott's funeral."

I nodded, jaw clenched. "Yeah."

"I looked in the mirror this morning and realized… I don't even recognize the dreamer I used to be."

"You look like a machine," I said.

"That's what I am. I work with 'em all day. Figured I might as well become one."

We stood in silence again.

James broke it with a smirk. "You still got your license?"

I chuckled. "Full of fuckin' points… but valid."

"No, it ain't," James said. "It's only valid 'cause it's no longer full of points. Motherfucker, I cleared 96 over the past few years. You only get 12 before they take it."

I blinked. "Damn. I always wondered why I never got hit with those surcharges they said I would."

"You wanna know how else to never see them?"

"How?"

"Slow the fuck down," James said. "You don't gotta speed everywhere just 'cause you got fast cars. In your line of work, no attention is the best attention. Cut that dumb shit out."

I nodded, eyes lowered like a scolded son.

"I graduate next month," James said, voice light again. "Top of my class. Didn't even try. Shit is boring, but I like the field."

"You already got a job?"

I smirked. "You gonna be my parole officer now?"

"Something like that."

I leaned back against the wall. "I met someone."

James raised an eyebrow. "Oh? What's her name?"

"You know her name?"

I laughed. "She's different. I might keep her around."

James rolled his eyes. "That's called having a girlfriend. Please don't tell her you're gonna 'keep her around.' Women like being chosen, not claimed."

We laughed—really laughed—and for a moment, it felt like nothing had changed.

James dug into a paper bag and pulled out a single cupcake and a pineapple soda.

"Happy birthday, brother."

I froze.

"No one even told me today. I've been in the mix so much... I forgot it was my birthday."

"Well, I didn't," James said.

"I can't believe we made it to 21," I said.

James handed me the soda. "Well, *I* haven't yet. But you're elder even if I will never do what you say"

We laughed. "Yeah, yeah. For a few more months."

We stood there in the hallway, holding court like they used to—not because we couldn't go anywhere else, but because the hallway *felt* like before. Before the guns, the bids, the weight, the loss. Before shit got complicated.

James glanced at his watch.

"I gotta bounce," he said.

We hugged again, and it felt heavier this time—like maybe we wouldn't get another one.

As James turned the corner, he looked back and said, "That mess with Marlon? Gone by morning. And slow the fuck down."

I smirked. "I appreciate you, like seriously Jay."

James vanished.

And CJ stood there, holding a half-eaten cupcake and the best gift he'd gotten in years—time.

I didn't go home after Lincoln Arms. I drove straight to MMC's spot.

The chef was already deep in the work. The windows fogged from steam, a damp rag under the door, the room alive with bubbling pots and low murmurs. MMC moved like a ghost in a lab— surgical gloves, old-school apron, and a focus that bordered on spiritual possession.

"You came to witness resurrection because I know you don't want a sample?" MMC asked, grinning without turning around.

I cracked a rare smile. "I came to see if the dead can rise." We dapped, and I dropped the brick onto the counter.

MMC peeled it open and sniffed. "Mid-tier Miami gas. Shit ain't platinum, but I can make it dance."

I gave him a nod. "Make it sing."

What started as dusty, stepped-on powder became baller-grade within minutes. MMC added weight, not excuses. That's why I trusted him.

"You bringin' the drought to an end, my boy," MMC said, stacking bags like sacred scrolls. "You about to get statues put up."

I didn't respond. I was already thinking four steps ahead.

The next day, the hydration began.

I called Cal into the back room of the old record store I used for planning. Just dusty vinyl on the shelves, an old turntable humming in the background, and a map of the city pinned to the wall. The empire was real now. But I knew how quickly real shit gets challenged.

"Start with our people," I said. "Get them right. MMC already worked it back to god-tier."

Cal nodded. "You want me to hit KP and MLK too?"

I shook my head. "Not directly."

He tapped a spot on the map that overlapped both territories.

"Use Cool Todd."

Cal raised a brow. "Rod?"

"Yeah. That slick motherfucker got hands in both pots. Let me be the source. Runners will talk anyway, but the work'll come through me."

"You want him to know where it came from?"

My eyes narrowed. "Tell him to keep my name the fuck out his mouth. I'm not the messiah—I'm just the river. He gets the glory. I get the silence."

Cal nodded again, this time slower. "You trust him?"

"No. But I don't need to trust him. I need him to owe me. That's stronger than loyalty."

I watched as Cal scribbled the instructions into my burner.

"Oh," I added. "Tell Cool Todd if anyone asks I… I hit a plug upstate. Ain't no need to say more. Feed 'em enough truth to believe the lie."

By mid-afternoon, the streets started to breathe again.

KP heads that had been damn near starving were moving again. MLK runners who had been talking tough were suddenly generous. Dopeboys with nothing to offer three days ago were now treating their crews to Chinese food and Henny.

I didn't show face. I watched from distance—from rooftops, tinted cars, corner shadows.

"Who got the water?" someone asked.

"Cool Todd been blessed," another answered.

I smirked to myself in silence. Just how I liked it.

Later that night, Cal and Barry met up with me back at the storefront.

Barry sat back, counting money without flinching. "Rod said folks out in MLK asking questions. They want to know why me and not them."

"Let 'em," I said. "Hungry mouths bark louder than full ones. Rod got the leash now."

Cal leaned forward. "C Shine and Ock B?"

"Treat 'em like us," I said. "No tax. They eat same price we eat. They got earned equity."

"And the others?"

I folded my arms. "15% bump. Still cheaper than anywhere nearby. Fair is fair. But favor ain't free."

Barry asked, "You still want me to circle back on Marlon?"

I didn't even blink. "I believe I already spoke on this once. Don't ask me again."

Silence.

Cal cleared his throat and shifted.

"I want the source that gave MMC the plug tracked down," I said. "Quietly. We pay them to shut the fuck up and never tell another soul."

"And if someone tries to cut in?" Cal asked.

"We negotiate with the plug. Offer a higher price. Not for exclusive rights—that's too rich. But just enough for limited access. Anyone else gets it secondhand. And no one's touchin' what MMC brings back."

They both nodded.

I grabbed a marker and updated the map on the wall. "We're here now," I said. "14th and cutting deep."

Barry walked out first, leaving Cal and I alone.

"You know this won't last forever," Cal said. "Feeding hyenas only works till they remember they hungry again."

I stared at the map. "I know."

He leaned back in the chair, silence settling like dust in the air.

"That's why we need more eyes. These motherfuckers might smile when they full... but they'll still rip a lion apart if the meat runs dry."

He didn't flinch. Just kept staring at the map.

Power wasn't earned once. It was maintained daily. I knew the water was running again. But I also knew the drought made people desperate. And desperate men don't whisper—they bite.

That was the last thought before the lights dimmed, and the night reclaimed the streets.

Chapter 9

There was no warning, just a faint shift in the air. I felt it before anything happened. The way a dog knows a storm's coming before the clouds even think about forming. It started with a runner getting hit. Not robbed for cash—just checked, like a temperature gauge. Whoever did it didn't want money, they wanted to see how my crew would respond. That's what told me everything I needed to know.

I didn't flinch. That was the thing about me. I let the streets breathe while I studied their breath pattern. I moved quieter the louder they got. I wasn't afraid of noise—I was allergic to wasted energy.

Cal and I were parked off 11th, sipping Pepsi, the car off, eyes scanning a stretch of real estate we already owned. It was about presence. "Feel that?" I asked. Cal nodded. "That's pressure in the wind," I said. "It don't scream. It whispers."

"Maybe it's nothin'," Cal said, though even he didn't believe it.

I gave him a look. "Ain't no such thing. Everything means somethin'. Even if it's just that somebody's watchin' to see how we move."

I had already made up my mind. I needed new eyes. Not just lookouts—but lookouts for the lookouts. Eyes with eyes. Ones that didn't need orders to know what they were lookin' for. The kind that didn't flinch, didn't flub, didn't fold.

That's when I made the call to Do Dirty.

Do Dirty was blood—first cousin, same roots back in VA. They always called him Party because he stayed down for whatever.

Always smilin', always with a bottle in one hand and an inside joke in the other. But all that changed when he moved to Southwest Philly. I had heard the whispers. That Party wasn't just holding it down—he was holdin' court.

Do Dirty's crew controlled seven blocks of row homes and a network so airtight not even the smoke from a Newport got out without clearance. Discipline. Silence. Movement. I respected it.

When Do Dirty pulled up two days later, there was no fanfare. Just a matte black Lincoln Continental with no plates and two brake lights that glowed like evil eyes. I stepped out in a black hoodie, Locs on my face, and a calm that could make a cop question my authority.

I walked up and we embraced. "You good?" I asked.

Do Dirty smirked. "I stay good."

"You heard anything?"

"Enough to know your name's ringin' loud. And not just around here."

I nodded. "Then let's tighten this bitch up."

We drove the perimeter—Cal in the backseat, Do Dirty riding shotgun. I laid out the zones. Streets. Corners. Stores. I talked about the stash rotation, the new heads, the ones I trusted, and the ones I needed watched.

"No more assumptions," I said. "I want three levels of watch. People watchin' the spots, people watchin' the watchers, and someone to watch them all."

"I'm that someone," Do Dirty said, plain. "Your vision, my system."

I nodded once. That was it.

That night, the temperature dipped. Not the weather. The climate.

He lit a cigarette for show — he never smoked. Just liked the fire.

Pressure had a scent. And I could smell it.

This time, I wasn't going to wait for the war. I was going to see it comin', and I was going to write the obituary before the first shot rang.

They say lions don't hunt when they full. I wasn't full. I was starvin'. And now, I had Do Dirty.

The whisper game was over. I didn't speak at first. Just looked out the window, watching the edge of my world in silence.

Do Dirty sat across from me in the back room of Cal's place— sleeves rolled, energy still calm, but eyes sharp. "I got something," he finally said. "Not what you wanted. But it's what you needed to know."

I nodded once. "Talk to me."

Do Dirty slid a folded paper across the table. It wasn't a report. It was a fucking name.

"Cool Skip," Do Dirty said. "That's your leak."

I didn't flinch. Didn't blink.

Do Dirty went on. "You said that name used to ring out. Before juvie. Back when you and James were still learning the game."

I nodded again. "He looked out for us. Always had clean hands."

"Not anymore," Do Dirty said. "He's using. Heavy. Lost control years ago. But you gave me a job. Put me on a team. Because you thought maybe I could bounce back."

I stared at the name for a long time. "He's got a cousin."

"Yeah," Do Dirty said. "Barry's been fucking her."

That hit harder than a bullet. I sat back, exhaled slow, calculating everything. Barry. His own man. Not malicious. Just… stupid.

"He doesn't even know he's the leak," Do Dirty added. "She listens. Talks to Skip. He pieces shit together and runs his mouth trying to look like he still matters."

I leaned forward, elbows on knees, head bowed.

Cal stood in the corner, arms folded. "So what now?"

My voice was steel. "Now? We tighten up. Quietly. Nobody knows we know. But the circle shrinks."

Cal looked over at Do Dirty. "You trust him?"

He nodded. "With everything."

I stood up. Walked to the window. "Barry ain't malicious. Just soft. That's worse sometimes. Makes a man think I deserves access just because he's loyal. Like loyalty makes you smart."

Do Dirty cracked his knuckles. "Want me to put him down?"

I turned. "Nah. That's not the play. We correct him. We educate him. But make no mistake—we reposition his ass."

Barry walked in a few minutes later like nothing had happened. I gave him the rundown, calmly. No yelling. No threats.

When Barry offered, "Want me to take care of Skip?"

My face hardened. "I believe I already spoke on this once. Don't ask me again."

Barry froze, nodded, and walked out. The room was still.

Then I turned to Cal. "Hydration begins tomorrow."

Cal smirked. "You calling MMC?"

I nodded. "He's going to bring this shit back better than ever."

I outlined the plan: hydrate their team first, then quietly feed C Shine and Ock B's crews. No premium—they pay what I pay.

Everyone else? 15% tax. Still fair, still cheaper than anything close, and it reminded people who kept them eating.

I added, "Even MLK and KP crews. I don't care what they've been whispering. You feed a man, he'll tell you the truth with a grateful mouth. And if I doesn't—he'll show you something with his actions." Cal nodded.

"And the source of the intel MMC got on this connect—find out who they are. Pay them. Not for loyalty. For silence."

Do Dirty said, "You negotiating exclusivity?"

I nodded. "Not full distribution rights. Too much heat. Just a premium to limit access. Anyone who gets product from somewhere else? It's secondhand. Stepped on. Not MMC quality."

I stared out the window. "Feed the block. Starve the whispers. And watch who starves loudest when they can't get a plate next time." They all understood.

I looked out the windshield again, then finally spoke—more to myself than anyone.

"Too many hyenas get brave when they smell confusion. We tighten the chain. No explanations. Just pressure."

Cal nodded. "You want me to pull Barry in tomorrow?"

I shook my head. "Nah. He'll come to me. Always hit the infection where it lives."

They all nodded. And then the phone rang. I didn't flinch. Reached into my coat pocket and checked the screen.

Maribel.

I paused a long second. And then answered, voice low, eyes softer than they'd been all night.

"Hey."

Her voice came through warm. Real. No questions, no pressure—just presence.

"You home yet?" she asked.

I exhaled slowly. "Not yet."

"I made that chicken you said you liked," she said. "Figured maybe you'd come eat it hot."

I leaned back, closed my eyes for a moment. Everything around me was spiraling—my team, my trust, my rules. But her voice? Her offer? That was gravity. That was grounding.

"That sounds good," I said. "I'll be there soon."

She didn't press. Just smiled through the line. "Drive safe."

When the call ended, I looked out into the dark again. The streets didn't stop. The danger didn't stop. The strategy never slept. But for a few hours tonight, I just might.

I didn't knock. I didn't need to. The door was already cracked just enough to let the world know I was expected.

I stepped into Maribel's apartment like a soldier returning from the front line. I wasn't bleeding, but my silence told the story. She didn't greet me with questions, just a quiet nod and a Pepsi poured over ice, already sweating on the table. Dinner was on a warm plate, covered, waiting.

I sat, stared at it for a moment, then began eating in silence.

Maribel watched from the kitchen doorway for a while before walking over and placing her hand gently on my shoulder. "You don't gotta tell me a thing," she said. "But whatever you choose, choose it like you mean it. The real ones feel your moves before you make 'em."

I looked up, eyes heavy. "You solid as fuck. Don't think I don't see it."

She kissed the top of my head and walked away without another word. She didn't ask me to stay. Didn't ask where I'd go next. She just made sure the door stayed unlocked if I ever came back.

The meeting was set for the next evening—neutral ground. Concrete walls, steel table, folding chairs. Pudge. Cal. Do Dirty. Barry. All seated when I walked in.

I didn't speak at first. Just looked around the room like a judge scanning the jury. Calm, cold.

"We got a leak," I said.

Barry blinked. Cal sat forward. Do Dirty folded his arms. Pudge sipped from his soda and didn't flinch.

I continued. "Unintentional. But a leak's a leak. Skip's cousin been running her mouth to Skip. Skip's been running his mouth to the streets."

Barry's jaw tightened. "I ain't know—"

Do Dirty stood up so fast the chair screeched.

Cal followed. Pudge put his soda down and cracked his knuckles.

I held up one finger. They all sat down.

I walked slow toward Barry. No yelling, no threats. Just the truth.

"Delilah ain't need a blade to bring Samson down. She just waited 'til he was asleep. Wake up, motherfucker."

Barry swallowed. I didn't stop.

"This ain't betrayal. But it is weakness. And weakness ain't something I negotiate with."

"You out the inner circle. Welcome to the outer one. You work for the circle now. Not in it."

Barry tried to speak again. I gave him a single look, and every voice in the room turned to silence.

I turned to Do Dirty and nodded. "Let's go."

They found Skip leaning against the wall outside a check-cashing spot on Ridge Avenue. Frail. High. Wearing a smile like it still worked for him.

Do Dirty pulled up in a nondescript van. Cal stepped out first and grabbed Skip by the collar, dragging him inside.

I climbed in last, and sat across from the man who once looked out for me when I was just a teenager trying to figure out the weight of my own name.

"You had a code once," I said. "Back when we ain't even know what a code was. You was solid then. And I loved you for it."

Skip's mouth trembled. "Ceej, I ain't mean—"

"But now," I cut him off, "you background noise. You leaking over pussy and powder. That's not a fall from grace, that's a choice. I should kill you for it."

Skip dropped his head.

I stared for another moment. "I said 'should.' But I ain't. You get one pass. Use it wisely."

Do Dirty opened the door. They let Skip stumble out, bloody and limping. Message delivered.

Back at HQ, I stood over the table, eyeing the map. Blocks. Corners. Arrows. Names. Circles. Crossed-out territories. It was war, only no one called it that.

Cal walked in. "That's handled?"

I nodded. "That part is."

Cal stayed quiet.

Then, almost carefully, Cal said, "You still got Do Dirty, though. He's solid."

I looked up. "Of course I trust Do Dirty. But I got my own empire. Seven blocks. Row homes. An entire machine. I need someone who's embedded here—on the ground, in the mud, living this side of the game."

I looked back down at the map, eyes narrowing.

"Loyalty ain't about hugs and handshakes. It's about consequence. Barry was lucky. Most don't get that kind of grace."

Cal nodded.

I stepped back, hands behind my head. The room fell silent.

"You let the hyenas eat too long... even lions gotta sleep with one eye open. And when they eat? They get strong. A pack of full hyenas don't just hunt—they take over the whole fucking jungle."

The lights flickered slightly. The room felt colder.

I walked out without another word.

Chapter 10

I sat in the dark with no sound but my thoughts—and they weren't kind.

The betrayals didn't come from strangers. They never had.

The first real one came from Rich. Not the loud kind with guns or shouts. The quiet kind. The "I'm your brother" kind. The "let me eat first" kind. The kind that made you question yourself before you questioned them.

Then came the Mortons. Grimy bloodline, fake honor, and smiling eyes that waited until your back was turned. Different names. Same disease.

I gave them loyalty. Covered for them. Fed them. Let them breathe inside my operation like oxygen. And they exhaled poison.

It was never outsiders. Outsiders were easy. They knew the rules. They stayed at a distance, understood the line. But the ones you showed love to? Real love? Day-one loyalty? That's when the trouble came.

"A stranger never got close enough to cross me," I muttered, tightening the strap on my watch. "It's always the ones I let sit at the fucking table."

They'd miss the wolf I used to be. That version had patience. That version had principles. That version wanted peace. But the wolf was gone.

What stood now was something colder. Something permanent.

"The wolf gave warning," I said under my breath, stepping into my sneakers. "The monster don't."

I drove in silence. Not because I didn't have music—just no need. I wanted to hear the engine, the road, the way the tires hummed against the pavement. That was language too.

In the rearview, I spotted Cal trailing behind in a dark Impala. Not too close. Not too far. Just how he'd been trained.

I respected that.

I'd sent a short text: Barbershop. Ride behind me. Don't say shit unless I ask.

Simple. Cal was sharp. Grew up quiet, learned quick. Still green in certain ways, but I didn't flinch in pressure. That mattered now more than ever.

We parked down the block from Double G's. I stayed in the car a minute longer, watching through the windshield. The shop was lit up, full of noise. Laughter spilled into the street like smoke from a grill.

Cal slid into the passenger seat without invitation. "You want me to go in first?"

I shook my head. "Nah. You don't walk in before me anywhere."

Cal nodded, checked his mirror. "Anything I should be listening for?"

I looked over. "Only thing I need you listening for is hunger."

Cal blinked. "Hunger?"

My eyes stayed cold. "Yeah. Anybody out here acting too hungry when they should be full… or full when they should be starving. That tells you everything."

Inside the shop, it was exactly what I expected—chaos, cologne, clippers, and comedy. The three usual barbers were posted up, talking fast, cracking jokes, and moving razors like magicians.

G-Money looked up and grinned. "Well damn, the King himself. What's the word, CJ? Come to get trimmed or just hear the gospel?"

I smirked and dapped him up. "A little bit of both."

Cal stayed posted by the door, leaning like furniture.

Tone, the heavyset barber with no filter, pointed at Cal. "Aye, that your shadow? Boy look like he waiting to audition for The Wire."

Laughter erupted.

I chuckled. "He hears everything. Speak less."

"Well I hope he hear this," Tone said, "because I'm about to drop knowledge."

He pointed at the TV in the corner. A Knicks highlight reel was running.

"Let me tell you why the Knicks cursed. You trade a dude named Ewing? A man named Patrick? That's Irish and Catholic at the same damn time. You don't trade holy people."

The barbershop exploded. One of the old heads on the side bench slapped my knee so hard I dropped my soda.

I sat down in the back, hood still over my head, letting the noise wash over me. This was how you caught whispers—by not looking like you were trying to catch them. I tuned in without speaking. I heard everything:

- A story about a man from the KP Projects who got caught cheating and tried to escape through a third-floor bathroom window—naked.

- A debate about who was finer—Lisa Bonet in A Different World or Jada Pinkett in Low Down Dirty Shame.

- A kid claiming he saw LeBron at Freehold Mall, eating Chick-fil-A in full disguise.

But what I didn't hear?

Nothing from MLK. Nothing from KP. No whispers about drought. No fake flex about who had the plug now. No warning shots wrapped in gossip.

Nobody acting starving. Nobody acting too full.

That told me everything.

Cal showed up twenty minutes later, slipped in quiet and dapped him and leaned close. "Everything feel right to you?"

Cal nodded. "Tighter than a drum. Nobody's blinking."

I didn't respond right away. Then: "Good. Let's keep it that way."

As Cal went to get my cut, I leaned closer and whispered, "You think Barry ever finds his way back in?"

I didn't hesitate. "Fuck no."

Cal paused. "You think he knows that?"

I cracked my neck. "He will."

Cal waited, then asked, "So what's the plan?"

I exhaled through my nose. "I give it thirty days. Barry's going to get weak. Slide toward another crew. Desperate. I ain't got the patience to rebuild from scratch, so he'll try to flip position. What I want—what I need—is for anything I hears out there to be poison. Misinformation straight from our mouths to his ears. We write the script, he's dumb enough to follow."

Cal looked slightly stunned. "So you're going to...?"

I cut him off. "Yeah. We know what he'll move on. We know where the whisper came from. That means we know who dies first.

No guessing. No second shots."

I paused. "And if that sound like mercy… it ain't. That's calculation." I got my shape-up. The laughter rolled like thunder. The heat outside made the air inside feel sacred. I let myself enjoy it. Just a little. But I never stopped listening.

At one point, a barber pointed at Cal. "Yo, you seen that chick with the thick thighs working at the DMV?"

Another barber shouted, "He seen her thighs — he measured 'em!"

I smirked. Even the peace was familiar. But that's what made it dangerous. Peace had a scent. And this one smelled like setup.

As the last joke landed, I looked at Cal and said, "Everything feel tight?"

"Airtight," Cal replied.

I stood, checked my watch. "Time."

I walked outside, the heat slapping me in the face like a dare. The car started. I let the windows stay down, letting the air slap back.

KRS-One dropped in immediately: "So you think that hip-hop had its start out in the West? Nah. It started with the East…" I leaned back in the seat. My Philosophy. The soundtrack of a different era. A sharper era. I wasn't reminiscing, though. I was remembering who I'd always been.

As the beat rolled and the highway lights stretched out like veins under the dusk sky, I merged onto the turnpike. Destination: Newark Airport. No flight bags. No tickets. Just a time and a gate.

I wasn't flying anywhere. I was picking up death, and I was bringing it home with me.

The airport lights hit different when you're not traveling. I wasn't there for departures or arrivals. I was there to collect shadows.

Three of them.

No names. No bags. Just presence. Each one moved like they'd killed before and didn't need to prove it again.

I nodded once. The one with the tight eyes and slow blink climbed into my car without speaking. The other two peeled off—one into Cal's ride, one into the backseat of Do Dirty's truck.

No greetings. No orders. Just proximity.

I spoke low. "These ain't people to introduce. They're not here to chat when you bored. They stay far enough to observe, close enough to end something. If they can hear you, you talking too loud."

Cal gave a short nod from the mirror.

Across town, Cool Todd had everything quiet. MLK and KP were humming like tuned engines. No noise, no complaints.

Cal had been laying ground for a new alliance. Sean—a player from High Point—was solid. The complex I ran had two exits, a full view of the lot from a single corner, and enough runners to move product from Connecticut to Florida using backroads that took longer but stayed off the radar. No tolls, no plates, just movement.

It was a slow line—but damn near bulletproof. And that's what mattered now. I respected it.

"Long routes don't lose," I muttered.

They met in a quiet spot behind a closed laundromat.

Sean was lean, clean, and didn't smile much. That was perfect. I explained my network—drop-offs at mechanic shops, pickup crews disguised as landscaping trucks, stashes in vacuum cleaner boxes and old boombox shells.

Cal nodded. I just listened.

"We don't move weight," I finally said. "We move peace of mind." The partnership was sealed in silence.

Later that afternoon, I watched a familiar car roll up near 8th Street. Maribel.

I tensed instantly. She stepped out in tight jeans and a flowing top —smile on her face like nothing in the world was dangerous. I moved quick.

"Get in," I said, popping the door on my blacked-out ride. My personal shadow stepped out the moment she got in. She looked surprised. I leaned toward her.

"Things a little hot right now. I can't afford to hurt anybody that looks at you twice."

She raised an eyebrow. "That supposed to be sweet or scary?" I smirked, reached into my other pocket. Pulled out a fold of cash. "Grab something for us to eat. I'll meet you there soon."

She stared at the money, then at me. "Put that away," she said, serious now. "Don't ever put me in the view of needing that shit. Not when I got the man, and I ain't even made it back yet."

She opened the door. "I'm cooking." He blinked.

She paused, turned back, and held up my keys. "I got it." I watched her walk off, hips confident, keys flashing in her fingers like victory.

I smirked—but it wasn't my usual cold grin. That woman made me feel something. Something I didn't have a word for.

Night fell. I walked into my place and found the lights low, the scent of garlic and spice in the air. Her heels were by the door, music low in the background—some soft Spanish guitar and drums.

She was in the kitchen, barefoot, humming. I stood still for a second, just watching her.

"You hungry or just going to stare?" she asked, smiling without turning around.

"I'm both."

She walked over and looked at me for a long time. "What you did today," she said softly, "grabbing me like that, caring like that… it cracked something inside me."

I looked down. "I care about keeping things calm."

She stepped closer. "No. You care about me. You won't say it, but I see it."

I opened my mouth, but she touched my lips. "If you was going to make me your girlfriend," she said with a smirk, "you coulda just said so."

I exhaled. Then she undressed. Not playfully. Not slowly. Deliberately.

Top. Bra. Shorts. Panties. All on the floor. All at once.

Her eyes didn't leave mine. Her body wasn't perfect—but it was real. Curvy. Soft in the right places. Sharp where it counted.

She walked to me, grabbed my shirt and pulled it up. I let her. The couch caught us first.

She pushed me back, climbed onto my lap, her thighs pinning me down like velvet steel. She kissed me deep, then bit my lip and whispered, "You still trying to act like you ain't mine?"

I didn't answer. She pulled me out, wrapped herself around me without warning, and rode me until I growled. "Fuck," I muttered, gripping her hips hard enough to bruise.

"Say it," she hissed. "Say who owns this moment."

I flipped her without warning—face down, cheek against the armrest. Entered her again, this time slower, deeper, with a hunger I hadn't ever admitted to having.

I whispered in Spanish—words I didn't even know I knew. She came hard, back arched, teeth clenched.

We barely made it to the bedroom. There, I took my time.

I went down on her like I was searching for revenge. She pulled my head harder, moaning, gasping, then laughed and whispered, "Now I taste us."

That line broke me. I flipped her, kissed her, fucked her like the world outside didn't exist.

We moved from bed to wall to hallway—leaving clothes, sweat, and scratches behind.

She marked me with nails. I left bite marks on her collarbone. No performance. No script. Just need.

Later, she lay on top of me, heavy breathing slowing, cheek pressed to my chest. Her arm draped across my stomach, fingers twitching in sleep. I didn't move. Didn't twitch. Didn't reach for water or the blanket or my phone. I just held her there.

Still. Perfect. And that's when it hit me. Not thought. Not theory. Not maybe. I was in love. And I loved the feeling, but it scared me to death.

I was up before the sun. Maribel still lay across me, breathing slow, one leg tangled in the sheets, her fingers half-curled against my chest. I eased her arm off gently and moved slow. Didn't want to wake her—not because I couldn't handle the conversation, but because peace like this was too rare to disturb.

I got dressed in silence, grabbed keys, and left without breakfast. My morning ritual wasn't new. I ran my rectangle like a king patrolling the outer walls—8th to 14th Street, clean turns, slow rolls, no music.

This time I added one more stop: a lazy pass by High Point.

Sean's crew moved like clockwork. A new drop truck, white with a landscaping decal, was loading up without anyone breaking pace. No yelling. No urgency.

Even the Laurel Ave crew had stopped posturing. The Lynn brothers on Kennedy weren't barking either.

I didn't trust peace. It moved too much like a setup. But the money was flowing.

Weeks passed like water: smooth, quiet, profitable. The call came on a Thursday. Blocked number. I answered.

"Two-thirty." Click.

No pleasantries. No need. That was the call.

I told Cal, "Hold things down. Leave my shadow on post." Then I rolled solo.

——

The warehouse up north was colder this time. Same faces. Same silence.

The connect didn't waste words. "It's hot. No more deliveries. Only pickups. Limited crew. You're one of 'em."

I nodded.

"Bring one," the man added. "No teams. One."

"I'll bring Sean."

The room buzzed with quiet approval.

They packed the car in front of them. Tore it apart. Bricks got wrapped, foamed, sealed, slid into molded panels. The dashboard was practically rebuilt before my eyes.

Sean was watching like it was magic. "Damn," he muttered. "They pack like surgeons."

I didn't even look at him. "Shut the fuck up and pay attention."

Sean also accepted a separate backpack—pills and bundles. Not my lane. But Sean handled it like a side order.

I didn't trip. I was focused on the return. They were twenty minutes from home when hell opened.

Three black Suburbans boxed them in at a red light. Sirens lit up. Doors swung open. Badges flashed. Guns out.

Task force. Three counties deep."Out the car! Hands where we can see 'em!" I didn't blink.

"This ain't heat," I muttered. "This is a fucking setup." But no one had known. Not even whispers.

They ripped the car apart again. Every bolt. Every panel. Nothing. But then they hit Sean's backpack.

Inside: prescription pills, unlabeled. Two bundles of dope. Loose. Enough to charge.

They cuffed us both. At county, I said the one thing I always said: "Don't waste your breath. Lawyer."

My rep meant my lawyer was there within the hour. Bail hearing would be in a few days. No big deal. No priors, nothing found in the car. I was clean.

Sean? Not so much. But I didn't worry. Until I did.

The lawyer returned with a strange look. "You're not being released."

I stood still. "Why."

"Your co-defendant. He's talking." I didn't flinch.

The lawyer sat down. "He gave them everything. Said he's got kids. A wife. He didn't sign up for this. Told them how the car was packed. Even guessed at your stash spot."

I looked past the lawyer. Not angry. Just... cold.

"He didn't even wait," the lawyer said. "Could've let me speak for him."

They tried to re-cuff me quietly.It didn't matter. In my mind, the outcome was already decided.

"Weak men always talk," I thought. "They don't betray to win. They betray to breathe."

The holding cell smelled like rust and sweat. Unlike juvie, I had no allies here. I sat on the edge of the bench, hands loose, back straight.

Fourteen men. All of them watching me. Word had spread. I was in county. No lawyer. No guards. No Cal. No Maribel. No Do Dirty. Just me and whatever came next.

I recognized none of them—but they knew me. Or thought they did. "That's him," one whispered. "East side boss."

"Got shooters in Philly and VA." I ignored it. I mapped the cell like a battlefield.

Two cameras. One guard station, 50 feet out. Three men watching too long. One kept smiling.

I had seen it before. That wasn't friendliness. A smile in here meant something had already been decided.

I leaned back. Let them watch. They were thinking: if they get me now, before bail, before I walk, they become legends. I let them think.

When chow came, I stood first. Tray in hand. Balanced. Quiet.

The three men shifted. I stepped toward them. "If y'all gon' do it, do it now."

I paused. Looked each one in the eye. "Just know… one of you not going home tonight."

They didn't move. They weren't cowards. They were just smart enough to understand what wolves smell like.

I didn't bluff. He never had. I sat down and waited for morning.

County was its own animal. And I had never been caged in it before.

But even behind bars, real power leaked. And out there, I fed enough wolves to be remembered—even by those who didn't eat directly from my hand.

Everyone inside seemed to know better. Except the ones who didn't.

The Laurel Ave crew didn't. They came in loud—half-rumor, half-resentment. Their mouths moved faster than their minds. They didn't get the memo.

The Kennedy Blvd clique did.

Before I was fully processed, Divine had already moved.

Light-skinned, slim, face like an R&B singer—but deadly from birth. Divine had once stabbed a man twice in the same lung just to hear the difference in his screams.

I saw my name on the docket and moved fast—aligned my entire pod with my presence and spread the word. Loud, early, surgical.

"That man? Off-limits. That man? Protected. That man? One of us now."

The Blvd was twice as deep as Laurel Ave in county. Their numbers alone made the air shift.

And before Laurel Ave could even whisper about checking me, a message came through: "Any action taken against CJ will be viewed as personal disrespect to Ock B."

That was enough. Because Ock B's word wasn't a threat. It was a prophecy.

His people weren't just in county. They were in state. In fed. In jail transport. In booking. In laundry.

Crossing me meant bodies dropped—from your newborn niece to your grandmother during a church prayer.

Ock B didn't retaliate. He erased. And he made it loud enough the streets could still hear it a year later.

The Laurel Ave boys went quiet after that. I moved with calm.

I recognized faces—old runners, minor crew heads, a few that once dapped me up at block parties. None I trusted. None worth remembering. I wasn't silent, though.

I spoke with the ones who kept their heads down. Men humbled by the system, not hardened. I never moved like a god. I was always down to earth.

But inside? I was building mental blueprints. Because bail was coming. And the moment I walked out, the war restarted.

The hearing came. The judge tried to posture, but my lawyer carved through it quick. No priors. No direct evidence. Nothing but association and panic.

I walked free by noon.

Outside my building, Maribel waited in her car. Engine off. Window down. Calm.

Cal met her at the door. Took her old key. Changed the lock without a word.

Maribel didn't ask questions. She just looked at Cal and said, "He good?"

Cal nodded. She stayed parked. She knew he'd come.

Inside, I didn't sit long. Sean's crew was dismantled within forty-eight hours.

His transportation routes were rerouted or wiped. His allies? Gone or converted.

Sean himself was marked—but how I would go out was still under debate.

I brought together Do Dirty, Cal, C Shine, and Big Abe—blood family, and the only loyalty left untouched.

The roundtable was quiet. Strategic.

Do Dirty didn't blink. "We make his bitch watch. His kids cry. And then we let him live to see it. Just for a while."

Cal kept it steady. "He gotta go. That ain't up for debate. But you burn a family, sometimes it gets messy."

Big Abe added, "We touch the wrong person, it'll scream louder than it lands."

C Shine nodded. "If you really want him to suffer… don't kill him. Starve him. Ruin his name. Make his kids grow up on the same corners he tried to avoid. Make them curse his name."

The room got still. I leaned back. I didn't raise my voice. Didn't tap the table. Didn't ask permission.

I just looked at Do Dirty, and he stood up.

It was done. I walked out. Because in that circle, once a decision was made, it didn't get unmade.

Indecision killed men faster than bad intel ever did.

I got home that night. Maribel was barefoot on the couch. I sat next to her. The silence between us wasn't awkward—it was heavy.

"I might have to do time," I said. "If this don't shake right, now would be the time to run."

She didn't blink. She leaned in, kissed me once on the cheek, and whispered: "I don't even fucking jog, baby."

I smiled. For the first time since county.

And somewhere across town… Sean's mother found her car stripped and her rent overdue.

His daughter got sent home from school for the third time in a week—no lunch, no ride, no homework.

His son got beat up for saying my daddy used to run things.

Sean got the message loud. Because I wasn't rushing his death. I was composing it.

Every ripple. Every consequence. Every drop of misery.

By the time Sean hoped for mercy at Do Dirty's hand, there had already been seven funerals—with Sean's being last and most humiliating.

His death wasn't quick. It wasn't clean. It was slow, intentional, and unforgettable.

Word spread across every county and crew: Since Sean wanted to be a bitch, he was treated like one—gang raped by men Do Dirty had on tap, his ass left as wide as his mouth.

And just like that, I wasn't just the monster. I was the silence.

The stories in the movies never painted war right. They added music. Cut to black. Gave villains backstories and heroes redemption.

But out here? Out here there were no directors. No edits. No second takes. Only decisions. Only pain. Only consequences.

And when Do Dirty delivered that final act—when Sean's body was dumped like a warning too explicit for news coverage—the streets didn't just talk. They wrote myth.

Months passed. Crews shifted. Corners bled. Babies were born. Mamas cried. But under it all... I waited.

I wasn't waiting for court because I feared prison. I waited because discovery was the only place where truth had to be printed.

No more rumors. No more whispers. No more "I heard—" Paperwork didn't lie.

Names had to be listed. Tapes had to be logged. Moves had to be explained. Fake gangsters rapped about that shit.

I read it. Because I didn't want to just beat the case. I wanted to know every snitch, every cop, every conversation that dared circle my name.

Most men fold with a pretty plea deal. Most walk out and let the leaks keep dripping. Me? I was willing to risk it all in trial—just to know.

Because winning the case was freedom. But knowing the full truth? That was power.

That's where we begin.

Chapter 11

Courtrooms pretend they run on law. They really run on choreography. You learn the steps the way you learn a block— where the security wand lingers when a man's heart is too fast, what kind of cough makes a judge look over glasses, when the stenographer stops typing because the truth got shy. The gallery is a weather report: relatives make storms, girlfriends make fog, quiet men make wind.

I sat where I could see the clock without seeing myself in anyone's eyes. The DA smiled like a man who thought he'd already convinced the room; the bailiff didn't smile at all, which is how you know he'd seen too many endings. Even the benches creaked their opinion. Rules help when the room respects them. When it doesn't, you need reading, not volume. I read

I never flinched.

The charges were heavy—conspiracy, trafficking, kingpin status— but I moved like a man accused of nothing at all. There was no fear in my eyes, no twitch in my jaw, no wasted energy. Just the quiet command of a man who knew the system and never trusted it. You didn't make it this far in the game thinking truth alone would set you free.

The streets were still breathing. And me? I was still conducting the orchestra, even with a courtroom in my future.

Cal stood in the living room going over the latest numbers. His growth had been undeniable—once a soldier, now a shadow general. I had groomed me for this moment over the past year: how to read moves before they were made, how to speak less and learn more, how to run an empire without ever needing to raise your voice.

"Money's still coming in clean," Cal said. "Barry's keeping the drop-offs tight. MMC's cookin' like I got angels in my gloves. Ain't nobody hungry."

I nodded. "That's how it's supposed to be."

Do Dirty had relocated two months earlier—on paper, it was temporary. In practice, it was wartime positioning. His own lieutenants still controlled the Southwest Philly blocks, but Do Dirty was here now. Eyes, muscle, and history—nothing I valued more. I didn't say much, just leaned against the wall behind Cal, arms folded, watching.

"You get a read on the MLK crew?" I asked, without looking up.

"They still whisperin'. But Cool Todd got the weight now. Told me keep your name out his mouth. He understood."

"He better." I didn't care about noise—I cared about motive. The drought had passed, and my grip on the region hadn't loosened. If anything, it was stronger now. Not because I flooded the streets. But because when the streets were dry, I fed the hungry without ever showing my face. Silence had power. It forced them to guess. And guessing made them nervous.

Every move was calculated. Every call was layered. The phones weren't traced, but the language had changed. People didn't ask questions anymore—they waited for instructions. I had created a kingdom built on discipline. When discipline disappeared, so did you.

The case against me had all the usual fingerprints: junk science, doctored surveillance, and snitches with names redacted so many times the transcripts read like riddles. But it was the discovery process that mattered now. I sat with my lawyer three days a week reviewing every file, every timestamp, every so-called "confession."

Sean had been under surveillance for months—paranoid, reckless, doing side deals with loose ends. He was sloppy. And he was the weak link that the feds had tried to weaponize. But their timeline had holes. The evidence wasn't clean. The government had tried to force the puzzle together, but the edges didn't match.

My legal strategy was surgical. Expose every misstep. Destroy credibility without theatrics. Weaponize precision. My attorney, a bulldog with clean suits and sharp instincts, respected one thing above all else: He never lied to me.

"You're not a saint," he once told me. "But they're painting you like Satan."

I just smiled. "Let 'em. Even the devil gets an appeal." Behind the smirk, though, I was clocking everything. How the arrest report didn't match the video footage. How the timestamps on two phone calls were exactly the same—down to the second. How a signed statement came from someone who was, at the time, dead.

These were not mistakes. These were fingerprints of desperation. The kind of thing desperate prosecutors created when they needed a win and had nothing clean to stand on.

The trial was days away. The air around me was tightening. But I didn't break routine. I still ran every morning at 5 AM, silence in my headphones. I still stopped by MMC's kitchen every Wednesday, just to nod and taste a grain of uncut powder. I still took meetings at the pool hall off Bangs Avenue, where the lights flickered and the eight-ball never sat right.

I still saw Maribel. We didn't speak about the trial. We didn't speak about much, honestly. But when we were together, the world fell quiet. I watched her move around the kitchen like she had all the time in the world. I liked that about her. She never rushed. She never panicked.

That night, she made rice and beans, slow-roasted chicken, and mango juice from scratch. I didn't say thank you. She didn't expect it. We both understood that gratitude lived in presence.

When she placed the plate in front of me, I reached for her hand and squeezed once. She squeezed back. No words.

Do Dirty stayed at the apartment two doors down. Always close, never intrusive. I rotated my lieutenants every 48 hours, made sure no one knew my exact pattern.

When she asked if I trusted them, Do Dirty just grinned. "They loyal enough to die," he said. "But they know he'd kill 'em first."

I respected that.

Back inside, I spread paperwork across the dining table. Surveillance screenshots. Traffic stops. Snitch statements that contradicted themselves in four different fonts. Cal leaned over one shoulder. Do Dirty over the other.

I circled a name. Then another. Then one more.

"Witnesses?" Do Dirty asked.

I shook my head. "They won't show their names on paper. Nobody with a spine signs it."

Cal pointed at one line of blurred transcript. "What about this part?"

I stared at it. "That's Sean. Talking like I ran shit. They'll try to use it. But he's dead. And the only thing louder than a lie is a body that can't confirm it."

The room went quiet. Then Cal spoke. "What happens if it goes left?"

I didn't blink. "You lead."

Cal straightened up. "You know I will."

"I do. That's why I'm sayin' it out loud."

Do Dirty broke the silence. "You sure about this lawyer?"

I leaned back in my chair. "He ain't the best. But he knows how to lose small to win big."

Do Dirty nodded once. That was enough.

I turned back to the files, my voice low but unshaken. "Don't panic. Don't pivot. Hold."

Courtrooms were built for control.

Every echo. Every robe. Every pause before a verdict. It was theater wrapped in concrete and ego. I understood the stage, but I wasn't here for a performance. I was here to measure the system's reach. To see if its hands were long enough to pull me under.

I sat motionless as the judge entered. My lawyer stood with measured calm. In the gallery sat ghosts from my life— my mother, spine straight and eyes rimmed with quiet fire. My sisters, still as statues. And Grim, arms folded, watching everything like a wolf daring someone to make a wrong move.

Do Dirty and Cal sat in the back row, separate from the family. Cal wore his usual all-black. Do Dirty looked like muscle dressed in thought.

The prosecution came in hot. "This man operated an empire," the lead prosecutor declared. "A kingdom of silence. But we've pierced that silence with proof. We have the video. We have the audio. And we have the names."

The jury didn't look at me—they looked at the screen being wheeled forward.

The first exhibit: video surveillance.

The prosecution cued it up confidently, fingers clicking across the keyboard. The room dimmed. The judge leaned forward slightly. I didn't move.

The screen flickered once. Then again. And then…

☐ "I'll house you… You in my hut now…" The opening of the Jungle Brothers' "I'll House You" blared across the courtroom. A perfect loop. No faces. No transactions. Just a blank black screen and that infectious bassline thumping like it was 1988 all over again.

The prosecutor froze. He tapped the spacebar. The track continued. He fast-forwarded. Rewound. Nothing changed.

No matter where he jumped, it was the same loop. The Jungle Brothers. Over and over.

He muttered something to the clerk. They unplugged and reloaded. New flash drive. Same result.

☐ "I'll house you… You in my hut now…"

The judge raised an eyebrow. "Is this supposed to be surveillance footage, counselor?"

"Yes, Your Honor. We're—this is… This isn't the file we submitted."

I sat still, but inside, a switch flipped. Because I knew that loop. Not just the song. The looped section.

It was James's favorite track growing up. His anthem when they were teenagers. Back when I swore he'd be a rapper, back before the street swallowed them whole.

The courtroom waited. The judge leaned forward again. The prosecutor straightened his tie and tried to recover.

"Your Honor," he said, "we will now submit audio surveillance, collected via wiretaps over the course of several months. Hundreds of hours of conversation. This is our clearest evidence of intent."

He nodded to the tech. This time, a different file loaded. Different timestamp. Different source.

The room went silent.

□ "Educated man from the motherland…" A new track played. Not "I'll House You". This was deeper. More raw.

"Straight Out the Jungle." The Jungle Brothers again. And once again, nothing but the music.

But it wasn't just the song—it was one specific line, looped with surgical precision:

"Educated man from the motherland. Some people call me a star, but that's not what I am. I'm a Jungle Brother, a true blue brother. And I've been to many places you'll never discover."

The courtroom froze. The jury stared blankly. The judge squinted at the screen. The prosecutor walked to the bench.

"We—Your Honor, this was not what we submitted. This file was cleared. We've confirmed chain-of-custody logs—"

The judge cut me off. "You're telling me every audio file—every hour of wiretaps—now plays the same song?"

The tech clicked again. Another file. Same loop.

Another. Same loop.

No voices. No dealers. No strategy. No codes. Just James King's favorite quote, layered inside the Jungle Brothers' anthem. Over and over. On every track.

James didn't walk in. He never does when a room thinks it's the main character. But the building felt him—just enough. The evidence cart paused; a screen froze on a buffering wheel no one in the first three rows understood. The clerk frowned at a form that suddenly needed a second signature it should've had already.

Nothing dramatic. Just five small delays that made two big assumptions bump into each other: chain of custody, and chain of confidence. The DA's smile tightened half a tooth. The judge adjusted glasses without looking anyone in the face.

I didn't move. James doesn't send messages; he adjusts margins. When a room tries to rush you, the right margin gives you back your breath.

And me? Still didn't blink. I didn't need to. Because at that exact moment, I understood what had happened. James had intervened. Without showing his face. Without calling in a favor. Without leaving a fingerprint.

This wasn't a glitch. This was a message. That no matter how far things went... no matter how high the charges stacked... James would always be there.

Not with words. Not with presence. But with action.

There would never be a time that I got hit and James didn't fire back from the shadows. And me? I'd burn the world down twice for him.

The judge dropped the gavel. "Court is in recess. Effective immediately. All surveillance files are to be reviewed by third-party forensic teams. This court will not move forward with corrupted evidence, no matter how many hours were logged."

I stood calmly. As I turned to exit, I saw them—his family. My mother. My sisters. Grim. None of them cried. None of them smiled. But their eyes never left me.

That was all I needed.

Outside, Cal pulled the car up. Do Dirty was already on the phone, speaking low.

Inside the ride, ten blocks passed in silence.

Cal finally spoke. "What the hell just happened in there?"

I looked out the window. "James happened."

Cal glanced at me through the rearview. "He looped a track into federal evidence?"

I shook my head. "He looped us into it. Nobody else could've done that."

Do Dirty asked, "They going to refile?"

"They'll try. All that's left is the accessory charge. Lawyer says I turn myself in next week. 18 months, maybe less."

Cal nodded. "That's better than life."

I leaned my head back. "That's better than them thinking they won."

No one said a word after that. But I kept hearing it, over and over, like it was stitched into the air:

"I'm a Jungle Brother, a true blue brother… And I've been to many places you'll never discover."

The night before I turned myself in, there was no sendoff. No drinks. No toasts. No goodbyes.

I didn't answer the phone. Didn't check the corner. Didn't brief the team. I drove to Maribel's.

The house smelled like garlic and rain. She had candles lit—not for romance, but because that's what she did when the world felt unsteady. I stood in the doorway, soaked in silence, watching her from across the kitchen as she stirred a pot she didn't plan to serve.

She turned and saw me. No smile. No words.

She simply walked over, placed her palm on my chest, and left it there for a full minute. Like she was checking if I still had a heartbeat. If the man in front of her was still flesh and not marble.

"You hungry?" she asked softly.

I shook my head.

She nodded once, turned off the stove, and walked to the bathroom. I heard the water start. The steam rising. The night pulling itself tighter. I followed her without a word.

The bedroom was candlelit, windows cracked just enough to let the storm-slicked air creep in. Maribel stepped out of her clothes like she was shedding everything false. Skin smooth and golden, curves made by god and grit. Her breasts were full and natural, the areolas a perfect brown, but the nipples carried a faint pink that made me pause. They looked like warm secrets, exposed only to those who'd earned the right.

She climbed onto the bed and waited. I undressed in silence. Laid beside her. And for the first time in years, I didn't take. I gave.

My hands moved with reverence, not possession. I kissed every inch of her, slow and deliberate. She gasped when I sucked her nipples—soft moans escaping in Spanish, like her body had its own dialect for being touched like this.

"Dios mío…"

"Así, así, mi amor…"

"No pares…"

They weren't dirty words. They were sacred.

She arched for me, her hands tangled in my hair. I took my time working my mouth down between her thighs, breathing her in like oxygen. When my tongue met her, she nearly cried out—but instead grabbed my shoulders and whispered through clenched teeth—

"You're mine tonight. You fucking understand me? You're mine."

I looked up, eyes locked with hers, and nodded once before sliding inside her.

And from there, everything else burned away. There was nothing soft about it now.

She rode me with fury, hips snapping, thighs clenched tight around my waist. Her Spanish returned, more urgent this time—"Maldito, no te atrevas a parar… hijo de puta, dame todo…"

I grabbed her ass, flipped her over, and took control again— driving into her with full-body precision, the way I used to work corners: no rush, no waste, all power.

She scratched my back. I bit her shoulder. Our sweat soaked the sheets. She screamed my name, then sobbed it. I said nothing— only grunted low like a man trying not to give myself away.

Her climax hit hard, legs trembling as she cursed and cried into the pillow. I didn't stop.Not until I knew she had nothing left to give.

Not until I was emptied inside her and the storm outside matched the one they just survived.

After, she lay on my chest, her breath shaky, her body slack. One arm across me like she was holding on to something more than a man.

I stared at the ceiling. And only then—when I was sure she was asleep—I whispered it.

"I love you too."

I didn't say it to her face. Not because it wasn't true—but because truth came with gravity. With consequence. And what she deserved wasn't promises… it was proof.

I watched her sleep for another hour before easing out of bed. I walked to the bathroom, splashed cold water on my face, and stared at the man in the mirror.

Still standing. Still silent. Still my own.

When I came back into the room, Maribel was awake, sitting on the edge of the bed.

In her hand was her birth control pack. She looked at me. Then at the trash can. She dropped it in without a word.

I didn't move. Didn't ask. Didn't react. Because I knew what that meant. She wasn't begging for a child. She was declaring a future. A seed planted in the dark, with or without me.

And me? I wanted it. I never said that out loud, but I wanted it.

Not because I needed a baby to feel whole—but because this was the first time in years I'd felt worthy of creating something, not just destroying it.

She stood, kissed my chest, and held my face in both hands. "You walk in that prison a man," she whispered. "You walk out a legend. But don't forget who you were before either."

I nodded. We made love again. Slower. Deeper. No talking. Just soul.

Her tears didn't fall until after. She didn't sob. Just wept quietly, her cheek pressed against my chest while my hand rested on her lower back like an oath made in silence.

When dawn came, I dressed without sound. She made coffee. Poured one cup. I didn't drink it.

At the door, I looked back at her. "You gon' be alright?" I asked.

Maribel nodded. "You already knew that."

I kissed her once—forehead only. Long and deliberate. Then I walked out the door, leaving no promise except the truth that lingered on her lips and lived inside her now.

By the time she closed the door, I was already gone.

They called the day a win for whoever needed a headline. I don't read headlines; I read posture on the way out. The gallery emptied like a tide that knew which rocks to miss. The DA didn't make eye contact with the hallway; the hallway noticed.

Outside, the city didn't change its temperature for us. It never does. I put my back to the stone and let the noise walk by without taking any of it home. Spectacle feeds stories. Outcomes feed families. I'm here for outcomes.

Chapter 12

State time wasn't a wake-up call. I had been awake my whole life.

The van ride to the facility was silent on my end. Other inmates talked nervously, cracking jokes that no one laughed at. One dude kept tapping his foot and whispering about which gang ran the block. Another tried to ask I where I was from.

I didn't answer. Didn't even look at him.

That silence did more than any threat could've. The man turned his head and didn't try again.

When the van pulled up, I stared out the window. The gates opened slow—like they wanted to remind you that they didn't have to open at all. Just heavy-ass metal sliding back on rusted tracks. No fanfare. Just state steel and second chances for sale.

Inside, intake was a machine. Strip. Cough. Turn.

Fingerprints. Photos. Forms.

My clothes were bagged and tagged, replaced with state-issued grays and boots that felt two sizes too big. The CO who processed me didn't say much—just looked at my name on the file and raised my eyebrow slightly before stamping the paperwork.

The name had clearly traveled.

My cell was clean but aged. Cinderblock walls with peeling white paint. A steel sink. A toilet too close to the bed. The mattress was thin, the blanket thinner.

I sat for a moment and just breathed. Not fear. Not regret. Just calibration.

I was inside now. And inside had its own rules.

Word had already hit the yard before I stepped foot on it. Ock B's name had done the work weeks earlier—pushed through the system like contraband, whispered from tier to tier: I ain't to be touched. He solid. Real. Got people.

In prison, that kind of whisper was louder than a CO's orders. So when I made my first walk to the yard, heads turned—but no one stepped.

I kept my stride slow, my shoulders loose. Didn't look for anyone. Didn't avoid anyone. Just walked like I always had—grounded, silent, and watching.

The yard was a storybook of every corner of the streets—folded into one space and left to boil. The Latin Kings still had presence, but they moved quieter now. 5 Percenters were still here too, though their numbers had thinned—shadows of the righteous ranks they held in the 80s. And now? Bloods and Crips had made their way east.

I always wondered how that shit even got here. How something born in the alleys of L.A., from Hoover to South Central, ended up duplicated on Jersey soil.

I'd met a few real ones from Cali back in the day—dudes who weren't mimicking anything. Their hood ties stretched back generations, down to grandfathers that had died for colors before the internet even existed. That shit was confusing… but real. And real had to be respected.

I never picked a side. If you were in it, pick one and live with it. If you weren't? Mind your fucking business.

I didn't say much to anyone, but a few familiar faces gave head nods. Some spoke with quiet respect. I returned it. Brief words. No long conversations. No lunch-table reunions.

I didn't want anyone thinking I was affiliated. Because I wasn't.

That first week was observation. Yard time, chow hall, count time. Same rhythm, same tension. I stayed alert but never tense. I watched who held court on the yard benches. Who got food and who gave it. Who pressed and who folded.

I noticed quick—real predators weren't loud. They watched, waited, picked targets with surgical patience. And the young loudmouths? They usually got tested fast.

One day, a kid bumped into me by the weight station. I didn't move. Didn't say a word. The kid mumbled something but walked off. Minutes later, that same kid bumped into someone else— someone smaller.

The smaller guy got pressed.

I watched the whole thing from the pull-up bar, eyes calm, arms tense. I wasn't there to save anybody, but I saw the game clearly. Some motherfuckers only hunt where they think prey won't bite back.

Later that week, during yard cleanup, a CO tapped me on the shoulder and pointed to a rack of tools.

"Take that one to the back fence."

I nodded, grabbed a rake, and walked it over. That's where I saw him. Big Josh.

6'4", maybe 250. Stocky, but smooth. Not an old head—but known. Ran Trenton like a silent rumor that never needed proof. Clean-cut, clear-eyed, and quiet.

Josh had his sleeves rolled and was raking with calm rhythm, like he actually gave a shit about the leaves.

I didn't say anything. Neither did Josh.

But I felt it—recognition without history. We hadn't done business. Never shared corners. But we'd both moved in silence long enough to know when another wolf stepped into view.

We kept raking. Two men with no need to speak. Not yet.

That night, I sat on the edge of my bunk and replayed the day. I wasn't waiting for an opening. I wasn't looking for allies.

But if I had to shape something behind these walls, I'd need men who understood why silence matters. Josh might be one of those men.

Maybe not MMC. But maybe something close enough.

I leaned back, folded my hands behind my head, and stared at the ceiling. I hadn't come here to serve time. I'd come here to reshape what waited on the outside.

I didn't get prison big. I got dangerous.

Every morning started the same—before count, before chow, before the block got noisy. Pull-ups until my lats screamed. Dips until my chest turned to stone. Squats, planks, slow push-ups with perfect form.

I didn't touch the weights unless the yard was empty. I wasn't here to look tough. I was here to stay carved, lean, ready. Every rep was a message to myself: stay sharp, stay small, stay lethal.

The COs started calling me "The Phantom."

I never missed a day. Never said a word. While some worked out for intimidation, I moved like a man at war with time itself.

I turned my cell into a temple. A space of sweat, silence, and discipline. That's where Big Josh took notice.

I would be hanging from the bar, body soaked, breathing calm, eyes fixed on the sky like I was reading scripture written in clouds.

Josh would be a few yards over, folding towels near the CO's post, watching.

One day, after a set of 100 straight push-ups, Josh walked by and nodded once. "Body built for war," he said.

I didn't answer, just nodded back.

That was enough.

The politics in the yard were constant.

Not just gangs—ZIP Code politics. If you were from East Orange, you stayed there. If you were from Camden, you didn't sit with Trenton unless invited. No matter your set, your street mattered. Your corner mattered.

Crossing those lines without clearance? That shit could cost you teeth.

The White boys weren't like the ones I remembered from back home. These dudes had numbers, muscle, and political weight. Some ran car crews like corporations. They weren't afraid of anyone just because their skin was darker. They weren't stupid either.

You played stupid in here, you got played for real.

Deals were made daily. Weak men became property. Some were turned out willingly, then acted like it wasn't what it was. I never judged. I'd seen enough to know that a man's breaking point wasn't always loud.

"Do you," I told myself. "But don't bring that shit my way." And nobody did.

They saw how I moved. They respected how I didn't move.

One loudmouth on the block tried to test me in the yard. It wasn't even serious—just bumped into me near the pull-up bars, didn't apologize. I let it go once. The second time? I caught him slipping behind the laundry unit. Quick, quiet, efficient.

A choke and a trip. The guy hit the ground hard. I leaned over him and whispered, "Now you know."

That dude didn't speak for a week. He didn't get tried again after that.

I stayed out of card games. Didn't touch dice. Didn't hustle food or favors. I loved basketball, but saw too many fights break out over a missed call or a lost bet. Fists flying over nothing. It was childish. I didn't have time for childish.

But chess? That was something else.

I played daily. Sometimes twice. Sat with the men who didn't talk much but ran whole blocks through whispers. The kind of men who didn't get loud—they made moves that echoed.

I wasn't just learning the board. I was learning men. I saw things through the game that no shrink ever could've pulled from therapy.

If a man protected his queen too much, he was weak for a woman. Couldn't think straight.

If he overused his pawns, he was too involved in day-to-day operations—micromanaged, couldn't delegate.

If he never used his knights, he was scared of risky moves.

If he ignored his rook, he lacked long-range vision—couldn't see past the block.

I watched, played, and adapted. I didn't talk shit. I didn't celebrate wins. But men started noticing they couldn't rattle me. Couldn't predict me.

That made me dangerous without lifting a finger.

At night, when the block got quiet, I would lay back on my bunk, arms crossed, replaying games in my head. Not just chess. The streets. The crew. The fall. The case.

Time didn't drag. It played like film reels.

I thought about Cal. Barry. Do Dirty. Even C Shine and Big Abe.

I thought about Maribel—not in lust, but in silence. In stillness. The way her body curled into mine after everything had burned out. The weight of her breathing when she finally fell asleep.

I wondered if she was still off birth control.

I never got letters from James. Not one. But sometimes I'd see him on the news. A local tech story here. A clean-cut expert on a national panel there. I would pause the rec room TV when it came on. Stare at it like I was watching a ghost of the boy who once ran beside me with a duffel full of street dreams.

And sometimes… money would hit my books. Never a large sum. Never enough to raise flags that would get it seized for court costs or restitution. But just enough that I never needed anything.

I knew where it came from. I never spoke on it. Not even to myself. The jungle had its way of speaking.

And James King never stopped protecting me.

One night in the yard, while I was finishing my workout, Big Josh walked over again. This time with a half-smile and two apples—rare, decent ones. He handed me one.

"Still ain't talkin'?" I took the apple. Bit into it. Chewed.

"Talking gets you seen. Listening gets you fed."

Josh laughed once. "Facts."

We sat near the back fence, watching the sky turn purple with dusk.

Josh leaned back, arms across the bench. "You know you ain't gotta survive this place. You can shape it."

I looked over. "What you mean?"

Josh tilted his head toward the yard. "These boys out here—they looking for rules. For real ones. Not loud shit. Codes. Ain't too many left."

I nodded slowly.

Josh continued, "You one of them. I see it. The way you breathe. The way you don't chase nobody's approval. You move like legacy matters."

I stared straight ahead. "Only thing that does."

Josh smiled again. This one wider.

"You ever cook?"

I shook my head. "I know a man who did. Precision was my god."

Josh tapped the bench. "Maybe when you touch down, we talk."

I didn't answer. But the look in my eye said maybe.

Months had passed. And although it felt like every single day of that 19 months, 20 days, and 14 hours, it went quick enough that I was glad it was almost done. State time wasn't easy, but it wasn't hard either. Not for someone like me. The hardest part was the thinking. The silence. The waiting.

He never got into trouble. Never had to.

I moved through time the way I moved through the yard—clean, disciplined, and untested.

Then one day, just before my release, Felix found me. He had heard my name on the yard weeks earlier. Wasn't sure it was the same Felix until now. But when I walked into the corridor outside one of the maintenance rooms and saw Felix's back, I knew.

The woman on her knees in front of him sealed it. She was a CO, pretty, uniform unzipped halfway down, wiping her mouth with the back of her hand like it was part of her shift. She stepped past me without flinching, didn't even make eye contact.

Felix zipped up slow and smiled wide. "You still raw as ever, CJ. Never thought I'd see you in this joint."

I smirked. "Wasn't the plan."

Felix shrugged. "It never is."

We dapped up hard. No handshake. A hug that said: I remember. I respect. I see you.

"You moving good in here," I said, nodding toward the door.

Felix grinned. "Some people play cards. I play people."

I chuckled once. "Still grimy."

Felix reached into his waistband and pulled out a slip of paper.

I shook my head. "Don't hand me shit in here."

Felix nodded. "Right. We don't write in here. Remember it—it's going to make you rich."

I leaned in. "I'm listening."

Felix gave me an address. North Jersey. I repeated it under my breath three times. Locked it in.

"That's a storage unit. Locked under a bullshit name. Inside, there's keys. A condo, a car, and a book of names—people who owe me. I can't touch the streets no more. But you? You could make it flip."

I didn't say yes. Didn't say no. But I nodded once. It was enough.

Then Felix, always the showman, offered me one last bonus. "You want a little sendoff before you go? I got a guard who owes me two more favors. She good with the mouth."

I considered it. Then she coughed—three times, rough.

That was enough. "Nah. I'm good." We both laughed.

Later that week, I ran into Scott. Hadn't seen me since juvenile. The dude looked the same—big, thick-shouldered, still had that Mississippi energy even though I was Jersey born and bred.

"CJ," Scott said, approaching with open arms. My face lit up. "Scott, damn."

We embraced like two soldiers who survived different wars. Scott grinned, then looked serious. "I got something for you."

I shook my head before I even heard it. "Nah. I don't need nothing, Scott. Whatever you got, I don't want it. Good to see you, though."

I started to walk away. Scott placed a heavy hand on my shoulder. That stopped me.

I turned around, saw the weight in his eyes. "He's in here."

I squinted. "Who?"

Scott nodded once, slow. "The Muslim motherfucker. The one that killed your boy's brother. New name. Supposedly reformed. Rolling with the righteous now. But he still muscle. Still active."

My mouth didn't move. My jaw clenched once. "I guess he's in the right place then," I said. "Just served."

Then I walked away. Didn't say another word. But inside? My mind was racing.

I hadn't touched the streets in over a year and a half. Hadn't made a single call to anyone connected to the life. Only spoke to my mother and my brother. No soldiers. No crews. No bosses. Just blood.

But now? I made one call. To Ock B. When he picked up, I didn't waste time.

"It came from me," I said. Then I hung up. Didn't explain. Didn't ask. Just gave the signal.

Three days before my release, a CO tapped on my bunk. "You got a message."

I stood, followed the guard into a side hallway. No cuffs. Just quiet tension.

The CO pulled out a picture. Laid it flat on the table. It was Bigg Ken. The man who killed Elliott, James's brother. Lying face-up in my cell. Dead.

Dick stuffed in his mouth. Stabbed at least 40 times—in non-lethal places. He bled out slow. He suffered.

The CO didn't blink. "Ock B said... you're welcome."

I stared at the photo. Not in horror. Not in anger. Just stillness.

A tear slipped down my cheek. Not for Bigg Ken. For Elliott. For justice. For a brotherhood that never folded.

I wiped the tear away with the back of my hand and nodded once. "Tell him I felt that."

My final days passed like minutes. The yard felt different now. Lighter. The countdown real.

I ran into Felix once more—this time across the yard. He shouted, "Don't forget that address!"

I threw up a hand. "It's already mine."

On my last night, I didn't sleep much. I thought of my mother. Of Grim. Of Maribel.

I thought of James. I thought of the jungle. The games. The silence. The empire.

I hadn't lost myself. I'd just paused.

Now? The pause was over. Time to press play.

Chapter 13

The gate didn't slam behind me. It clicked. Soft. Precise. Like it was whispering, You'll be back.

I didn't turn around. I just walked. Two bags. One light, one heavy. My steps were silent, but the silence around me felt different now. Less sacred. Less powerful. More forgotten.

A black Bonneville sat near the corner, engine humming low. Cal was behind the wheel.

No music. No words.

I opened the passenger door, threw both bags in the back, and got in. We didn't speak for three blocks.

Then Cal said, "You look lean."

I looked out the window. "I am."

Cal nodded like that answered something. Maybe it did.

The town hadn't changed. But everything felt off.

The corners still had motion—bodies moving, deals floating—but the rhythm was noisy now. Sloppy. Loud voices. Slouched shoulders. Nobody looked sharp. Nobody looked like they earned anything. Just standing around, waiting to be somebody.

My eye twitched. I saw a young dude walking with a TechnoMarine knockoff, belt loose, laughing too hard. No discipline. No weight. Just surface.

We passed the old barbershop. Still open, but quiet. I clocked it. G-Money probably moved out or moved on. The energy wasn't there.

Up the block was my building. Still there. Still mine. Cal pulled into the back. I stepped out and looked at it like it was a memory somebody had repainted in the wrong shade.

I climbed the stairs alone. Keys still worked. The door opened like it never missed me. Inside, the apartment was clean. Sparsely furnished, but it didn't smell abandoned. Cal had kept it tight.

I set the bags down and sat on the edge of the couch. Let the silence stretch. The floorboards didn't creak. The heat kicked on soft. I was home. But it didn't feel like it.

That night, I rode with Cal. No purpose. Just movement.

We rolled past Congress, 14th Street, Monmouth. I took it in. Noticed more young faces than familiar ones. The names I remembered were now ghosts or whispers. Some gone. Some hiding behind newer masks.

"Where's Barry?" I asked.

"Low," Cal said. "Real low."

I didn't press. I could smell guilt before it spoke. "Who's runnin' what?"

Cal gave me the rundown. Eighth was still ours.

Tenth to Twelfth? Faded. New kids pushing bullshit. Uncut, noisy, and weak. Cal said they had bodies behind them, but no structure. No backbone.

I nodded. "And the rest?"

"C Shine and Big Abe still here. Still solid. But Shine got a case pending. He moves... different now."

I grinned for half a second. "Still got the bowlegs?"

Cal laughed once. "Ain't changed."

The laughter died quick.

Later that night, I sat in the kitchen alone. Poured a glass of tap water. Held it in my hand like it was wine.

The fridge hummed. The hum turned into a rhythm. The rhythm pulled me back.

The weight of time sat in my bones like iron. My shoulders had changed. My breath, deeper now. More controlled. My hands no longer reached fast. They moved like they measured every second.

I had watched empires rise and fall in prison—from chessboards to cell blocks to CO whispers. Now I was back in a kingdom I built. But it no longer felt like mine.

I remembered what Big Josh told me: "You don't survive this place. You shape it."

I had. But now? I had to reshape the outside.

The next morning, Cal picked me up again. We went to a tucked-away garage—formerly a stash spot, now a half-dead front.

Inside were two familiar faces and four strangers. Cal introduced them all, but I didn't commit the names. I committed the posture.

One youngin wouldn't make eye contact. One kept shaking his leg like he was wired on caffeine or fear. One smiled too much.

Only one stood still and didn't speak unless spoken to. I nodded at that one. "You the only one I might not bury," I said.

Silence.

I turned to Cal. "Let's talk alone." We stepped into the back office.

Old maps. A whiteboard. A dusty couch. I stood while Cal sat.

"Tell me everything. Start with the paper flow. Then the bodies."

Cal did.

Nothing added up. There were leaks—small ones—but enough to bother me.

"Shine and Abe?" I asked again.

"Still loyal. Just had to pivot a little while you were gone."

I didn't respond. I was calculating. Not paranoid. Not angry. Just awake.

I turned toward the map. Ran my finger down 14th. Across Congress. Back to Monmouth. Then down to the waterfront.

"We start over," I said.

"Same name?" Cal asked.

I shook my head. "No name. Just order."

The Elks Club looked like it hadn't been touched since Reagan left office.

Paint flaked from the window frames. The wooden sign hung crooked, half-lit, like it couldn't decide whether to announce itself or give up. But it still stood. That was enough. Everybody who mattered had passed through here. And those still moving right? They came through often enough to remind the block they hadn't died.

It sat quietly on the corner of 4th and Monmouth, and I pulled up just after dusk. Alone. No music. No words. Just memory riding shotgun.

Across the street, the old record store was boarded up. Faded posters for cassette release parties still clung to the window like ghosts. I used to post outside that spot with James—arguing over tapes, soaking up game from the old heads who used the front steps like a porch throne. That store was where the pulse of the street lived back then. Now it was silent. Dead.

I didn't mourn it. I respected the loss.

Inside the Elks, it smelled like old wood, menthol, sweat, and respect. Tables were half full. A DJ spun soul cuts off vinyl, blending it with faint R&B and New Jack edge. The walls were yellowed with memory. Neon lights buzzed. A few heads turned. Most nodded. No one interrupted.

I grabbed a Pepsi from the bar, nodded at the bartender I half-recognized, and made my way to an open pool table near the back.

I didn't shoot. Just stood there. Cue in hand. Eyes scanning. Watching.

There were wolves in the room—you could feel them before you saw them. But most of the crowd? Hollow-chested, over-accessorized, and loud.

The jewelry was brighter now. Not better—just more.

The mouths were louder. Not sharper—just thirsty.

I watched as three dudes argued over who had more connects, louder than the DJ. I didn't recognize a single one. I could tell by the way they gestured, by how they moved, that they wouldn't have survived the blocks I came from. Not just because of violence. Because of principle.

This wasn't power. It was performance.

I sipped my Pepsi slow. Observed. Said nothing.

Cal arrived late, like always. No entrance, no posturing. He just walked up, grabbed a chair by the table, and nodded once.

"They don't know you're here yet," he said under his breath.

I didn't answer. I just leaned on the stick. Cal knew better than to fill the silence.

We watched together for a few minutes.

A man across the room clowned loudly, spinning a tale about "how the whole thing flipped" and how I "held down the East Side solo" while others folded. I looked at him, and I saw it.

Fraud.

The wolves were still here—but they moved quieter now. Like survivors in a world that forgot to respect them.

Most of the new players had skipped pain. Skipped process. Went straight from internet instructions to the corner with nothing in their chest but ego and imaginary enemies.

I whispered, more to myself than to Cal: "Shootings used to mean something. Now they happen with mouths. Or drive-by texts. Motherfuckers posting clout and calling it consequence."

Cal nodded slowly, unsure if it was agreement or acknowledgment.

I continued. "Ain't about power no more. It's popularity. Who got seen. Not who put in."

I turned and looked directly at Cal. "But I'm lookin' for the ones that got overlooked. The quiet ones. The ignored. I still see 'em."

Cal stayed quiet. I respected him. Trusted him. But I never confused Cal with someone like me.

"You always been diplomatic," I said. "Always fair."

Cal smirked. "You sayin' that like it's a flaw."

I looked around again. "It is … depending on the temperature."

There was no malice in my tone. Just truth.

Cal wasn't built from lack. He didn't grow up clawing for breath, dodging raids, sleeping in two rooms with five people and no father.

I came from necessity. I wasn't trained. I was forged.

Cal nodded toward a younger dude in the corner—dressed light, posture sharp, mouth closed.

"That one right there," I said. "He don't laugh much. That's the one I want."

The room moved around us, oblivious. I stayed posted. Calm. No chain. No flash. Just that silence that made real ones uncomfortable and suckers nervous.

I didn't need to reclaim anything. "Whatever's lost," I muttered, "we don't want it back."

Cal looked at me.

I tapped the edge of the pool table. "Let the hyenas eat the carcass. Even if it's mine. I ain't fightin' for dead flesh. Let it go."

That line hung in the air.

Cal stood up, nodding. "You done?"

I grinned faintly. "Just starting."

We left together. But only one of us was walking with war in his heart.

Almost a month passed. No welcome-back party. No loud reentry. Just presence.

I had returned, but unless someone saw me with their own eyes, they didn't know. And I loved it that way. No fanfare. No court to rejoin. If my name didn't echo anymore, that was fine. I wasn't there to chase an echo. I was there to build something new. Or burn down what stood in its place.

I drove slow that morning—no music. Just memory. The streets hadn't changed much in appearance. But the soul? Gone. It moved different now. Corners were louder. Eyes darted more. Hunger had become more reckless than strategic.

I'd already heard the news. MMC caught a case.

High-speed chase from 118th and Morningside to the Tremont in the Bronx. It made the local news, but word spread faster on the street. They said he had enough weight in the car to bury himself in time. I didn't flinch at the news. MMC knew the rules. If he didn't make it out, it wasn't because the game changed—it was because the game never gave favors.

I parked and walked upstairs. Cal was waiting.

"Morning," Cal said.

I nodded. "Any word?"

Cal shook his head. "Nothing new. MMC's hearing pushed back. No bail."

I leaned against the windowsill and looked out. "It's not about them falling," I said. "It's about what we keep standing."

Later that day, the inner circle met—what was left of it.

The room felt different. Divine was there, quiet as always. The Blvd had been dismantled. I was the last one breathing from that camp, and I brought him in without hesitation. Loyalty wasn't about trend. It was about survival. Divine knew how to move with code.

AB showed up right on time. Pretty boy. A little louder than I liked. But he had discipline, and more importantly, he knew structure. When he was given a job, he executed it clean. I didn't need mute soldiers—I needed ones who knew when to speak and when to disappear.

Big Abe walked in last. He held down the rooming houses while I was gone, and left word the properties were mine until further notice. No ego. Just respect. Abe was still muscle, but now he sat a little closer to command.

"Where's C Shine?" I asked.

Abe shook his head. "Gone."

"What you mean gone?"

"He took a plea deal. Quiet. No words. Just… gone."

I nodded. That was Shine. Always surgical. If he needed to disappear, it was for a reason. No sendoff. No drama. Just dust in the wind. I respected it.

We got to work. Maps laid out. Corners redrawn. I didn't want to expand—I wanted to refine. The play was simple: Let everybody eat. Wherever they eat. However they eat.

But the moment they cross lines into my domain — There was no hesitation.

And if it could be handled discreetly? Even better.

I stared at the names on the whiteboard. Any name that had ever violated, even if forgiven, was circled in red. "This ain't revenge," I said. "This is housekeeping."

Barry stood to the side, listening.

I turned to him. "That includes you, Barry." His posture shifted, unsure.

I didn't raise my voice. "Your muscle ain't needed. Ain't nobody fist-fighting out here anymore. Trust never comes twice in my eyes. You here because I let you be. Keep it tight. Or disappear."

Barry nodded. Nothing more needed to be said.

Then came Do Dirty. Not a phone call. Not a heads-up. Just his presence, storming through the front door like he never left. He had a duffel bag in one hand and a smile on his face.

"Don't play with me like that, fam," Do Dirty said, walking toward me. "You know I'd end up with life if we got caught bringing this arsenal over the Benjamin Franklin."

I smirked. "Anybody knows anything you doin' sideways, you never take the bridge, motherfucker."

We laughed. Hugged. But when we pulled back, it was all business. Do Dirty looked at the map on the table. "We building or burning?" he asked.

I answered without hesitation. "Both. But only when necessary." I laid it out again: keep the peace. Let people move. But if they so much as step onto what's mine—past, present, or promised—it's war. Not performative. Not poetic. Just final.

Ock B wasn't there. He'd caught 30 days—smacked the shit out of a car wash attendant who wouldn't acknowledge a scratch on his car. Would've walked away with nothing, but he had light work in the glove compartment. Enough to get sat down. Not enough to matter long term.

Still, it was classic Ock. No restraint. I made a mental note: when he's back, we talk. Until then, keep his seat warm.

The room sat quiet.

Divine stood still, waiting for instruction.

AB nodded like he was already strategizing.

Big Abe leaned back, calm but coiled.

Do Dirty cracked his neck and pulled a burner from his waistband, checking the clip. I raised a brow.

"Relax," Do Dirty said. "I ain't pullin' unless you say pull."

I nodded.

And Cal? He sat near the back, watching. Not trying to lead. Not trying to fade. Just… observing. Still trustworthy. Still diplomatic. I respected that.

But I also knew… Diplomacy has limits.

That night, I walked out alone. The moon was low. The streets soft. But my silence? Unforgiving.

I wasn't back to reclaim a throne. I was back to redraw the blueprint. And every whisper in the city would soon learn the difference between being quiet and being untouchable.

I caught her two weeks later, midday, when the city thinks it's off-duty. Monmouth's storefronts yawned open, and the mall turned the air into conditioned forgetting. She stood outside a window the way she always did—like time was hers to pace.

I hadn't seen Maribel in weeks. We'd had a date and a bed and a promise shaped like breath, but after I came home the house felt different. I don't give a thing a name it hasn't earned.

"Still moving while you stand still?" I said.

She looked at my reflection before she looked at me. "Still leaving fast?"

"Only when the room deserves it."

We walked without agreeing to. Past the fountain that never worked on time, out to the strip where buses exhaled. She didn't fill the quiet. She tuned it.

"Real date," I said. "Not my place. Not yours."

She weighed it without dramatics. "Tomorrow, 2:30. Daylight. I work nights."

"Where?"

"Cross Street Café." She smiled once, small. "On the good side. Two blocks from the line nobody talks about unless they had to cross it."

"What's the dress code?"

"Breathing. And shoes."

Her name was Christa. I'd known it already, but I let it arrive in my mouth like something I wasn't rushing. She grew up past that invisible border—upper-middle calm, parents who didn't give speeches about dreams; they drove her to them. If a school had the better lab, they filled out the form before she asked. If a coach had the right season, they found the fee. That kind of help doesn't brag. It just shows up on time.

"People think it's all the same town," she said. "It's not. If you never crossed Cross Street, you never learned the other language."

"I speak both," I said.

"I know," she said. "That's why I said yes."

I got there early. Sat where I could see the door and the mirror. Cross Street Café pretended it was indifferent to money, which is how you know it loved it. Chalkboard menu. Good coffee. Cups that break quiet without being loud.

Christa walked in on time, not early. Hair pinned back, eyes clear, posture honest. She didn't dress for attention. She dressed for weather and purpose.

"You eat?" she asked.

"I do."

"You pray over it?"

"I read it first."

She smiled. "Same."

We ordered small things and let them cool while the room taught us how to be in it. "You seeing someone?" she asked.

"Not sure I can call it that," I said. "We used to like each other a lot once upon a time. Haven't seen her in a while."

Christa nodded like an answer she respected. "Then we're choosing in daylight," she said. She didn't ask about prison. She asked about sleep, and whether mine listened when I told it to. I asked about work. She served nights—drinks, plates, sometimes patience. She liked the cash and the rhythm. Didn't love the noise. "The trick," she said, "is not letting volume pretend to be truth."

"Most tricks are like that," I said.

She told me about the house she grew up in—one step from the hood, two steps from the polite lie that the hood didn't exist. Parents who didn't work themselves to the bone; they worked smart and left stretch in the day to drive kids to the thing that might become a life. No posters on the wall about greatness. Just calendars with boxes full of action.

"Some parents root from the stands," she said. "Mine put gas in the car."

"You still cross the street?" I asked.

"Daily. Or I forget my manners," she said. Then, after a beat, "And I like remembering."

We walked after, no destination. She matched my pace without studying it. I told her I didn't bring people to my place, and she told me she didn't bring people to hers. "We can still be seen," she said. "Seen isn't the same as known."

"Tomorrow night?" I asked.

She shook her head. "Late shift. But I can do the day after. Same hour. Same table. If either of us breaks the rule, we say it first."

"What rule?"

"No pretending we're not choosing," she said.

I nodded. "Deal."

We stood at the corner where Cross Street made the town honest. She looked both ways out of habit, even with no traffic.

"Keep your map," she said. "Just don't let it make you forget you're allowed to draw."

She left me with the quiet cleaner than she found it. Not a favor. A perimeter.

I hadn't lied about Maribel. Once we were two people moving the same direction. Lately we'd been two people respecting the silence between us. Daylight was a fair place to start something else

I watched the street breathe. Then I went back to building what I came back to build.

Chapter 14

Weeks had passed since my return. Word hadn't spread. No announcement. No street whisper. No crown placed back on my head. Just presence.

Quiet. Watchful. Intentional.

Things were falling back into place, but it was like handling broken glass—sharp, delicate, and unforgiving if you weren't careful. The streets still moved like they were looking for a father figure. I wasn't interested in parenting. I was back to study the soil. To see what grew in my absence and what needed to be uprooted.

AB pulled up early, as instructed. Summer league basketball at the community center smack right in the middle of 4th Street, was known for its pull—players, shot-callers, thirsty girls, and would-be hitters trying to look like hitters.

I had no plans to play politician.

"You sure we want to be out here?" AB asked.

I nodded. "We not here to be seen. We here to see."

We parked right up front. Tinted-out. Engine low. I leaned back in the passenger seat, unbothered. Just another man watching the game with a plate of wings in my lap.

To anyone else, we looked like regulars. But I was processing every detail like a criminal psychologist—body language, jewelry flash, tone of voice, who laughed too loud, who moved with tension in their spine.

Cool Todd was out there, shining like the damn sun. Brand new Lexus coupe. Neck heavy enough to give him spinal issues.

His wolves were all around, and his hitter never sat more than five feet away. I respected the structure, not the flair. Flash made you visible. Visibility made you vulnerable.

Cool Todd was too outside. Too often. That only ended one way. Still, he had the city's attention now. For the moment.

Then there was Puerto Rican Knowledge. Everyone called him Papi before it became the popular thing to do. OG since '86. Product of Lincoln Arms.

Still clean, still feared, still carrying heat. I never dealt with him, but I watched him.He was the type you didn't bother unless invited.

The court was surrounded by red—less blue than years past. Bloods had momentum. Crips were quieter.

Women were everywhere, prowling for the next man to make their come-up—or their setup.

I didn't speak much. Just watched.

I watched patterns more than people. Who checked mirrors when they didn't need to. Who laughed with their mouth and not their eyes. Who scanned the edges like they owed somebody money. The ones you worry about aren't the loud ones—they're the men who stand still for too long and the women who keep a bag they never put down.

I studied my own affiliates too. How they greeted others. How often they smiled. How much mouth they had. Who smoked too casually. Who stayed chasing women that weren't chasing them back.

"If everyone shakes your hand, you ain't feared."

"If no one moves when you walk toward them, you ain't respected."

"If you move first, you're the one with fear."

I collected all of it. Like a scientist. Like a predator.

AB leaned back, chewing on a toothpick. "Yo, we should hop out. All these bitches out here today."

I didn't even look AB's way. "I'm good. I'm just here for the food and the view."

"You sure? I see a few old joints from back in the day—"

"I'm sure."

I stayed in the car. Tinted. Hidden. My kingdom still moved. I didn't need to.

Then — I saw her. Maribel. Walking with her girls. Laughing. Summer dress hugging her just enough to hurt.

Hair down, bouncing with every step. Sunlight hit her like it had been waiting all day. And in that moment — I didn't see the game. Didn't see Cool Todd. Didn't see any wolf, OG, or hitter.

I saw her. And something in my chest cracked open. I hadn't breathed right in weeks. Hadn't touched peace.

But there she was. Breathing like oxygen I'd been holding out for.

Without a word, I opened the door and got out. Maribel saw me. She froze. Then ran. Full speed. No hesitation. She hit my chest hard—hugged me so tight my feet shifted.

I wrapped my arms around her and just inhaled. She smelled like memory and promise. Like everything I didn't know I missed.

Then—slap. Right across my face.

"What the fuck, CJ?!" she barked. "How long you been home?"

I didn't flinch. "You know I show more than I tell."

Her lip trembled. Her eyes flared. But she smiled through it.

She tucked a curl behind her ear and missed. Hands usually that sure don't miss. Twice she checked left—same spot each time— like a person waiting on a signal she hoped wouldn't come.

I noticed her glancing over her shoulder. Too often. Too alert. "You looking for somebody?" I asked.

She shook her head fast. "Nah. Let's go home. Now." Her urgency didn't hit me as odd—not yet. I was too high on her presence. Too flooded with love I'd been pressing down like trauma.

I turned to AB. "I gotta roll."

AB tossed me the keys. "I'll catch a ride. Catch up tomorrow." I nodded, barely hearing him. All I saw was her.

We walked off hand in hand. But if my guard hadn't been so low, if I'd been watching her the way I watched the game... I would've seen it.

The signal. The unease. The guilt masked as urgency. But I wasn't watching the signs. I was back inside something soft.

And for the first time since state time— I felt love. I just didn't know...It was the setup before the shatter.

We went back to my place like two people carrying a glass sculpture between us—delicate, unspoken, and liable to shatter at the smallest misstep.

I let her in first. The door clicked behind me like a clock restarting. Time had passed—nearly two years—but this house should've frozen something in place. Her scent, her slippers by the door, the old playlist we used to laugh to in the kitchen. None of it remained. Her presence didn't feel like a homecoming—it felt like a walkthrough.

She didn't move like before. Back then, she'd take her shoes off without thinking, check the fridge without asking. She used to own this space with her spirit. Now, she walked like a visitor trying not to knock anything over. I noticed. I always did.

We talked, but the conversation limped. She laughed, but it didn't rise from her gut—it barely made it to her eyes. Her gaze drifted around the room like she was searching for a version of herself that used to live here.

I didn't press. I chalked it up to time and distance. Damn near two years was a long stretch. But the real truth was heavy in my chest. She hadn't waited for me.

And if I was honest, I never really expected her to.

We didn't mention prison. I had no desire to explain what 700 days behind concrete felt like. And she wasn't asking. That was fine. What could I say? That time in a box teaches you what parts of love are real and what parts are just dressed-up loneliness?

At first, her letters came weekly. Then every other week. Then once a month. Each envelope lighter than the last—fewer pages, fewer updates, fewer feelings. I never complained. What was there to say? A woman in her 20s writing a man locked down wasn't something to bet your future on.

Still… some nights, I bet anyway. I clung to the sentences she scribbled about staying tight for me. About dreaming of our baby. About counting the days. Now, in the flesh, none of that lived in her tone.

We ordered food. She didn't ask what I liked anymore. Just grabbed the menu, said she wasn't in the mood to cook, and ordered her usual. I nodded. I ate out of habit, not hunger. Then she showered, came out in my old tee like a memory trying to smile its way back into reality.

We fucked. That's what it was—fucking.

Not lovemaking. Not reunion. Not passion.

It was an obligation. A performance. A nod to the version of us that used to be wild for each other. I finished, rolled over, and stared at the ceiling. Not cold, but not held either.

She curled against me like she used to, but her touch didn't settle anything. If anything, it unsettled more.

"Ever been to an island?" I asked suddenly.

She propped herself up on one elbow, confused. "What?"

"Any island. Doesn't matter which. I been hearing about 'em. Readin'. Jamaica. Bora. Aruba. Turks. I thought maybe we could go."

"Yeah…" she said slowly. "That sounds nice. Let me check my schedule this week and see when's a good time."

Back then, she'd have pulled out her phone, rattled off three locations, argued about which one had better sunsets. Now she responded like someone trying not to commit to anything.

I didn't look at her. Just stared at the ceiling fan. "Just tell me," I said after a long pause.

"Tell you what?"

"If you been fuckin' with somebody. I ain't one of these street clowns who go outside killing behind lies. But if you welcomed disrespect into my house while I was in a cell… that's a different story."

Her silence cracked something. "I didn't want to tell you this while you were in there," she finally said. "But yes. I was seeing someone. It wasn't love. It wasn't real. It was just something to help me not fall apart while you were gone."

I sat up, elbows on my knees. "You ain't break me, Maribel," I said. "But you did make me question if I should've ever tried to believe in somethin' soft."

She reached for me. "I swear, I ended it."

"I didn't ask you that."

Tears filled her eyes, but I didn't flinch. "I don't judge you," I continued. "I ain't dumb. You young, beautiful. I was gone almost two years. But don't gaslight me into thinking it was still us. That man ate at our table, even if I wasn't here. Don't tell me otherwise."

She nodded. "I love you, CJ," she said again, quieter this time.

I stood, walked to the kitchen, and opened the fridge just to cool my face with the open air. I didn't drink. I grabbed a cold Pepsi and cracked it. Took a long sip.

"I used to tell my brother James," I said, "that you don't need proof when it comes to people. You ain't a cop. You don't need affidavits and receipts. If your gut says it's different, believe that shit. It'll keep you alive."

I turned back to her. "I ignored mine for you."

She was crying now—barefoot, vulnerable, wrapped in the same towel she used to joke was her throne.

"You're home now. Let's build again," she whispered.

I walked over and kissed her forehead. "If you love me the way you say you do… you'll go clean that up. Quietly. Permanently.

I'll be here. But not if it lingers."

She looked up. I saw pain. Regret. Maybe even real love.

"I mean it," I added. "If I gotta kill somebody, it won't be cause I was lied to. It'll be 'cause I was invited into a lie."

She nodded and gathered her things. No big scene. No screaming match.

As she turned the doorknob, I finally said it—not on paper, not in a cell. But in person. "I love you."

She turned, eyes wide, lips trembling. And for the first time since I came home…she believed me.

She left. And I sat in silence, holding the ghost of what almost was.

Outside, the streets were calm. Inside, I was rearranging the pieces of a heart I didn't know was still breakable.

Later that night, long after she left, I sat on the edge of my bed with one of her old letters in my lap. It was creased at the fold, smudged slightly with something that could've been tears or sweat. I had read it a hundred times inside, but now in the quiet of freedom, the words stung different:

"I know you miss your freedom, baby, but know that I'm your freedom waiting for you. We going to get through this, and when you home, I want you in every room of this house. In me. Around me. Baby-making, vacation-taking, future-having, all of that. I love you. Don't let time change you."

It was signed with a lipstick kiss back then.

I folded it back up slowly and slid it into the shoebox of old memories I thought would mean more now than they actually did. I wasn't angry—not in the way people imagined rage. What I felt was more mature. Deeper. Sadder. It was the mourning of something that wasn't dead, but clearly wasn't alive either.

I remembered sitting on the edge of my bunk, rehearsing lines that would sound honest and still protect me. Jokes I'd pretend were spontaneous. The way her hips would fit my hands, the way her laugh would bounce off my kitchen walls. I played those fantasies like a favorite song. Freedom changed the key. Too many notes missing.

I laid back, eyes open to the ceiling, hands crossed on my chest like a man preparing for burial—not of my body, but of a hope I didn't know I was carrying.

Love, I realized, doesn't kill you. It makes you wish you could die softer. Tomorrow would come. It always did. And me? I'd still be me. Just with one less illusion to carry.

She was back. And for a little while, it felt good. Not perfect—but real, and real was rare enough. I moved like a man who believed again. Not just in her, but in the possibility that maybe, just maybe, I wasn't destined to walk alone forever.

Maribel didn't just have my heart—she had my care. My provisions. My protection. Every unspoken promise a man could make without saying a word, I kept.

Anything she needed, anything her family needed—I handled it.

Her brothers didn't ask for nothing, but I still made sure their barbershop chairs stayed full. Her little sister? College applications got paid for in cash. No explanations. Just silent security, the kind that said, "I got you."

All I ever asked in return: "Tell me what you took, and I won't ask why." That was my only rule. No lies. No guessing.

And the streets? They were quieter than ever. That silence I once built with violence was now maintained by structure.

The rules were simple: If you had dealings outside the circle, you were out. No second chances. I knew better than anyone—the downfall of most crews wasn't betrayal.

It was blurred lines. You stop knowing who your brother is, and worse, who I isn't.

Violations weren't met with blood. They were met with exile. For the top brass—those closer to the vault—punishment was swifter, colder, and far more permanent.

Big Abe had become the muscle of my will—never needing instructions, always knowing the mission.

Do Dirty? The flame on the end of the fuse, waiting.

Divine, diplomatic and disciplined, navigated the shadows with grace.

And Pudge? Always watching, always aware, the unofficial voice that whispered truth before it became a headline.

I had begun to believe in the idea of legacy again. A child. My heir.

Not a soldier, but a scholar. Someone who wouldn't need to shoot their way through a neighborhood just to be respected.

I pictured myself in the driver's seat of a low-slung coupe, my son riding shotgun, teaching him the rules of a kingdom he'd never need to conquer.

I never brought up the past again. Never mentioned the other man. If she said it was over, that was that.

I believed her. Not because I was naïve—but because she had always been solid. And sometimes, the people who showed up the strongest deserved the most grace.

I gave it freely. Until that day.

It was Pudge who first brought the whisper. One of my top lieutenants — Rell D — had been spotted making side deals. Word was, he'd been recruiting a chef to cook outside the network. Not just foul. Dangerous.

Big Abe verified it. Said he was cooking up at the Rivera Motel. A ragged joint just outside my zone. Not deep into enemy territory, but far enough that it felt like betrayal.

I didn't get mad. Didn't raise my voice. I just nodded.

Big Abe picked me up from 8th and Clifton. As we pulled up to the motel, Abe cracked the silence with a simple line: "Simba made his way to the elephant graveyard." It was an old Lion King reference between us. Translation: someone just crossed into where they didn't belong.

I didn't plan to confront him. Just show my face. A quiet reminder that there were boundaries you didn't test. But as we idled near the lot, watching Room 212 like it owed us rent, my world split in half.

Maribel. She walked right up the stairs. Didn't hesitate. Keyed in the door. Room 212. I didn't speak.

Big Abe didn't look at me, but reached over and rested his hand on my shoulder. "Seeing is believing, C. Let that be enough. You ain't got the stomach for what's behind that door."

I didn't move. Just stared at the number like it was carved into my soul. When Abe went to pull off, I held up my hand. "You strapped?"

Abe looked at me. "Always."

I took a breath. "You think I'm 'bout to kill somebody over a misdemeanor to the game?"

"No," Abe said. "But I think we need to overdo it."

I nodded. "Family affair. No need to loop Do Dirty." We waited. Thirty long minutes.

Then—Boom. Big Abe kicked in the door like it was made of paper.

Inside, it was exactly what I feared. Maribel bent over, Rell holding her hair like reins, one hand around her throat.

The sounds, the sweat, the betrayal—all of it screamed louder than any gun ever could. Rell froze. Begged.

I looked at Maribel. "This what you couldn't let go?"

No answer.

I tapped Abe twice. "Let's go."

Rell was spared. Not out of mercy. But because I didn't spill blood for what was freely given.

Back in the car, I said nothing. Abe saw the tears. Just a few. Didn't say a word. Didn't dare.

I asked to be dropped at my mother's house. Grim opened the door. "You good?" I didn't respond. Just walked in.

And when Abe pulled off — I broke. First, soft. Just breathing. Then sobs. Then howls. My brother held me. No questions. Just love.

That was the last time I would ever love with my whole heart. From that moment forward, my care would come with armor. No more naked trust. No more "maybe."

If there was a doubt—I'd walk. Not because I was heartless. But because the only way to keep standing—

was to stop letting love knock me down.

Chapter 15

Three and a half weeks.

That's how long I had been gone—not missing, not hiding, just silent. No calls. No movement. No explanations. Only two people had seen me since the betrayal: my mother, and Grim.

The world hadn't stopped turning, but it had slowed—just enough for me to feel each click of the clock like a weight pressing down. And that's what I wanted. No distractions. No women. No vices. Just the clean pain of clarity.

My days began before the sun. Joggers were still in bed. The city hadn't stretched yet. But I was already up—sweat dripping, breath steady, hands wrapped in cloth as I punished the heavy bag in the basement of my mother's house. There was no music. Just the thud of fists and the sound of my lungs catching rhythm.

Each hit was a lesson. Each round, a sermon.

Don't get attached. Don't assume love means loyalty. Don't ever lower your crown for comfort.

Upstairs, my mother didn't ask questions. She made me tea every morning and left it near the door without saying a word. Some days I didn't drink it. Other days I finished it before it cooled. Either way, I knew what it meant: I still believe in you.

After my workout, I showered, changed, and stepped out with my hoodie up, shades on, and headphones in—though nothing played. I wasn't listening to music. I was listening to the streets.

I walked everywhere. No car. No soldiers. Just my own two feet.

Around 7th and Monroe, I passed a couple kissing inside a car. The girl laughed, and I kept walking. Not slower. Not faster. Just forward.

At Lincoln Arms, a kid on a beat-up BMX bike flew past me, nearly tipping over the curb.

I called out softly, "Stay clean, lil man."

The kid looked back but didn't recognize me. That was fine. I wasn't out here for recognition. I was retracing steps. Mapping every alley, every fence, every light pole like I was preparing for war. Because in a way, I was.

Love had made me soft. Not weak—soft. And softness had a cost.

I passed the Rivera Motel. Didn't flinch.

Looked once—long enough to register the moment, short enough not to relive it. That part of me was gone now. I wasn't chasing ghosts. I was building monuments.

By the time I returned to the house, Grim would already be outside, folding up the last of a newspaper like an old soul. We didn't speak right away. Grim set the board, and I sat across from him, hoodie still up, body still warm from the walk.

Chess was our language now. I didn't play to win. I played to observe—my brother's eyes, my rhythm, the way I anticipated betrayal across sixty-four squares. It reminded me that everyone has a pattern. You just have to sit still long enough to see it.

"Knight takes bishop," Grim said one morning.

I nodded. "Saw that coming."

Grim smirked. "But you didn't stop it."

My response was a whisper. "Didn't need to."

I took his queen five moves later. No celebration. Just strategy.

That afternoon, I stood in front of a cracked bathroom mirror, trimming the sharp edge of my beard with steady hands. The man looking back wasn't broken. I was sculpted. Older. Colder. Alive in a way most people never experience.

My phone sat on the dresser. Off. I turned it on. One bar. No service yet. But it didn't matter.

I picked it up, went into my contacts, and scrolled past names that no longer deserved space in my world. Deleted six numbers. Blocked two more. Then, finally, I tapped the name that mattered:

Big Abe.

I didn't say hello when the line connected. I just said: "I'm ready."

There was a pause. Then Abe's voice, warm and thick as ever. "You sure?"

I stared out the window. "Never been more."

Later that day, Big Abe pulled up in a matte black pickup—no logos, no noise. I got in the passenger seat, no handshake, just a nod.

We drove in silence through the city's pulse. Past shuttered bodegas, neon-lit barbershops, street corners still haunted by ghosts in oversized jeans and cracked Timbs.

"I kept things running," Abe finally said. "No changes. No chatter."

"I know," I replied.

Abe looked over. "You really back?"

I turned toward him, eyes hidden behind dark lenses. "I'm something better."

We didn't speak again until we reached the old pool hall on Bangs Avenue. The place had been gutted since last winter—new flooring, fresh lights. But the walls still carried the scent of chalk and cigar smoke.

I stepped inside like a man entering my own legend.

Every cue stick, every light fixture—it all whispered stories back to me. I had built this life one lesson at a time, and now it was time to edit the circle. No more softness. No more seats at the table for sentiment.

As Abe racked the balls for a quick game, I walked toward the window and looked out over the street. Rain had started to mist the glass.

Behind me, Abe spoke without looking up. "You planning on bringing her up?"

I didn't respond. Didn't move. Didn't blink.

Finally: "She's gone. The man she knew is too."

Abe didn't press it. He broke the rack and sank a stripe.

I turned, picked up a cue, and lined up a clean shot on the eight-ball—out of turn. I hit it anyway. The ball dropped with a satisfying crack.

"No more playing by rules that weren't mine."

That night, I returned to my mother's house. I sat at the kitchen table, poured a bowl of cereal—no milk—and ate in silence. No TV. No music. Just the hum of the refrigerator and the rhythm of my own breath.

I thought about Maribel once. Just once. Then buried the thought deeper than memory.

This wasn't numbness. It was precision. The kind that only comes after you've been shattered and decided you'll never break again.

Several weeks passed. I still didn't touch the phone unless work required it. I wasn't answering to the streets. Mornings were the same—early workouts, quiet walks, sharp discipline. The only people who had regular access to me were my mother and Grim. Neither asked about the streets, the betrayal, or the name that hadn't been spoken out loud since the motel.

They understood me. I wasn't gone. I was building pressure.

Still staying at my mother's house, I moved like a ghost—hoodie up, head down, shades on even before sunrise. I walked through the neighborhood like I was taking inventory of the world that once tried to break me. Past the Rivera Motel. Past the old corner store where we used to post. Past Lincoln Arms where a kid sat on the steps eating sunflower seeds with my cousin.

I kept walking. Mapping the silence. Feeling the weight of memory but never letting it distract me.

This wasn't grief anymore. It was precision.

Black coffee and dry cereal. Pigeons from the kitchen window. Chess with Grim, who didn't ask questions—just made moves. And I studied him. Not the board. The man. His tells. His tempo.

Because that's what life had become again: tells and tempo. I was ready. Not for revenge. Not for love. For order.

The first ripple came when Big Abe called. "Got some movement," he said. "And B's home."

I paused. "Ock?"

"Yeah. Just touched down yesterday."

"Tell him I said nothing. Yet."

"Understood."

I hung up without another word. The meeting wasn't called with noise. It was summoned with silence.

I sent word through Cal to only five men. Do Dirty. Divine. Big Abe. Cal. Pudge. That was the circle.

We met at a warehouse on the south side—neutral ground, no eyes, no echoes. Second floor. No signage. Just an iron door that looked like it led to nothing. People showed up anyway.

One of the younger lieutenants tried to slide in. He wasn't invited. Thought maybe if he stayed quiet, kept his back to the wall, he'd earn a stripe just by being in the room. He didn't make it to the second sentence.

"Yo, anybody heard from Maribel?" That was it.

Big Abe turned slow. Didn't blink. Didn't curse. He stood and pulled the young man close by the collar like he was about to whisper a bedtime story.

"Since when is anyone in CJ's mouth or presence a concern of yours, mothersucker?"

The room went still. Abe didn't swing. Didn't yell. He let the silence slap him.

The lieutenant didn't argue. He apologized with his eyes, backed out the door, and was never mentioned again.

I walked in seconds later, eyes sweeping the room. I didn't ask who had been there before me. I already knew. I nodded once at Big Abe, then turned to face the circle.

I didn't call it a meeting. I called it a structure check. No chairs were assigned. No agenda was read. This wasn't politics. This was purification.

I stood while they settled. "This ain't a family," I began. "It's a structure. And structure doesn't forgive."

No one moved. "We had a good run. But grace made us lazy. Made some of us think friendship was a shield. It's not. That's over."

My voice stayed steady. Not angry. Not emotional. Just factual. "Going forward, it's simple. Anyone caught negotiating outside? Cut off. You eat with us, or you die out there hungry. No middle ground."

I looked at Do Dirty, then Divine. Paused on Cal. Gave Big Abe a slight nod. Then landed on Pudge.

"No more friendly affiliations. No conversations with ghosts. Streets aren't about flash. They're about flow. Anyone disrupting that rhythm? Gone."

I turned to Pudge. "Give me the word."

Pudge unfolded a single sheet. "Cool Todd's name been coming up. Flashy. Loud. Not direct. But I got weight on him."

I nodded. "Watch. Don't move."

Divine raised a brow. "Could sit him down. Feel him out."

"Let him earn his seat first," I said.

Then Do Dirty brought up southern expansion. "Weight's moving clean down there. Could eat heavy if we move fast."

I didn't hesitate. "You only grow what you can protect. We're not God. We're gravity. We pull what belongs close. Let the rest orbit till it crashes."

Ock B, who had arrived late and sat without being acknowledged, let out a dry laugh. I didn't look at him. Not yet. The structure check closed with silent nods. No handshakes. Just understanding. One by one, they filed out.

Cal. Divine. Do Dirty. Pudge.

Big Abe lingered, but I nodded. He left without a word.

Only Ock B stayed. I turned to him and walked closer. "Listen, brother," I began. "I know you have your own thing. Your own energy. Your own style. I respect it. But we're allied in this. And the only way this works is uniformity."

Ock tilted his head, unreadable.

I didn't blink. "The way your crew acts. The way mine acts. They act like the purchase acts. That's the bar."

He let that marinate.

"I love you, B. I trust you. Those words don't float off my lips easy. But you have to check this. You can't slap everybody. You can't beat everybody. I understand the place of fear—it matters for what we do. But let the fear come from what you don't do. That's when it's real."

Ock stayed silent.

I kept going. "You're not a sucker. They always know that. But if you treat disrespect, war, and ignorance the same—you waste your weight. Penalize it all the same? Then raise the level of who you let walk through that door."

My voice dropped. "We need to be silent as church mice. Businessmen. Moving like businessmen."

I paused, then gave him the last piece. "They think you've gotten soft? Good. Let 'em try. That's when you overreact. That's when you make an example. But not everybody, brother. Come on, B. I need you."

Ock finally nodded. "I got you. For real."

We dapped. One hard grip. "Good."

He left. The door closed behind him. I stood in the empty room a moment longer. The silence wasn't heavy anymore—it was clean. The house was in order.

Seven weeks had passed since I reemerged. The machine ran smooth. Business was organized. Crews were quiet. The city had adjusted.

But something else started whispering through the alleys. Not about power. Not about turf. About her.

It came from Cal one night, said soft like a man unsure whether to speak at all. "She not gone," Cal said. "But she out there."

I didn't look up from my plate. "What business is that of mine?"

Cal nodded once and said no more.

I didn't bring it up again. But the seed was planted. And on a night with no plan—just silence humming behind the wheel—I saw her.

Outside. Standing under a streetlight in a short coat with her hair pinned back in a way that used to mean elegance. Not now. Not tonight.

I slowed the car. She was posted like a woman with no home and no time. The kind of woman you don't want to see outside after 10 o'clock unless she's waiting for someone to save her—or sell herself.

Her eyes caught my headlights. She squinted.

Then she smiled. It wasn't the same smile. Not even close. It was aged. Tired. Thin around the edges like a memory folded and unfolded too many times.

She walked up to the passenger window. I rolled it down. "CJ?" she asked like she wasn't sure it was real.

I didn't answer. I looked her over. She looked like six years and just under two months had dragged across her face since the last time we touched. Still beautiful—but not in the way that makes men jealous. In the way that makes them sad.

"You got a second?" she asked. I tapped the passenger seat. She got in.

The cabin filled with a scent that wasn't hers—cheap perfume over a long day and a longer week. Her nails were chipped. Lipstick imitated the outline it used to keep with ease. When she tried to sound playful, her voice broke in the middle like a bridge that forgot how to carry weight.

"I'm sorry," she said. I stared ahead. "I ain't... I ain't been right," she continued. "I didn't mean for things to go like that. It just—"

"You need money?" I asked, flat.

Ashamed, she nodded once.

"You want me to just give you money?" She swallowed. "Maybe I could give you something in return."

I put the car in drive and pulled away from the light. I didn't take her to my house. Not to one of my rentals. Not to a quiet spot with warmth.

I turned down an alley off Clinton Street. Wet brick. Sour-sweet trash day. A single bulb humming like a bad memory. Tight, dark, empty—the kind of place no one parks unless they've got nothing left to lose.

I killed the engine. Stepped out. Opened her door. "Come on," I said. She followed. We faced each other in the pool of light. Cold needled through my sweatshirt; steam lifted from the hood like a tired spirit leaving a body. I tucked a stray piece of hair behind her ear. That was the last gentle thing I gave her.

"Don't kiss me," I said. "Just look."

She lifted her eyes. There was the girl I knew and the woman life had made at the same time. Hope crowding against apology. "This isn't about us," I said. "This is a burial."

She nodded, a small, breaking motion. I leaned back on the car, palms on the metal, and kept my gaze on her face. No tenderness. No rescue. Just witness. "Alright," I said. "Pay your debt."

Heat moved through her as if she'd swallowed a furnace and it had chosen the wrong room to warm. She lowered, slow, without bargaining. Not seduction—penance. The alley thinned to breath and the grit under my shoes. Her hands shook once and then steadied. I didn't close my eyes. I didn't touch her hair. I held her in my sight and let the last of my love burn itself out like a wick meeting glass.

My head hit the metal behind me, not in pleasure—release. Years of letters and kitchen laughter and made-up futures left my chest one inch at a time. I let them go. I made myself watch.

When it was over, she stayed still a heartbeat longer, as if time would give her back a second she could spend better. It didn't.

I stepped off the fender and reached into my pocket. I peeled bills until the roll felt lighter—maybe three, maybe four thousand—and let the money fall to the concrete. It slapped the wet ground like a verdict.

She flinched.

I lifted her chin with two fingers so she had to meet my eyes. They were dry and so were hers.

"Even when I spend on someone who stopped deserving me, I'm still generous," I said. "That's the last kindness with your name on it."

I dropped my hand. She gathered the money with small, clumsy motions, the way people pick flowers after they've trampled the garden. I stepped around her like a puddle, got in the car, and pulled off.

I didn't tell Cal. Didn't mention it to Grim. Didn't log it in the ledger of what had been lost.

There was nothing to process. No heartbreak left. Just a grave in an alley and a few folded bills in someone else's pocket.

That night, I didn't shower right away. I sat in the dark. Didn't cry. Didn't drink. Didn't feel.

It wasn't about Maribel anymore. It was about memory—and how sometimes, to move forward, you salt the earth so nothing old can grow there again.

Grace was gone. And mercy? Mercy died in that alley.

Chapter 16

Ten days after the alley, I hadn't said a word about what happened that night. Not to Cal. Not to Grim. Not even to myself. Whatever softness I'd once carried for Maribel had been carved out in silence and dumped behind me like trash in the wind. There was no eulogy. No regret.

Only pressure. The kind that builds in quiet spaces.

And just like pressure always does—it made something crack.

Do Dirty slid into my car outside a print shop. No greeting. Just a short sentence. "Rell D talkin' again."

I didn't turn my head. I kept chewing the toothpick in my mouth. "Where?"

"Dice game off Spruce. Said you was locked up while she was crying in his chest. Called her 'his now.' Loud. Twice."

I blinked slow. "Pull my card."

We watched him for two days. Rell was predictable. Loud in the afternoon, buzzed by nightfall. He moved like he wanted to be seen—chain out, shoes loud, phone always pressed to his ear like he was managing some imaginary empire.

I didn't speak much while we followed. I was saving my words for the right moment.

On the third night, the window opened. Rell was parked outside a chicken spot, leaning back in the driver seat with a toothpick in his mouth and old Jadakiss playing low through the speakers. Alone. Laughing on the phone.

Do Dirty approached first. Calm knock on the driver-side window. Rell turned, confused. Then he saw Do Dirty. Then the passenger door opened—and I slid in like I'd never left.

"Yo, CJ—" I cut him off before the smile could finish forming.

"You were given grace." I stared ahead, not at Rell.

"Not a warning. Not a pass. A pardon."

He blinked. I kept going. "'Cause I don't believe in mind tricks. The mind does what it does. It beats every muscle in your body—including the heart."

Rell swallowed. I turned toward him now, voice like polished glass. "So let's be clear—this ain't about that chick. She yours. Or anyone else slick enough to trick the fiend you made her."

That was supposed to be the period. The last word. But Rell wasn't done. He tilted his head, half-grinning. "How you think I knew to f —your girl?"

My eyes narrowed.

"One of your own set it up." He leaned in, voice lower, meaner. "Barry's cousin. Which makes her Skip's cousin too. Family on both ends. All that 'solid' you brag about? It's got holes." He smirked. "Loved knowing I made her get that abortion."

I didn't breathe.

"You think you top dog? You in a kennel, motherf—"

I moved before the word finished. Not with a gun—my hands. Two stiff jabs to close the distance. A hook to take breath. Do Dirty reached over the wheel and yanked the door open; we dragged Rell halfway out so the sill could teach his ribs a lesson. Elbow. Knee. Palm to nose. He folded and I caught him before he hit the pavement so his skull didn't make decisions I hadn't made yet.

He coughed, spitting blood on his shirt. Tried to laugh through it. I gripped his jaw. Not hard enough to break. Hard enough to remember. "Keep my name out your mouth."

He gurgled a chuckle. "Or what—you'll shoot me behind a—"

I leaned closer until he smelled the no in my breath. "Or I'll make it business."

I let him go. Do Dirty drove his forearm across Rell's chest one more time—enough to set the lesson. Then we sat him back in the seat. I took both of his phones, scrolled quick, noted who glowed in the recent list—Rod, a Laurel number, and one saved as 'Cuz.' I powered them down, broke the first, pocketed the second.

"Walk home," I said. "And don't call mine again."

We closed his door. Left him hunched over the wheel, coughing apologies he thought I couldn't hear.

In the car, Do Dirty didn't speak. He started the engine and pulled off slow. No music at first. Then I clicked on something soft—old Earth, Wind & Fire. Something I used to play when things were calm.

I leaned back in the passenger seat, hand on my thigh, eyes out the window. Didn't blink for a full minute.

Finally, I spoke. "Turn it up. I don't want to hear sirens tonight."

Do Dirty did. The music swelled. We passed under streetlights that blurred like old memories.

I didn't say another word. But in my mind, the noise was deafening.

I don't pray for peace. I budget it. Ten minutes with my eyes closed. Twenty with my phone off. A full hour where I let no one's name enter my chest. Order is subtraction before it's a build: subtract the impulse, subtract the witness, subtract the need to be understood. What's left can lift weight.

I wrote three rules on a receipt and folded it into my wallet.

1) Don't swing where memory is asking. Swing where math says.

2) Reward silence louder than I punish noise.

3) If I must hurt something, let it be my options, not my men.

The city looks different when you carry rules instead of rage. Streetlights stop being warnings and turn into metronomes. Every red is a count. Every green is a cue. I drove inside that counting until my heartbeat matched it, and the urge to correct the world with one hard act finally sat down and listened.

I didn't call meetings anymore.

If you saw me, it was because you were supposed to. If I spoke to you, it was because you mattered. Silence wasn't just my weapon —it was my circle.

Tonight, it was Elliott's on Route 9.

The pool hall looked like time had stopped just inside the door. Wood-panel walls, dusty Bud Light signs, cue chalk so old it might've known my father. The old man behind the bar knew not to speak unless spoken to.

I leaned over the table. Lined up a corner shot and sank it soft. I wasn't playing anyone—I was measuring the angles of the night.

Cal and Big Abe sat in a booth, quiet until I walked over.

"Word's out," Cal said. "Rell ain't makin' the week."

I chalked my cue. "Then we make sure what's heard ain't just noise. It's a lesson."

Big Abe leaned in. "Two names floatin'. Not enemies. Not friends. Just... off."

I raised an eyebrow. Cal answered. "Griff. From Jackson. And that pretty boy Johnny Ross."

I stared through the table. Then said it slow. "Griff..."

I chuckled once. Not from humor—from memory. "Tall brown-skin punk from Jackson. Only child. Spoiled since birth. Raised in privilege, but a couple cousins on our side gave him just enough street dust to pass."

"Made noise in the suburbs 'cause he was the only Black boy in a classroom full of soft hands and piano recitals. Wore his skin like a trophy." I walked to the rack and racked up again.

"Then he popped up here like he had stripes. Like the wolves forgot he only had one day on the block—and that day was years ago."

"One day. That's all. Back when the streets still bit you for standing wrong. But people forget. Fast."

"Griff don't move. He orbits. Always close when it gets loud, never close when it gets bloody. Dangerous... for a different reason."

Cal nodded. "What's the play?"

"No body," I said. "We isolate him. Let him feel invisible. That kind of silence screams louder than a pistol."

Big Abe cleared his throat. "Second one? Johnny Ross."

I exhaled. "Pretty-boy with light eyes and a fresh fade like he thinks the world owes him something."

"His pops got political weight. Some suit outta Princeton. Johnny? He orbits too. Never claimed the life. Loves the smell of it."

I cracked my neck. "I used to think he was a standup cat."

Then added: "Until I found out he's a kitchen bitch."

Cal squinted. "Kitchen bitch?"

I let a small smile show. "The type who, when the fellas outside playing spades, gossips in the kitchen with the aunties. Stirring tea. Whispering. Wearing cologne like he trying to impress somebody's mother."

Big Abe laughed once, deep and short. "Dangerous?"

"Nah," I said. "Just weak. But weakness spreads."

I leaned in close. "Send word. Tell Johnny this ain't the side of town for soft mouths. Either keep it pretty and distant… or we paint ugly and close."

Cal raised an eyebrow. "Translation?"

I finished my rack. Sank the 8-ball. "Tell him enjoy his view. But stay the fuck off the lawn."

They left Elliott's without fanfare. I stayed behind for one more Pepsi. The bar was quiet. The regulars gave me space like instinct.

I took my drink outside, leaned on the hood, and watched headlights pass like ghosts that never stopped to ask directions.

Inside the booth, a few younger heads were laughing too loud. One looked up, saw me, and immediately shut up.

I didn't smile. I sipped and let the silence speak for me. They used to fear my name. Now they wonder if I'm watching. That wonder? That's the leash.

Abe tapped once on my window as I sat in the Elliott's lot finishing the Pepsi. He didn't open the door until I nodded. "Say it," I told him.

"We got ears in places, but not where you want them yet," he said. "Boys from Laurel keep drifting two corners past their boundary like they can't read street signs."

"Good," I said. "Let them drift."

I waited for the rest. I gave it to me slow. "There's a re-up tomorrow—Monmouth underpass, 11:45. You bring two. No calls. If anybody else shows, they weren't invited."

Abe's eyes said he heard the capital letters.

I leaned closer. "Tell nobody but the two you bring. Not even Cal. Not Pudge. If a third body wanders in, we'll learn who talks in their sleep."

I almost smiled. "You want me to seed it?"

"I want you to protect it," I said. "Seeding is my job."

I cracked my knuckles once, a quiet amen, and stepped out into the night. I watched his shoulders disappear around the corner and marked the time. If watchers appeared tomorrow at 11:15, the leak wasn't his. If they appeared Wednesday at 2:15, the leak was somewhere else entirely.

Later that night, I walked past a mural. Not of me. Not of James. Of someone new—some local rapper who'd been killed over a chain and a comment on social.

I didn't stop. I just looked. Let 'em paint what they want. The ones who matter? They remember.

The next morning I put on a plain gray hoodie and walked into the courthouse like I was running an errand for a neighbor. Downstairs

—Records. Fluorescent hum. Paper and toner for perfume.

"Help you?" a voice said that already knew the answer.

Kelly. We met after court months back. Sharp without being sharp-tongued. The kind of woman who can move a room with a stapler and a raised brow. I slid a slip across for certified copies—nothing heavy. She stamped, glanced at the case number, and didn't let her face move.

"Long time," she said.

"Been keeping quiet," I answered.

She stacked my papers, squared them twice, then lowered her voice just enough. "Quiet's good. But your file wasn't."

I held her eyes without asking.

"Pulled yesterday," she said. "County task force login. Then a detective from the city asked for audio from a hearing that doesn't need audio."

"Curious detective," I said.

"Nosy," she corrected. "And sloppy. I left the request number on my counter. I put it where it belongs."

"Trash?"

She blinked once. "Inbox. I follow rules. But some things take time to route."

I nodded my thanks with my mouth, not my head.

As she handed me the envelope, she added, "If you're still a two-phone person, stop. They're listening wrong and will still hear you."

"I study," I said.

"Good," she replied, already on to the next window. "Then study faster."

I walked out with papers that meant nothing and information that meant everything. The city wasn't only whispering in alleys; it was rummaging through drawers.

The whispers wouldn't stop.

First it was a faint rumor. Then came the whisper: that someone inside had been feeding Rell D crumbs. The moment outside Room 212. The abortion. The shame. The betrayal. Rell didn't know all that on his own.

I tried to dismiss it. My mind is sharper than paranoia, and my circle is handpicked. But the words refused to leave.

Barry knew pieces. Big Abe had casually mentioned a cousin months ago. Cal once nodded knowingly. And that lieutenant—the one who asked about Maribel without invitation—that stuck too.

I wasn't spiraling. I was tightening. "You get the truth from mouths that don't think they need you anymore," I told Cal one night as we rode through town. "If you listen long enough, the truth always slips."

I didn't call for violence. Not yet. But I did make moves.

Barry was removed. Not harmed. Just out. Not even outer circle. Gone—vanished from the tree like he never existed.

The lieutenant? Quietly reassigned. "If I'm wrong, I restore," I said. "If I'm right… I want him to suffer slow." But I needed clarity.

That's when Skip called a meet. Skip wasn't a friend, not a foe. A man who stayed useful and unremarkable for two decades—an art in itself. We met in the wash bay of a closed carwash, the hum of the idle brushes covering more than words.

He didn't waste time. "That cousin you think belongs to Barry?" he said. "She belongs to me, too."

I waited.

"She been layin' up with Rell. Months." He slid a folded list on the workbench: dates, corners, two fake re-up windows I'd only told to one person... and there they were in his handwriting. "He's been selling knock under your stamp outside the circle. Not my rumor. My eyes. And the dumbest part? He bragged your name made it move."

I didn't reach for the list. "Why are you handing me this?"

Skip shrugged. "Because business ain't gossip. And a man selling under your name without your blessing is a fire that burns all our houses. Also," he added, "it'll make you happy when the day comes."

I looked at the list without touching it. Barry's cousin. Skip's cousin. Rell's mouth. My stamp on packs I never blessed.

"Keep your cousin out of my mentions," I said. "And if I'm happy one day, it'll be because you stayed out the way."

He nodded, picked up his own paper, and left with it. I didn't need a souvenir. I had what I came for: the reason this would be business when the time arrived.

An hour later the phone buzzed with a number that lives inside steel. Fifteen minutes, recorded. MMC.

"Brother," he said, voice thinner through the county line.

"You breathing?" I asked.

"I'm good," he lied like a professional. "Heard movement. Heard you back."

"I'm a schedule, not a rumor."

He chuckled, then coughed. "They keep asking me about Monmouth. About underpasses. About who pays who."

"Answer none," I said.

"I been answering air." He paused. "Need me to password to anyone?" There it was—the temptation dressed as help.

"Yeah," I said, keeping my tone flat. "Tell your outside to avoid **Wednesday, 2:15, the Laurel triangle**. Police like symmetry."

He exhaled. "Copy."

I let a beat pass. "And if you hear an underpass at **11:45**, that ain't ours. That's a story they're telling you to see if you repeat it."

"Say less," he said. "Head up."

The line clicked. I stared at the wall until the dial tone quit bragging. If watchers showed at the triangle on Wednesday, it wasn't Abe, and MMC's circle just volunteered its outline to me on a state-issued recording.

Fly and Mani came in next—cousins, young, not broken in but loyal.

"You two remind me of us before we had something to lose," I told them. "Stay around the wrong people and you'll lose your chance to even matter."

I pulled them close. Simple orders: fresh eyes, quiet ears. Watch everything. Report only to me. Fresh eyes see what you've been looking at too long to recognize. And Laurel Ave? It was making noise again.

I knew Rell had roots there. I fed Cool Todd when no one else could. Even though the alliance had faded after the drought, favor has residue.

I asked Cal, "Rod been talking?"

Cal shook his head. "Not loud. Sometimes silence is just fear hiding in plain sight."

I nodded. "Then let's see if fear remembers where it came from."

Rod got pulled into a meet—low-key. I didn't threaten him. I watched. He eventually spoke. "Rell was wild. Said you got soft. Said people only follow you because they scared, not 'cause they believe."

My jaw clenched. "And you?"

"I ain't say nothing," Rod said. "But I ain't stop it either."

I leaned back. "You ever seen a church burn? They say the cross stands last. That's what people remember. I want every story that gets told about me to end with that picture."

Rod nodded. "What you want me to do?"

"Eat with us or die with them," I said. "And if anyone in your camp mumbles wrong—your name dies first." Rod left smaller than he arrived.

Later that week, Fly returned with news. A small group—two lieutenants and a runner—had been seen talking with some Laurel Ave affiliates. Laughter. Gestures. Loose talk.

I said nothing. Instead, I sent Big Abe and Do Dirty.

That night, those three men were beaten, duct-taped, and dropped outside the hospital parking lot with a sign that read: KEEP LAUGHING.

The next day, Fly whispered, "They ain't laughing no more."

"Good," I said quietly. "Then the music can start."

I drove the rectangle once without stopping, just so the streets could see me and remember how to behave in my presence. Not fear—function. Expansion is a thirsty word; it makes men sprint. Order is patient; it makes empires last long enough to raise children who don't need guns to introduce themselves.

By midnight, I had two watches going in my head: **11:45 underpass** and **2:15 triangle**. One of them would attract moths. The other would stay dark. Either way, I'd know which window my future betrayal liked to open.

I rolled past Cross Street and caught a glimpse of Christa through a storefront reflection—head down, hands busy, nothing dramatic. I kept rolling. Some things deserve daylight and a name you can say without bleeding. Tonight was for math.

The city exhaled around me. I didn't mistake it for peace. It was just the breath a body takes before it gets disciplined.

Chapter 17

Amanda's Soul Food Spot off Highway 37 had the kind of seasoning that spoke in tongues.

I sat in the corner booth near the window—facing the street like always. Cal was already halfway through his catfish platter. Big Abe had a mountain of smothered turkey wings in front of him, but I still made room on the table to rest my elbow like the king of the block I am.

I wore a clean, well-fitted navy blue sweatsuit. Nothing loud—just sharp. Tailored by movement. Muscle showing just enough to remind people I don't just run things—I can move them.

Cal looked me over and whistled. "Damn, C. That joint look custom. Got the wrist and the waist tight—like you paid extra to not look like the rest of us."

"You wish you could afford this, don't you?"

Cal laughed. "C'mon, C. I ain't broke at all—I can afford that."

I leaned back, flipped my sleeve, and turned the label outward. South Pole. Forman Mills.

Cal's jaw dropped. Abe nearly choked mid-laugh. "Ain't no way!" Cal said. "Man, you lyin'."

"Dead serious," I grinned. "See, labels don't mean anything."

I leaned forward, still playful but with steel underneath. "Real talk? A chick'll take a neat, well-fitted Forman Mills suit over some weird-ass YSL sweatsuit where she gotta lift your fat stomach to suck your—"

Abe hollered. Cal shook his head, laughing. "Nah, but that's facts," I added. "Half of y'all dress like saggin' still in style.

Five-hundred-dollar gear that make you look like a lost teen at a middle school dance."

They laughed again, and I let the sound hang a beat. Then I wiped my hands, put the fork down, and let the air change.

"I ain't never been sloppy. Never chased the fanfare that comes with this little bit of power we hold. I watched that be the downfall of everybody before us. With us. Even the ones we used to look up to."

The table went quiet.

"Think about the formula. We grind and climb to get a little money. Then we want things. Once we get 'em? That ain't good enough. Now we gotta show we got it. Perform like the whole world's watching. And maybe they are—but not how you think."

"Most people don't take that home with them. They see your car— one you can't afford to keep—and forget it the second you turn the corner. You'll hear your name in whispers, but it don't change a single life. Don't rewrite what anybody really thinks about you."

"Now that you up here, you gotta stay up here. That chain around your neck? That's part of your persona now. And all it's really saying is, 'Look at me. I spent a lot. Please see me.'"

"Meanwhile hunger is real. And you shining so bright, you don't see the wolves growling. Then what happens? You get got. Or you get locked. Or you die protecting some dumb thing you were going to lose anyway."

"And no disrespect to true grandmasters—Rich Porter, Alpo, Big Meech… all the American gangster stories we grew up on. You know what they all got in common?"

"You can find them in the spotlight. Dripping in jewels, dancing like they were free. And yeah, they had it—but they were temporary. Same clubs as a dude trying to make a Christmas list work for his daughter. Christmas two weeks away, and Santa don't show unless a.45 does."

"You can't live like that unless every single person in your circle lives the same way. Nothing works like that. Somebody always at the bottom. And if he's looking up at you? That ain't admiration. It's resentment."

"You so high up, you can't see past your presidential Rolex. And the second they stop seeing you as someone to envy, you disappear. The spotlight stays on the dummy with the shine... and off the wolves waiting for that shine to blind him."

Silence. Just the fryer humming.

Cal nodded slowly. "Damn, C... You got that one filed away or that came off the top?"

I picked up my fork. "A little of both."

We finished the plates without talking. The food sat right—grease baptized in purpose. When we stepped out the side door, the cold slapped the steam from our collars. I busted off down the alley alone, needing four minutes with myself before we turned the day back on.

—

Back-lot nights behind Neesha's Custom Kicks always felt like secrets settling into the gravel. Pudge was already waiting, arms folded, leaning on my old Monte Carlo like it still had value. In a world where loud meant weak, Pudge stayed permanent.

"Appreciate you coming out," Pudge said.

I watched the flicker in the busted streetlight above us—half-lit, but always enough to see the wrong thing coming.

"Talk to me," I said.

"Word is… somebody sniffing near your old lines. Ain't made moves yet, but they being loud in soft spaces."

"Who?"

"One of them retired types. Used to rock with you. Nothing concrete. Felt like you should know."

I nodded once. "Let 'em sniff. Make sure the trail leads somewhere I already swept."

He grinned. "Housekeeping."

"Structure," I corrected. "Housekeeping is what people do after a mess. We don't make them."

He tapped the Monte once like it just agreed.

Late morning, I was on the roof two buildings off Monmouth, the underpass in view through a chipped pair of binoculars that looked like they'd watched the moon landing in person. Big Abe rolled up.

At 11:36, with two men I picked specifically for their quiet—no phones, no jewelry, no opinions. They staged like city workers, vests over hoodies, cones out near a pothole that didn't need saving.

At 11:44, a stray dog crossed under the bridge and shook off last night's rain. At **11:45**, nothing happened, which was exactly what was supposed to happen. I exhaled the kind you can only hear inside your own skull.

At 11:52, a silver sedan crept by, eyes in the rearview, antenna naked. County, not city. It didn't stop. It didn't need to. Seeing nothing teaches as much as seeing everything. Abe didn't flinch. Neither did I.

My man pulled the cones back in at 11:58, and the roof felt a shade lighter. I broke the binoculars down and drove to the triangle early, parking two blocks out so I could walk the last stretch on foot like I was counting trees. The Laurel triangle had always been a pocket of bad geometry—three streets meeting at the wrong angle, where sound bounced and men forgot how to calculate escape routes.

At 2:07, a gold Acura I'd known in another life cruised through slow. Not Rell's—one of his boy's old cars re-sold twice in the last year, still wearing its past like cheap cologne. It rolled past and didn't stop. At 2:12, a DoorDash throttle idled right where we'd said avoid. The kid didn't deliver anything. He unfocused his eyes like a man pretending to be invisible.

At 2:15, a plain sedan stopped on the far edge of the triangle. Two men inside with haircuts that said "policy," not "corner." New antenna cluster on the trunk, the kind that tries not to brag. They didn't even look at me. They looked at the shape of the intersection, the way you look at an equation you plan to cheat on.

Pudge—who I had posted a block back—clicked the plate twice with that tiny camera that pretended to be a key fob. I kept walking, made the corner, and stared at a half-torn flyer for a church fish fry like it was a map. The sedan pulled off first. DoorDash left next. The Acura circled again and gave up.

I didn't smile. But something in my chest sat up straighter.

It wasn't Abe. And it wasn't my house. The triangle conversation existed only in a state line, exactly where I placed it. If watchers arrived anyway, they were either listening to MMC's call or listening to the person who listened to his call. Either way, the circle I needed to shrink just told me where to cut.

I let a beat pass. "And if you hear an underpass at 11:45, that ain't ours. That's a story they're telling you to see if you repeat it."

"Say less," he said. "Head up."

The line clicked. I stared at the tree until the dial tone quit bragging. The circle around MMC wasn't my enemy; the system listening to both of us was. I cut the call volume in my life down to one voice—mine.

That night I rode through Country Circle with Cal. No music. No talk. Just observation. Old women sat on stoops with robes over sweats. A couple kids threw a football in the dark, like nostalgia itself was trying to breathe. I scanned faces—not for guilt, but rhythm. Who moved too fast to wave? Who didn't wave at all?

A car passed. Slowed too long.

"Paranoid?" Cal asked, watching the mirror.

"Prepared," I said.

I shifted in my seat. One hand on the door, not because I was reaching—but because I always could.

"You ever think about how quiet it got after the car?" I asked.

"Quiet how?"

"Not grief. Not loyalty. Just… quiet. Like people waiting to see if lightning strikes twice."

Cal didn't answer.

"People think storms make noise," I continued. "They don't. Rain makes noise. Wind makes noise. A real storm creeps in smooth. You only know it hit after it breaks your house in half."

I met Do Dirty later that night outside a closed laundromat on 13th. Lights off, but the security bulb blinked every six seconds like a clock counting down.

"Saw Johnny Ross over on Clinton," I said. "At a dice game I ain't playing in."

Do Dirty frowned.

"Maybe he just passing through."

"People don't pass through rooms they don't speak in," I said. "You post where you study."

Do Dirty said nothing. I looked out into the darkness.

"Start watching who disappears when the lights go out. Not just who steps forward when the crowd claps."

Cal's phone buzzed. He handed it to me. AB.

"You might want to circle back with Barry," AB said.

"What about him?"

"Getting real comfortable again. Acting like his spot don't come with expectations."

"He talking?"

"Not reckless. But loose. Soft-mouth. Like the people around him supposed to hold water he can't."

I ended the call. Didn't speak. Memory crept back like it paid rent.

Rell D's voice from the car returned in full color: How you think I knew to touch your world? One of your own set it up. Barry's cousin—and Skip's cousin. Family on both ends.

"Cal," I said quietly. "You still got eyes on Barry's movement?"

"Somewhat."

"Double it. Then triple it. I don't want to hear anything—I want to see everything."

"Say less."

"And that lieutenant?"

"Keeping quiet since Abe stepped to him."

"He gets pressure," I said. "Just enough to remind him of gravity. No harm. Distance."

"And Barry?"

"He's out," I said. "Not outer circle. Out."

Cal raised an eyebrow. "Completely?"

"You get the truth from people who think they don't need you anymore." I let the sentence settle. "If I'm wrong, I'll restore him tenfold."

"And if you're right?"

"I want him to suffer slow."

I never liked doubling back. Tonight I did—pulling into the east lot behind a beat-up bodega at the edge of Laurel Avenue. Too close to old lines. Too many stories woven into brick. But that's why I was here.

Waiting in the shadows were Mani and Fly. Cousins. Blood thicker than hustle. I'd been watching them dance on the edge, rocking too close to the wrong crew. The kind of mistakes that don't get corrected; they get carved into murals.

Fly stepped forward first, tall with cornrows and a chipped tooth that gave him a permanent smirk. Mani was more compact—thick beard, diamond stud, and eyes that didn't blink enough.

"Unc," Fly said, giving me the title reserved for respect, not family.

"Don't call me that when you're on borrowed time," I replied.

They went quiet.

"Y'all ain't here because I trust you. You're here because I don't. And the way you moving? It's going to get you killed by people who won't send flowers."

Mani raised a brow. "We wasn't doing nothing—"

"Exactly," I snapped. "You were just there. 'Just there' gets you caught in fire you didn't light."

I stepped closer, voice steady but darker. "Fresh eyes see what I've been looking at too long to recognize. I'm bringing you in because I'd rather use you than lose you. Don't twist that into forgiveness. I'm watching you both harder than the rest."

Fly nodded. Mani said nothing.

I turned to Cal, who stood off to the side the whole time, arms folded. I didn't speak. Just logged everything.

Back in the car, I lit the engine but didn't drive. Laurel had changed—loud boys with nothing to say. Too many weapons, not enough wisdom.

"The last torch just went out," I muttered. "Now the wolves are circling. The question is who's letting them in."

Two days later, I met Cool Todd at an old warehouse lot near the tracks. Just two chairs. No entourage. No music. Just rust and wind.

Rod came smooth, as always. Black hoodie, gold rope, a cigarette that never burned out—he just replaced it every few pulls.

"Ain't seen you in a minute," Rod said. "Thought maybe you forgot your old friends."

I didn't smile. "Didn't forget nothing. I remember Rell kept you fed through the drought. I remember I had family on Laurel."

Rod shrugged. "Rell was Rell. Loud. Funny. Unpredictable."

"Unpredictable how?"

"Bragged about knowing things. Connections. Secrets."

"You ever hear specifics?"

Rod tapped ash. "Said you getting soft. Said people only follow you 'cause they scared, not 'cause they believe."

My jaw clenched. "And you?"

"I ain't say nothing," Rod said. "But I ain't stop it either."

"You ever seen a church burn?" I asked. "They say the cross stands last. That's what people remember. I want every story told about me to end with that picture."

Rod nodded. "What you want me to do?"

"Eat with us or die with them," I said. "And if anyone in your camp mumbles wrong—your name dies first."

He left smaller than he arrived.

I cut through Cross Street on the way back and caught a glimpse of Christa in a shop window reflection—head down, hands busy, nothing dramatic. She looked up at the same time and caught me catching her. No wave. Just a clean, almost-smile that said she had her own life, the kind built on calendars and habits, not chaos. I kept rolling. Some things deserve daylight and a name you can say without bleeding. Tonight was for math.

By the time the sky settled into bruise-purple, I was on the roof of one of my buildings, looking out. I thought of Barry. Thought of the lieutenant. Thought of Maribel. Mostly I thought of the silence —the specific kind that comes before a setup. The subtle shift when people smile too fast or move just slow enough to seem normal. I know the difference.

You can lock your doors. You can change your circles. The danger is always the bread crumbs.

Someone leaves just enough for wolves to follow. Just enough for them to find a way in.

My phone buzzed. Text from Cal: "Rod checked out. Nothing suspicious yet."

Second text: "Mani and Fly been clean. They listening. Watching."

I put the phone away. "Good," I said into the wind. "Let 'em keep watching."

Then I said it aloud, just once—like I was confirming it with God.

"If I'm wrong, I'll restore him tenfold. If I'm right... I want him to suffer slow."

The wind picked up on Laurel below. I didn't flinch. I was already listening.

Chapter 18

Barry didn't take the removal lightly.

I could tell by the way his smile sat too even, like a picture frame forcing a crooked wall to look straight. I tried to hang his shoulders loose and keep his voice calm, but his eyes did the talking. When I moved him to the outer circle, he nodded like it didn't sting, then stopped telling jokes, stopped seeking my eyes, started measuring rooms before he entered them. Distance grew its own spine between us.

I didn't accompany the move with a speech. That was intentional. I don't give explanations to men who feel entitled to forgiveness. Silence is the better accountant—it counts what noise tries to hide.

Within days two different pipelines carried the same flavor back to Amanda's. Barry wasn't moving reckless, but he was moving thirsty. That special thirst that shows up as revision—retold stories where he travels from soldier to savior, from background muscle to architect. He started calling people I'd let drift years ago— bargain hustlers, mid-tier hitters, washed-up names with loud mouths and soft hands. He set up small link-ups, talked vague, tested water like a man trying to convince the tide it used to obey him.

He wasn't plotting. He was positioning. And Cal was the first to bring it to the table. I walked into Amanda's with my hoodie up and my jaw tired. He didn't even sit before the words left his mouth.

"He out here acting like we betrayed him," Cal said. "Told one of my old peoples he don't even know what he did wrong."

I twisted the cap off a Pepsi and watched the bubbles climb. Cal kept going. "But he said it like a dude who definitely knows. You know what I mean?"

I nodded without looking up. "When people think they've been wronged, they either disappear quiet… or talk loud so they don't vanish." I let that rest. "Loud mouths ain't brave. They're scared of being forgotten."

The fryer hummed. The room exhaled. Barry's behavior wasn't surprising, it was textbook. Proximity to power tastes sweet; entitlement is the aftertaste. Survival gets mistaken for stature. Standing near the flame becomes the same as building the fire. Men start rewriting the script and expect the cast to clap on cue.

I walked to the back window and looked down on the block like a chessboard I designed. Cal followed, hands in his hoodie pocket.

"How you want to handle it?" he asked.

"Let me speak," I said. "Don't interrupt. Don't warn me. Make me feel free."

"No bump? No pressure?"

"That's when truth leaks—when people think no one's listening." I tapped the glass twice. "Put a man in a cage and he'll hold secrets. Put him where he thinks he's safe, where he thinks no one's watching, he'll confess without knowing."

"So you're going invisible?"

"I'm going to let the wind carry my breath back to me."

The plan was simple. No paranoia. No flex. No theater. Give him rope, not a stage. I'd call old friends. Reframe old battles. Convince one or two fools that moving him out was my mistake.

Eventually he'd say the wrong thing to the right set of ears. I'd be standing by the door the wind chose.

For a week I watched him move exactly like I drew it. I wasn't a rebel. I was a forgotten heir trying to build a throne from memory. I posted at neutral spots—diners, after-hours, the back room of a barbershop I once flipped into safe ground—and let my presence be rumor. I told stories just loud enough to be overheard, not bold enough to challenge me. Seeds, not swords.

"He did what he had to do, I guess," I heard him say to two outsiders at a cracked Formica table, Henny dark in a plastic cup. "But let's not act like I did it alone."

He wasn't factually wrong. It was the tone. The slide from brotherhood to bookkeeping, from loyalty to ledger. By week's end even Pudge had a version.

"He out here talkin' like he founded the church," Pudge told Cal, "but he forgot who wrote the scriptures."

I didn't correct a thing. I don't argue with whispers; I move them. My silence wasn't weakness. It was a countdown.

The slip arrived the way real fractures do—sideways, through a mouth that didn't mean to bring it back. Mani overheard it in the back room of an uptown shop where the clippers never cool, the dice are honest only because they're watched, and disrespect is considered safe if the audience laughs. Barry leaned in a faded vinyl chair, plastic cup sweating, ringed by hungry listeners— some new, some washed, all looking for an angle.

They joked about old codes, the "then" versus the "now." That's when he dropped it, easy as a yawn: "Yeah, I used to rock with him heavy... until I saw how it really was."

No threat. No malice. Just distance, delivered in the past tense—the grammar of betrayal. The room chuckled; someone clapped his shoulder. No one thought twice. Except Mani. I finished his cut, stepped outside like he needed air, and called the wind back to me.

Cal brought it to the back hallway while I checked invoices and let the quiet be armor. "Word for word," he said. "Didn't even blink. Smiled like it was a universal truth."

"A man who removes your name from his respect list," I said, "is already halfway to betrayal." I didn't say it angry. I said it like math. "That's the first break. Not the plot. The mouth."

"Done?" Cal asked.

"Not because he challenged me," I said. "He didn't do that. I stopped honoring the bond. When a man stops honoring, he already sees myself as free."

I sat alone after they walked out. Barry had been with me since early flips, pressure we retell as joke now but used to live like siren. Dependable muscle. Consistent. That was enough—until it wasn't. I don't hate men for wanting more than their assignment. I hate when they rewrite the assignment and expect applause.

Respect isn't begged. It's enforced. From the moment he put me in past tense, the cord was cut. No speech. No summons. Confirmation only.

Before I moved, I rounded the proof. The canary windows had already paid me in quiet: the 1:45 underpass stayed clean; 2:15 at the Laurel triangle attracted policy haircuts. Kelly at Records had underlined that somebody with county credentials was pulling my name like I was a vending machine. Skip—useful and unremarkable by design—added an extra note at the carwash: "My cousin is Barry's cousin is Rell's pillow for a hot month. Your stamp hit packs you never blessed. Not rumor. Eyes." I didn't take his paper. I don't need souvenirs. I needed motive that belongs to business and a conscience that doesn't need to burn afterward.

Big Abe asked to move when he heard the barbershop line. "Quick?" he said. There's tenderness under his hardness that only old loyalty knows how to hide.

"Not loud," I said. "Comfort first. I want him thinking he's writing the next chapter."

"Comfort is when men forget they're being watched," Abe said.

"Comfort is when they forget who gave them a name."

Two days later I met Do Dirty on a low-rise roof that overlooks the block Barry once helped us hold. He didn't ask why. He's a fuse; he waits for the flame.

"He's done talking like we're tied," I said.

"He said it out loud?"

"In front of people," I said. "With pride."

"So we kill the echo?"

"No," I said. "We kill the permission."

He smiled the kind that doesn't reach eyes. We both knew what that meant. Whispers don't need volume to travel; they need permission. Take away permission and echoes die on their commute.

I didn't choose a stage. I chose a place a man feels alone. A corner store lot off Stuyvesant, mid-afternoon, nothing glamorous. Chips under his arm. Phone to his ear. The same jacket I'd given him last winter like provenance. Divine slid in from the driver's side, Do Dirty bracketed the front. There was no speech, no argument, no wrestling with ghosts. Clean. Small. Final. The street swallowed the moment like it had practiced. Engines hummed. Nobody screamed. Pest control.

Back at my mother's, news sat on the kitchen table like weather. Expected. Unremarkable. Cal stood by the window and let glass reflect his shape instead of his thoughts.

"It's done," I said.

He didn't nod. He watched the street breathe and finally muttered, "That's the problem with using people from your own town. You ain't the only one they knew… just the only one they feared."

The rumor mill didn't ask who did it. It asked why I waited. That question told me my timing was right. People respect an execution; they study a patience.

Later that week me and Do Dirty ate outside a Popeyes off 33, early enough to avoid heat, too late for innocence. "You know what I hate?" I said. "Everybody who watched New Jack City and walked out believing they were Nino. A whole generation of stupid."

"Yeah, but it's entertaining," he said.

"So is fire," I said, "until it's your house burning." I let the grease sit on my tongue like a sermon. "We treat scripts like scripture, forget every ending is death or prison, remember the jewels and the cars and the women and the parties. That's the formula. That's the trap."

A teenager rolled past on a bike—hoodie too big, hat low, backpack bouncing. "You know what that kid sees when he looks at us?" I asked.

"Respect?"

"He sees what he could be," I said. "He doesn't know this life isn't meant to be lived in long. It's a costume. Even kings outgrow the robe."

I went back to the same roof that night. The circle had tightened; the air still leaned wrong. Not noise. A shift. The kind that doesn't knock. It slithers. I looked out at the skyline and let the rules in my wallet recite themselves without the paper:

1) Don't swing where memory is asking. Swing where math says.

2) Reward silence louder than I punish noise.

3) If I must hurt something, let it be my options, not my men.

4) Don't hire memory. Hire function.

"You can build a kingdom with whispers," I told the dark, "but make sure the walls don't talk back." I lit a match and let it burn to my fingers before sending it off the edge. "This isn't revenge," I said into the wind. "This is pest control."

The day after Barry, the triangle test paid one more dividend. Pudge handed me a photo—plate kissed by that tiny fob camera from across the block. DMV turned it into a name: a city detective who steals the county's login whenever he wants bigger ears than his badge. Kelly had given me the request number; the plate gave the request a face. I didn't call her. I don't make soft women feel like decoys. I just folded the information into my pocket like cash I don't spend where I earned it.

I cut down phones. Not lines—devices. Two only. One lives in a drawer in a room with no windows. The other lives in my front right pocket and only rings for four names. If your name isn't one of them, you meet my quiet and guess what my breath sounds like.

Ock B asked for a quick set of steps that evening—warehouse stairs, concrete cold enough to keep tempers honest. "You sure about slow?" he said. "Boys expect thunder."

"Slow is louder if your ears work," I said. "I don't want fireworks. I want funerals that feel like timing."

He grinned. "You always did like poetry."

"I like math," I corrected. "Poetry is what men use when they don't have proof."

I let the laugh fall down the steps. "I got you." He meant it. I still reminded him: "The way your side moves. The way mine moves. They move like a purchase moves. That's the bar." He nodded and we were done.

Night run of the rectangle after that. No music. Window cracked enough to let the cold slap the fog out. I rolled 8th, 10th, Monmouth, cut the waterfront and let silence get big. The underpass looked like a mouth that knew secrets and kept them for once. By the time I came off Congress, I'd budgeted my peace: ten minutes eyes closed, twenty minutes with the phone off, an hour where nobody's name enters my chest. Order is subtraction before it's a build. Subtract the impulse. Subtract the witness. Subtract the need to be understood.

Grim had the board out when I got back. We don't talk for openings. He pushed the knight like it was stretching before church. I met it with a pawn and watched his eyes, not his hands. Five moves later he sacrificed a bishop men cling to when they want to feel holy about poor coordination. "You saw that," he said. "I did," I said. "Didn't need to stop it." Three moves after I checked him and let the check breathe without finishing it; the point wasn't victory, it was tempo—reminding both of us I set it now without trying.

Amanda's lull between lunch rush and dinner crowd is where discipline hides. Cash drawers counted, vendor ledger signed, fryer oil changed.

I was rolling towels when a number that never had the nerve to ring me before tried. I let it die. It called back. I answered.

"CJ?"

"Speak like you respect your own name first," I said.

"Right," the voice said. "Johnny Ross." I could hear cologne through the phone.

"Why are you calling me?"

"Heard you said that lawn line. Wanted you to know it's all respect."

"Respect is distance," I said. "If you need a number to reach me, you're already too close."

Silence. Then the smaller voice men use when the performance bleeds out. "Understood."

"Good," I said. "Keep the view. Forget the lawn exists." I hung up and put him back in orbit where he belongs.

Fly and Mani came through later with three small things that weren't small. A corner I don't claim anymore got swept an hour after a car I don't drive crossed it on purpose. A Laurel runner asked the wrong question about an underpass he paid not to know existed. And a woman I've never met asked Kelly by her first name at Records like they share a kitchen. The first two go in the same folder the plate went into. The third gets a yellow tab. I don't like when civilians get named by men who don't own quiet hearts.

"Y'all doing better," I told the cousins. "But better is a floor, not a trophy." Mani bowed his head like he was hiding a grin. Fly didn't hide his. I let them enjoy the small win and reminded them of the bigger rule. "The day I need you to shout," I said, "I'll send you to a parade. Until then be the reason air conditioners get blamed for drafts."

They laughed their way out of the kitchen and took the lesson with them.

A text from Skip slid in after dark: "Carwash closed Mondays. If you need to talk to a cousin, choose Tuesday." I didn't answer. I memorize schedules, not opinions. I wants to be useful; I let him. Usefulness is a leash polite enough to look like friendship if you squint.

I took Cross Street instead of the highway on the way home and caught Christa in a storefront reflection—navy dress, flats, hair in a low twist, hands moving like a life built on calendars not chaos. She looked up at the glass the same second I did and almost smiled. I didn't wave. Not everything deserves a scene just because two people can read the same room. Daylight is its own kind of respect.

Night again. Roof again. The city breathing like a boxer in the seventh—steady, calculating whether to dance or clinch. My phone buzzed three short texts from Cal: "Laurel quiet." "Triangle empty." "Records not pulled again." I put the phone away and let my chest answer with silence. Peace isn't a prayer; it's a budget. I folded the rules back into my wallet and added the piece I never write down: If I'm wrong, I restore tenfold. If I'm right, the suffering won't look like vengeance. It'll look like maintenance.

Maintaining a kingdom isn't the same as keeping one. Anyone can keep what doesn't fight back. A kingdom fights. You don't win by shouting at it. You win by listening until the walls hum the song you wrote and then refusing to change the key.

The wind shifted—quiet, exact. Somewhere between 2:12 and 2:15 tomorrow there would be a test I didn't schedule. I'd be ready anyway.

I took the stairs slow, closed the door without a sound, and let sleep find me first for once. Pest control on schedule. The rest would arrive on time without an invitation.

Chapter 19

The storage unit sat off Route 130 behind a row of abandoned storefronts and a mattress outlet that hadn't seen a customer in a decade. It looked like nothing. That was the beauty of it. Chain-link rust. A keypad that glitched every third entry. Cameras too dusty to scare anyone honest and too obvious to bother anyone crooked. The kind of place you forget after you pass it. The kind of place I remember on purpose.

I'd had the address and the combo for months—since the day Felix pressed a folded slip of paper into my palm in the yard without breaking stride. No explanation. Just a number, a padlock code, and a nod. I slid it into the back of my Bible and didn't look again. I don't unwrap gifts until I'm ready to live with what's inside.

I parked two streets over, walked in with a baseball cap low and my hands empty, and let the gate complain as little as possible. The unit door rolled up with a throat-clearing groan. I stepped in and pulled it down behind me until the outside sound disappeared. The scent hit first—old rubber, dusty cardboard, cold metal, time. Dry air, heavy anyway. Secrets have weight.

My flashlight cut a thin triangle across stacked crates, two duffels, and a steel footlocker old enough to have seen wars I only read about. A gray plastic bin sat to the side with a strip of masking tape that read, in block letters, "TOOLS." I aimed at the lid and smiled. Tools are always the most interesting box in a room full of weapons.

I went to the first crate. Pried it up. Money stared back at me— hundreds, band after band, crisp bills packed so tight they moved like one thing. Labeled by hand. Dates on the paper sleeves stretched back years. I lifted a brick and flipped it to see the last band: "FEB-2004 50K." I put it down and opened the crate beneath it. More cash. Smaller denominations stacked like they knew their job wasn't glamorous but still mattered.

The second crate held product—bricks wrapped to a surgeon's standard. Twenty, maybe more. Clear plastic so clean it could hum. Purity is a sound when you know how to listen.

The footlocker had two latches and an attitude. I worked the key across both, lifted the lid, and let the smell of gun oil rise slow. Pistols lined in foam. Magazines wrapped in wax paper. A couple threaded barrels. A compact Uzi that looked like it forgot why history tried to bury it. No dust. Everything maintained like it was waiting for an order, not a handshake.

I kept the light moving. Keys on a steel ring sat in a shallow tray: an Audi fob, a condo fob with a Hoboken address, two mailbox keys, and one that looked like it belonged to an old elevator with a temper. Beneath the keys sat a slim, black leather notebook. No name on the cover. Inside, neat columns—first names, numbers, and three-letter codes only Felix and God could translate without a legend. I turned a page and saw a small square of paper taped in the center, like a compass rose in a map no one should own. "KITCHEN—JOSH."

Felix did everything without adjectives. Even his trust was quiet.

On top of the last crate sat a white envelope with my name. I opened it. Five words in block letters: "You stayed solid. This buys." No signature. No sermon. I stood there in the thin cone of light and felt a heat in my chest I don't usually allow. Felix was always flamboyant about his clothes and surgical about his moves. Loyalty cost him nothing to promise and everything to practice. He practiced when it counted.

I closed the footlocker and sat on it. Let the flashlight lay on its side so the beam cut the room diagonal. I thought about the first time I met Felix—the smirk like he'd cracked a joke and won the pot without showing his hand. I thought about the shower I stopped in the yard. I didn't tell anyone. There are things you do because your code won't let you watch a weaker man drown. Felix knew without being told. The jungle always knows. That's what they never teach in movies. Codes don't speak English; they speak pattern.

I texted one line to five men: "Warehouse. One hour." Then I put the keys in my pocket, the notebook in my waistband, and left the rest sleeping for now. You don't wake everything up on the first night you visit a graveyard of gifts.

The warehouse lights buzzed like they never forgave fluorescent for outliving fire. I put the crates on a concrete table that had seen deals and apologies and more than one prayer disguised as a plan. Stacks of money sat in front of five places—$386,000 each. Neat. Square. Honest. Two bricks each in a separate row. I don't make men guess about generosity. Guessing breeds theater. Theater breeds envy. Envy breeds knives.

When Cal, Do Dirty, Big Abe, Divine, and Ock B stepped in, I didn't shake hands. I don't turn generosity into a ceremony. I let them see it. I let them breathe it. Then I spoke.

"If you're in this room, you're not just with me," I said. "You're rich. You're anchored. You're family." I let silence sit where applause would ruin the lesson. "This isn't a loan. This isn't a front. It's yours. Every dollar. I kept more because I earned more. That's how it works."

I nodded to the bricks. "Two each. Uncut. Josh cooks it right and you'll be sitting over a million before you lift a finger."

Cal lifted his chin. "Josh?"

"Big Josh from Trenton," I said. "Met him inside. I watched him fold a day into discipline without telling the room he was doing it. I'm not replacing MMC—you can't replace a man with history—but I'm hiring precision. Josh cooks right, and he's paid to be silent."

Do Dirty grinned. "What's the catch, General?"

"Loyalty. Uniformity. Zero visibility," I said. "That means no new cars. No gaudy chains. No Gucci baby mommas on IG. Not for a year."

They chuckled. I didn't. "We go quiet. We invest. Barbershops, salons, food trucks, corner stores. Thirty percent of profits back in. When one location runs itself, you start another. One in the hood, one in the suburbs. Different faces on paper. We become the current. Everyone else just tries not to drown."

I paused, then set the hinge: "You know how white money got so far ahead? Free labor. Not smarter. A head start bought by bodies. Imagine everyone working for us, absolutely free, for generations. That's the edge. This is our free. We don't steal people. We steal time. We make our money work without needing applause. That's the only revenge that doesn't send flowers after."

The room went still like the lights had a say. "I believe in you," I said. "But belief is a compliment, not a strategy. Strategy is: all of us eat. Not on paper—real. Rich enough that none of you ever needs a favor again. Then when we stand next to each other, we don't stand on me. We stand together."

I let my voice drop. "No more getting wiped if someone catches a case. No scrambling to hold things. Even if one of us falls, the rest lift without wheezing." I looked at each man until I saw the line land behind the eyes. "I'm not on some 'exit the life' sermon. I want us to elevate this thing so high that we are the only way in."

Divine tapped the table. "Say less."

"Empire building starts now," I said, and the lights buzzed like they agreed.

Months passed and the current formed. Food trucks with clean logos and better grease parked where the day needed salt—business parks at lunch, school lots after practice, bus terminals when shift change made the air hungry. The smell of jerk smoke and whiting fry lines began to mark our borders better than graffiti ever did.

Barbershops buzzed with honest cuts and coded gossip. A sneaker boutique ran back-to-school discounts that paid for themselves twice before the first bell rang. Do Dirty's cousin signed for a nail salon in Rahway; Cal's old teammate did books at a smoothie shop where everything green tasted like discipline. We rotated storefronts and faces; the source never stood still long enough to be pointed at. Nobody flashed. Nobody got sloppy. my instructions were gospel because the tithes made sense.

I walked nights with my hands down and my head up. Sometimes I stood far enough from a truck to let the steam hit me without the money recognizing its father. Sometimes I parked by the warehouse gate and didn't go in because true order is when a room doesn't miss you. The system breathed; I counted its ribs.

One night I came home lighter than I'd felt in years. I stripped to my undershirt, poured a cold glass of water, and watched the sky from my small balcony. A real breeze touched the curtains. I didn't carry my piece to the bedroom. I lay across the bed with my hands behind my head and let peace stand on my chest without trying to weigh me down.

The knock came like a lesson. Not frantic. Heavy. Three measured pounds at 2:13 a.m. I walked barefoot to the door, grabbed the gun from the hallway shelf because instinct isn't a sin, and opened to a line of faces that don't visit at that hour without reason—Divine, Cal, Do Dirty, Ock B, Big Abe. Nobody breathed wrong. Nobody spoke. But the air had shape.

"What happened?" I asked. My voice didn't raise. I don't bargain with panic.

Cal looked at the floor. Do Dirty stepped back like he knew the room needed space. Divine said it the way a man hands you a folded flag. "You might want to sit, C."

"Say it," I said.

Big Abe's voice found gravel. "It's Grim. He didn't make it."

I kept my hand on the knob because muscles do what memory tells them. "Didn't make what?" I asked.

Silence stretched. I walked into it. "Didn't make what, motherfucker?"

Abe's eyes dropped. "Grim didn't make it. He's gone."

I didn't shout. I didn't throw or pace. I went to the back room, put on a coat, and came back. "Take me."

The ride was quiet until words could stand without breaking. "Everything," I said. "Who said what. Who watched. Who walked. Who called."

Cal nodded. "Wasn't a setup. Wasn't crew. Spanish cat, new face. Talking greasy. Grim don't take disrespect. He got off first. Beat him bad. Thought it was over. Walking away."

"Where'd he get cut?" I asked.

"Right shoulder. Deep. Artery. From behind."

"Cowards don't fight fair," I said.

We pulled into the hospital bay. Fluorescent tried to make mercy look clean. A nurse raised a hand and I looked at her like a closed door looks at a draft. She let me pass. The curtain was drawn. The tubes were gone. The sheet sat at his waist. Grim looked interrupted, not peaceful. I sat and took his forearm in both hands. "You weren't supposed to be here," I whispered. Then I let silence sit where wailing would have been about me instead of my brother.

When I stood, my phone buzzed. I didn't look. There are calls you let die because the person on the other end shouldn't have to hear the way you breathe.

Back at the warehouse the air lost patience. I stood at the same table where we'd stacked our future and let the room feel the subtraction. "Nobody lives," I said. "If this man had a fifth-grade crush, hurt her feelings."

Do Dirty leaned forward. "Parents? Siblings?"

"If they're in the way," I said, "yes."

Abe's face shifted. "C—if it's not necessary—"

"Then destroy what they own," I said. "Down to the tricycle. I want everyone who survives him to hate he was ever born."

Ock folded his arms and nodded. "If anybody gets picked up, I don't care what it costs. They don't live through the night."

"Done," I said. I wasn't angry; I was accurate.

Abe cleared his throat. "Internal. We handled it. But you should know."

"Go," I said.

"Barry talked to Rell," Abe said. "Confirmed. He's the one who gave up the Maribel play."

"You handled him?" I asked.

"We stripped him. Everything. Properties, cars, respect. He's walking, but he ain't breathing."

I nodded. "If I'm wrong, I'll restore tenfold. If I'm right, I want him to suffer slow." Do Dirty half-smiled. "Whispers will bring it back," he said. They do. They always do.

In the shadowed corner Fly and Mani waited like punctuation. "You're with me now," I said. "Laurel's humming. Rod may be making calls off someone else's name. Find me the echo, and I'll kill the singer."

"Say less," Fly said.

"They don't know what they did," I told the ceiling. "We'll teach them. Piece by piece."

I returned to the hospital room alone. The sheet held a brown bloom near the shoulder. Not much. Enough. I looked at Grim's knuckles—purple and swollen like they still believed in right now. I was twelve the first time I watched him drop a man twice his age for cursing in front of our mother. I told him for years after, "Stop doing that. Nobody fights fair anymore." He'd laugh and say, "Then make sure they need to cheat." I traced the ridge of a scar on his wrist from when he reached into a window and forgot glass has a voice.

"I needed more time," I said. I didn't cry there. I cried later.

In the car, Cal tried to fill a space that didn't belong to him. I held up a hand. "Not now." He nodded. The engine hummed. The silence sat.

"How'd the blade get in?" I asked finally. "Grim doesn't turn his back."

Ock answered. "It was clean. He faked a stumble. Came up swinging. Grim dropped him twice. After the second, he pulled when Grim started to walk."

"He finished what the man started," I said. "Then got stabbed for it."

"Yeah."

"He died with honor," I said. "Make sure no one else lives with it."

We stopped at Elliott's off Route 9. I needed noise nearby, not on me. I ran the table alone. The clack of cue on ball was the kind of math I could stand to hear. Cal sipped a ginger ale and counted how many times I blinked. Fly and Mani came through quiet. I motioned them closer.

"I shouldn't have to pull you in," I said, "but proximity to amateurs gets men like you killed. Fresh eyes see what loyalty looks past. From now on you don't work near me. You work for me."

"Already watching," Mani said.

"Good," I said. "Rod still has lines to Rell. The drought might've dried friendship, but favor leaves residue. I need to know what Rell told whom and when. Specifically, he fed me a line about 'one of mine' giving him the keys to Maribel. Told him how to catch her. Told him I made her terminate, and somebody close celebrated it. Find out who knew what—and who laughed."

They stood a beat longer than most men can. "This isn't about a woman," I said. "It's about betrayal. Bring me mouths, not rumors." They nodded and left the air the way they found it.

Back at the warehouse Abe caught me at the door. "You good?"

"As good as I'm going to be."

"You sure you want to scorch the tree?"

"I want the roots," I said. "Trees grow back." He didn't argue. Old loyalty knows when to keep its mouth full of teeth.

I ran the table again until the eight dropped like a period. "Grim taught me to shoot with a broomstick and a milk crate," I said to no one in particular. "Line it up. Shut up. Less talk, cleaner aim." Cal smiled like an old photograph. "Laurel's noisy but not reckless," he offered. "Rod's name fading. We may not need to heat it unless—"

I turned. "You think I'm lighting matches for the show?"

"No," he said quickly. "Checking the temperature."

"Keep your hand on the burner," I said.

Do Dirty zipped a duffel without looking at me. "You ready?" I asked. "I was born," he said. That's why he stays.

Two weeks held me hostage while the state did paperwork with my brother's name. Workouts in the morning until my lungs could count for me. Walks in the afternoon with a hood up and a phone off. Chess at night with Grim's empty chair in my peripheral vision even when he wasn't there. I didn't drink. I didn't touch. I sat with steel and let it teach me what bends and what breaks.

They finally released the body. Macedonia Church on John Street. Lemon oil and grief. Colored glass tried to turn sorrow into art and did a decent job for people who needed help. I arrived before the room did. The casket gleamed like an argument. I don't remember the service. I remember wood. I remember the air not moving. When it was time to walk by, I did. Tears fell and didn't derail my steps. I put a hand on his chest and told God a thing only brothers understand.

Elsewhere, James worked.

I don't take out anything that belongs to James's legend when I tell it. Some men plan with volume. James plans like water. He doesn't tell me all of it. He doesn't need to. Word came sideways first: the man who stabbed Grim had a condition—heart or seizures, no one could keep the story straight because none of them deserved clarity. He needed medication. James reached the nurse who touched the bottles. A cousin owed him a favor, the sort that lives in the family like a scar you choose to keep. Labels switched. Pills replaced. The man died three nights later, curled and clawing at a fate that wore hospital beige. The guards called it natural. It wasn't.

Then the father died. I didn't ask how. I heard "pacemaker" and "alert system" and "transmission" and let the words float away. Systems fail. Sometimes they are failed. James understands the difference and doesn't insult you with details.

The mother lived. James made sure of it. Eviction first. Then the car. Then the whisper that made certain circles look away when she walked in. Grief came through her door like a four-week notice that turned into a year. Every tree bears fruit. Some bitter. James made sure she tasted each.

Back to the church steps. The day was cloudless. Mercy took the morning off. I came out into a crowd that knew how to offer condolences without thinking they fixed anything. Then James appeared. He walks through people like he steps between raindrops. We saw each other and everything that happened to us since we were boys stood up at once. We embraced the way men do when apology and approval and anger and love all speak the same language for a minute. I wept. He did too. Grief has a dialect only certain brothers can pronounce.

"I miss him," I said into his shoulder.

"I know," he said into mine.

We stood in our own weather until time remembered it had a job. "Everybody dies," I whispered. "It's done." He nodded and slid something wrapped in black tissue into my hand. "For later," he said, and then he was gone in the way only James can be—present enough to fix the room and absent enough to keep it safe.

That night I went home alone. Cal offered to stay. I told him no. I put the tissue on the table and unwrapped it like it could explode. Jungle Brothers—Straight Out the Jungle. I laughed once, sharp and clean. I pulled out the old CD player, blew dust off plastic like a ritual, and let it spin. Track one crept in, then two. By three I knew the parts my mouth still remembered. Me and James. Bikes. Bars. Candy and corners. Ducking fists and dodging fate. The CD was a map back to who we were and a proof of who I have become.

Outside, whispers had already taken a breath. I hadn't been seen. No flash. No public vengeance. No parade of fear. Some said I'd softened. That the crown sat on a table somewhere, up for whoever reached first. People mistake quiet for vacancy when they've only lived next to noise.

I wasn't hiding. I was sharpening.

The next morning I drove to the unit again and counted slower, the way a man prays without telling God he's doing it. I closed the door and let the dark feel like an ally. Then I opened the notebook and, for the first time since I met Felix, wrote a word on a page he'd left mostly clean: "Grim." I underlined it once. Then I began a list with two columns—What I know. What I can prove. Revenge pays interest when you draft it like a ledger.

I left the keys where they were easy to touch. I took the notebook, shut the gate, and let the keypad complain. The world outside had the same bad paint and better intentions. I slid into the car and turned the Jungle Brothers back on. The city nodded along without pretending it understood. That was enough.

The work continued. Not louder. Cleaner. I tightened the circle until conversations could occur with my eyes only. Fly texted, short like I taught him: "Rod quiet. Rell louder." Mani added: "Two mouths put Barry and Rell at the same table last fall. Bar on South Trenton. Details soon." I replied with a period. Periods are all the instruction a good soldier needs when the sentence was written weeks ago.

I drove the rectangle once more, my peace budgeted, my anger accounted for, my brother's voice somewhere between a hook and a rule. The crown didn't weigh more. It sat truer. You don't lower it to feel comfortable. You grow your neck.

I took the long way home on purpose. Gravity felt hired. The city wasn't kinder. It was honest. That's all I needed from it.

I pressed play again. The beat came up like a memory you choose to keep. I let it run and I let it teach me one more time what the jungle had always taught: stand, or don't. But if you stand, don't flinch.

Chapter 20

Heat is a language if you learn to listen.

Big Josh worked the lab like a choir director who didn't need to raise his hands. Glass sang when it touched glass. Solvent curled in clear whirlpools. Thermometers steadied at numbers that meant something only to men who worship precision. I stood a step back with my sleeves pushed to the elbow, watching the drip find its rhythm. I don't intervene when craft is performing. I hold the room and let excellence talk to itself.

"Four degrees," Josh murmured without looking at me. "We're right on the line."

"That's where I like to live," I said.

He smiled in the reflection of the steel pot. Josh is a big man who moves like his shadow is his first audience—quiet, exact, unhurried. State time taught both of us the same sermon: you can make noise or you can make results. Results don't need choreography.

I kept inventory in my head while he cooked. Bricks asleep in the steel drawer. Reagent count halved since last week. New filters stacked in twelves. The table wrote its own ledger: product, process, profit. We were rebuilding a house without a front door. No visitors. No tours. Just rooms that kept the weather out.

"You still want the cadence we talked about?" Josh asked. "48 hours between any two drops? No matter how clean?"

"48 minimum," I said. "A week where I can help it."

He nodded and leaned into the steam. "It's slower."

"It's permanent," I said. "Fast feeds the graveyard."

I don't call it paranoia when the math agrees.

While the second wash bled clear, I ran the distribution for the month out loud so the room could hear me commit. "Northside is Tuesdays and Fridays only. Waterfront once, unannounced, between Wednesday and Sunday—never a pattern. Laurel gets starved until the echo forgets who started it. Suburbs are cashflow, not headlines. Cal handles the first line. Divine audits the second."

Josh kept his eyes on the mercury. "What about flash?"

"We don't wear a single new thing for a year," I said. "Not a belt. Not a buckle. If it shines, it sits in a drawer."

He chuckled. "You're going to break some hearts."

"I'm going to save some lives."

He cut the flame, waited three heartbeats, and lifted. The smell hit full and clean. He didn't have to ask if it passed. Work that good announces itself without raising its voice.

I sealed the first package and signed the corner with a dot only I would notice years from now. "Welcome to the choir," I said. "You sing; I'll keep the doors from getting kicked in."

We cooled the room back to neutral. I left Josh with the scale and stepped into the corridor that ran the length of the warehouse like a courthouse hallway no judge ever entered. My phone stayed on airplane until I was under open sky. I don't let signals stack inside a place that prints money.

Night had already pressed its forehead to the city. I drove Cross Street slow on purpose, windows down so the air could proof the dough of my thoughts. I wasn't looking to be seen. I was looking to confirm that the light still fell on things the way I remembered.

That's when I saw Christa. She was standing inside a half-gutted space two doors past a boutique that pretended it had Paris on speed dial. The storefront had fresh drywall and a hope I could feel from the street—blue tape lines, a folding table with catalogues, and a five-gallon bucket acting like a stool. She wore flats and a navy shirtdress spattered with primer, hair drawn low and neat like work didn't scare her clothes. I parked and stepped out without an entrance. The bell above the door tried to squeal; I put a hand up and made it behave.

She turned. Recognition lifted both her eyebrows before a smile arrived. "You're either here for a pair of paint-splattered handshakes," she said, "or you think this is still a bakery."

"I came for the smell of new walls," I said. "And the person braver than a timeline."

"Drywall doesn't judge," she said. "That's why I like it."

She wiped her hands on a rag and offered one like it still mattered to shake. I took it. Her grip was clean, firm, warm. People from the good side of town learn how to shake the way they learn piano scales—once, properly, forever. But I could see the stone-throw distance in the set of her jaw. Cross Street isn't a map line; it's a calibration. She'd grown up where parents made goals look like chores you finish, not dreams you perform.

"You seeing somebody?" she asked, not coy and not casual—just honest in a way that made the air feel less like a test.

"I'm not sure I could call it that," I said. "We liked each other once upon a time. I haven't seen her in a while."

Christa nodded as if she respected the precision more than the confession. "Good answer," she said. "Not because it's flattering. Because it's accurate."

"I don't traffic in flattering," I said. "It spends like counterfeit."

She laughed. "Then you'll appreciate this: we're over budget by ten percent, under schedule by two weeks, and my contractor wants to be paid in compliments."

"What is it going to be?" I asked, looking at the taped rectangles on the floor.

"A little bit of after-school, a little bit of before-care, a small-batch print shop so kids can see their ideas get made, and a boring revenue stream in the back so the front survives."

"Boring revenue," I said. "I speak that language."

"I figured." She picked up a paint stick and pointed at an empty wall. "This is going to be a calendar. Not for classes. For promises. If it goes up there, it happens. My father used to say goals are just things you schedule."

"Your father taught well," I said.

She looked at me for a second longer than a stranger would. "You moving okay?" she asked. "After… everything?"

I didn't ask how she knew. People who pay attention always know. "I'm vertical," I said. "The rest follows."

She nodded once. "Do you want tea?"

"Only if it's the kind that forgives the hour," I said.

"It is." She went to a small kettle sitting on a folding chair and poured into two paper cups. It tasted like discipline with honey. We stood without saying much. Quiet that wasn't awkward. Quiet that respected the furniture.

When I left, she walked me to the bell that remembered how to behave. "Text me when you get wherever you're going," she said. The fact that she didn't hand me her number made it land cleaner. I lifted my phone and she tapped hers to it. The contact appeared without a flourish: "Christa (Cross)."

"Tomorrow," she said, "I'm here till nine."

"Tomorrow is a moving target," I said. "But I'll try to land close."

"Close works," she said.

I stepped back into the dark and let the air catalog the new entry in my ledger: not weakness. Not relief. Just a note that the world could still place something gentle in a room without breaking the windows.

The city reminded me what it really wanted a mile later. I crossed Laurel and kept going until the strip bled into a lot behind a shuttered rental office. Two cars idled already. Two more slid in behind me. We didn't block the exits; we narrowed the decisions.

Griff arrived late in a coat that believed in itself more than he did. Johnny Ross stood next to a borrowed coupe like a mirror he wanted to admire him back. I collected phones in deli bags, zipped them, and placed them on the hood of my car without counting. I don't audit men before I correct them; the correction is the audit.

"Hands in pockets," I said. "Now out. Now in again. Good. That's the last command you'll enjoy tonight."

Griff tried hauteur and found he'd left it in the bathroom mirror. "We were just passing through," he said.

"People don't pass through rooms they don't speak in," I said. "You post where you study."

Johnny shifted his weight. "We ain't—"

"Stop," I said, not loud. "You can tell your friends how brave you would have been later."

I nodded to the meters that lined the back of the lot like skinny sentries. Zip ties whispered when they locked, plastic teeth taking small bites of stupid. Their wrists met cold poles. No blood. No bruises. Shame does more permanent work than a bruise.

I stood where all four pairs of eyes could find me without turning. "Repeat after me," I said. "Enjoy the view."

They stayed quiet the way men do when dignity has to choose between defiance and a longer life.

"Enjoy the view," I said again.

"Enjoy the view," Johnny breathed.

"Stay off the lawn," I said.

"Stay off the lawn," they chorused, softer.

"Louder," I said.

They obeyed. The lot learned the sentence enough to say it back later without us. I took one step closer so they could count my breathing if they needed a memory to keep them honest. "Phones get returned if the sentence stays true for ninety days," I said. "Break it, and you won't have hands to hold a phone with." I cut the ties and left them standing with wrists marked and faces learning the shape of humility.

We were gone before the lot remembered it had cameras that didn't work.

Amanda's was closed when I slid through the back door. The fryer had the good grace to be quiet. I wiped the stainless top out of habit and let the walk-in breathe cold on my face for a slow count. You learn the difference between clean and empty by standing still with doors open.

Kelly called on the line only three names know. "I shouldn't be using this phone," she said without hello. Her voice held its usual poise, but I heard the part where caution lives. "2:13 a.m., your plate again. Same credential tree at County. Same workstation time stamp."

"Who touched it?" I asked.

"A support login under Logan's subdomain," he said. "The DA's office has been leaning on him for ad-hoc pulls. He's good. And too eager to be useful."

"Is he curious or crooked?"

"Curious," she said. "Which can be worse."

"I won't touch him," I said. "I'll test the pipes, not the plumber."

"What do you need?" she asked.

"A canary," I said. "Put a harmless discovery into the scan stack that only that credential should see. Title it like a traffic memo— Monmouth Avenue municipal crap. Drop a line in the image notes: 'Traffic device offline 2:12–2:15 Wednesday, service ticket queued. Interim observation: unfamiliar Audi pausing twice at triangle.' Don't link a plate. Just the note."

"You want to see who shows up at the triangle between 2:12 and 2:15," she said.

"I want to see who believes their secret is unique," I said.

Kelly exhaled. "You'll owe me a story for this one day."

"I owe you safer clocks," I said. "And flowers on a day you don't expect."

"Make them boring flowers," she said, and hung up.

I put the phone down and let the note exist in the world without me watching it. That's how you see real movement. If you stare, you change it. I trust the wind to carry what needs to whistle.

MMC called from a number that knew my pocket but not my name. I took it outside because echoes behave better under stars.

"C," he said.

"You straight?" I asked.

"I'm breathing," he said. "Hearing is next week. They want the usual. I want different."

"You'll get freedom or less noise," I said. "Sometimes they're the same."

I half laughed. "I miss kitchens."

"We built a quieter one," I said. "Listen. I'm moving the Jersey window to the bridge on Thursdays after nine and the tunnel on Sundays before noon. You hear anything about that?"

"Nothing yet," he said.

"Good," I said. "Because the window is the opposite. If you hear the lie repeated, I know what wall leaks."

"You setting traps again," he said, not accusing.

"I'm checking weather," I said. "You keep your head above water."

"I always do," he said, and the line clicked to air.

At 2:10 the next night I parked two streets off the triangle and let the car idle the way a man listens to his heartbeat before running. At 2:12 a county sedan ghosted through like it wanted a cigarette and an alibi. At 2:14 another car I knew only by color slowed as if curiosity had brakes. Neither stayed long enough to be proof. Both stayed long enough to be named later if I needed them to be.

Fly's text landed at 2:18: "Got something you'll like."

I met the cousins behind a shuttered deli with a mural that lied about fresh bread. Mani had the look people mistake for menace when it's just concentration. Fly carried a laptop in a sleeve that used to be a binder, to make cameras think we were students. He propped it on a crate and played a clip. South Trenton. Bar neon trying too hard. Date stamp from months back. Barry's jacket, the one I'd given him before I took his name off the door, shining where it shouldn't. Rell sat across from him with a grin like gasoline.

No volume, but I didn't need the words. The body language made its own transcript. The slide of familiarity. The lean of men who think the table is private because their mouths are close. Barry's hand cutting the air when he is proud of a story. Rell's head thrown back at the laugh that follows cruelty.

Fly paused the frame when both sets of eyes carried the same hunger.

"More than rumor," Mani said.

"Residue," I said. "That's what betrayal leaves behind after it thinks it cleaned."

"We also got two mouths—separate—saying the abortion part wasn't Rell bragging," Fly said. "It was him quoting. Same energy. Same laugh."

I clenched my teeth once. Not anger. Alignment. "I don't need confessions," I said. "I need patterns. This is one."

"What do you want done?" Mani asked.

"Nothing yet," I said. "When a man hangs himself, you don't wrestle with the rope. You hand him silence."

I left them with cash for microphones and patience. On the drive back I thought about the math of grief. It doesn't add; it divides. I'd lost Grim and I'd lost the version of Barry I could have forgiven. Loss doesn't ask if the ledger is ready. It writes its own column. You balance it or you drown in arithmetic.

Near dawn the canary sang. Kelly's text came like a note slid under a door: "Triangle watchers = DA sedan + Logan's roommate's Civic (verified by campus sticker). Your phrase reached the right ears."

"Thank you," I wrote. "No more drops from your side. Let it breathe."

"Copy," she wrote. "Be boring."

"Always," I said, and meant it.

Amanda's opened slow that morning. I rolled towels and stocked lids because peace has chores. Cal came through with eyes that knew better than to ask questions first. We sat at the back table where grease turns into memory if you let it.

"Griff?" he said.

"Learning to love his view," I said.

"Johnny?"

"Watered the lawn with his own tears," I said.

Cal huffed a laugh. "You're insufferable when you're punished."

"Punishment is love if you survive it," I said.

He sobered. "Christa?"

"She builds calendars on walls," I said. "Her father taught her that goals are just things you schedule."

Cal smiled a small smile. "You sound like you needed to hear that."

"I did," I said. "And I will again."

His phone buzzed. He flicked a glance and looked back up. "Laurel thinks you're asleep," he said. "Every time you blink, someone gets religion."

"Good," I said. "Let them think I pray with my eyes closed."

That afternoon I drove to the water and parked where gulls audition to be alarms. I walked the rectangle the way I used to, not to check for enemies but to see if my shadow still paced the way it should. I counted steps. I cataloged faces. I let the Jungle Brothers run without skipping. That album is a map to a boy who built a man. I play it when I need the boy to nod in approval.

As the sun set, a newer kind of quiet slid into the seat next to me. A text from Christa: "Got out late. You safe?"

"Yes," I wrote.

"Good," she wrote. Ten seconds passed, then: "You don't have to carry everything alone."

I looked at the screen. The sentence stood there like a chair in an empty room—useful, available, not pushy. I didn't answer. Some replies are better made with presence than words.

I drove without music for a mile, then turned it back up. The beat remembered me and I remembered it. Tomorrow is always a moving target. I planned to land close.

The triangle canary ran for three nights. On the second, the county sedan drove slower. On the third, it didn't come. Logan's roommate's car wasn't brave enough to show twice. I logged both plates the way I log a heartbeat after a sprint—useful if I ever need to know whether I'm still alive.

I met Ock on a strip of concrete where kids learn to ride bikes and grown men relearn balance. He dropped a bag at my feet. "For later," he said. No theatrics. The metal inside had the weight of consequence and maintenance. I nodded. He nodded back. Two men agreeing to be necessary without auditioning for applause.

Night again. Warehouse again. Josh had left the room cleaner than he found it. The packages sat in three straight lines like a choir at attention. I put one aside for a purpose that didn't need a witness and labeled the rest with a dot only I respect. Distribution moves best when it looks boring enough to ignore.

Before I locked up I wrote on the corner of the whiteboard we never let guests see: "What I know / What I can prove." Under that: a small list of names and times and plates and lies. Beside it: another smaller list made of first names that didn't belong to enemies. Names like Christa. Like Kelly. Like Josh. Like Fly and Mani. I don't put James on boards. James lives where boards learn their manners.

You can build a kingdom with whispers if your walls don't talk back. Mine don't. They hold heat and keep recipes and remember the temperature where the mercury stands without a tremor. I turned the lights off one switch at a time and let darkness finish the last verse.

On my way home I passed the storefront where Christa's calendar was going to live. The bell didn't ring. The lights were off. The tape still held its blue promise. I pulled to the curb and sat for one minute longer than I needed to. Tomorrow is a moving target. I had already decided to land close.

And when I finally lay down, I didn't pray for safety. I budgeted it. Ten minutes with my eyes closed. Twenty with my phone off. An hour without anyone's name entering my chest. I've never needed sleep to survive. I've needed order. Heat knows when it's been obeyed.

Morning would ask for proof again. I'd show it without speeches. The choir already knew its part.

Chapter 21

The triangle sang.

Not loud—never loud. Just the kind of hum only a man who lives by rhythm hears. I parked two streets out and let the engine purr at idle. The clock on the dash rolled to 2:12 A.M., and the corner breathed like it had a secret in its mouth.

A county sedan slipped through first. No lights. No radio glow. The driver looked like every early-shift civil servant I ever studied —awake in the eyes, tired in the bone. I didn't stop. I hesitated. That's different. I gave him three seconds of curiosity at the apex of the triangle, then flowed past like traffic was the plan all along.

Two minutes later a Civic wandered in with a campus parking sticker peeling at the edge like a loose tooth. Hesitate. Roll. Hesitate again. Then gone. I memorized the plates without writing them down. I don't write anything down unless I plan to let it survive discovery.

The canary I asked Kelly to build had whistled exactly the way I wanted. "Traffic device offline 2:12–2:15." It's funny how words are cages when you lock them correctly. Men who believe their secrets are unique always circle the hour that calls them by name.

I waited until the street swallowed its own footprints, then moved. No rush. No chase. Just a quiet pivot and a slow coast back to air I trusted. The triangle did its job. Now I had to burn the pipe without burning the plumber.

Kelly picked the meet. She always does when the stakes are institutional. A parking deck with a broken camera and good echoes. Third level, east corner, where the wind makes you choose your words.

She was there first, hair pulled back, coat too light for the hour because she refuses to dress like she expects danger. I respect that. She doesn't perform caution. She practices it.

"Two hits," I said by way of greeting. "County sedan. Civic with a university scar."

She gave a once-nod. "The sedan's on a DA courier rotation— paper runners after hours. The Civic matches a roommate on Logan's lease. Logan's clean. His curiosity isn't."

"I don't want him," I said. "I want the pipe."

"We can salt the audit trail," she said. "Not to implicate—just to make the path cost more than the walk is worth."

"Do it," I said. "And no more canaries from your console. Let the wind work."

"Copy," she said. She handed me a small envelope like a woman passing a note to the past. "Permit thing for your friend on Cross Street. Expediter who doesn't like bribes but loves to be thanked on clean letterhead."

"You could've sent that by text," I said.

"I wanted to see if you were sleeping," she said.

"I don't sleep," I said. "I reorder."

She studied my face like a lab tech reading an instrument without trusting it. "There's a second leak," she said. "I can feel it and I can't prove it."

"You don't have to prove it," I said. "You just have to stop feeding the first one."

She tucked her hands into her pockets and looked off the edge of the deck toward a part of town that thinks it's too clean for consequence. "You sure you're not going to burn Logan?"

"I'm not in the business of killing messengers," I said. "I kill the belief that the message will be safe next time."

"That's colder," she said.

"That's quieter," I said. "Colder is noisy with cost."

She nodded. "Be boring," she said, her goodbye and her prayer.

"I'm allergic to exciting," I said.

Back on Cross Street the morning light looked like it wanted to apologize for the day before. I didn't accept. I parked in front of Christa's gutted future and stepped inside without ringing the bell that doesn't exist yet. She was on a ladder, pencil behind her ear, lines of blue tape crisscrossing the wall like she was mapping a city only she believed in.

"You don't sleep either," she said, looking over her shoulder with a smile that didn't perform relief. It offered it.

"I'm developing a brand," I said. "Insomnia & Order."

She laughed and climbed down. "You brought me something?"

I handed her the envelope Kelly had pushed across the night. "An expediter. Permit person. No drama, no envelopes, yes to correct commas."

"Where did you find a unicorn?"

"In a herd of horses pretending they weren't mules," I said.

She opened it and then closed it again without reading. "I'll look later," she said. "Tell me what you see when you look at this space."

"Revenue in the rear that never tweets," I said. "Promise wall in the front that humiliates lies. One calendar. If it makes the wall, it happens."

"Good," she said. "You remember."

"I don't forget where breath came from," I said. I pointed to the taped rectangles on the floor. "Drop zone for backpacks here. Parents don't cross this tape unless invited. Kids design the front window once a month. The best thing they make goes on a shirt and the proceeds pay for field trips."

She watched me and then watched the room. "You have the nervous system of a building inspector," she said.

"I build in places where the ceiling falls if you breathe wrong," I said. "I learned to breathe right."

The electrician came in then, wearing a belt that had seen more days than most men's convictions. She introduced me like I had a last name and a mortgage. I let the fiction sit. I walked the space with us and talked amperage and code like poetry no one bothers to memorize anymore.

"You're paying attention," Christa said when we were alone again. It wasn't a compliment. It was a fact.

"I'm learning how not to erase things," I said. "It's newer than it should be."

"Good," she said. "Stay new."

I left before the room learned my weight. I make it a point not to lean on things I want to stand without me.

Josh was already in the lab when I rolled the warehouse door high enough for the day to enter. He doesn't greet loudly. He nods like discipline is the only language worth speaking before noon. The room smelled like chemistry and math—my kind of church.

"Cadence?" he asked without lifting his eyes from the bath.

"48 hours minimum. 72 if the city coughs. No deliveries on the same weekday two weeks in a row. We're teaching boredom to carry us."

He grinned at the glass. "Boredom pays better than applause."

"Applause costs more than funerals," I said. "But it's the favorite bill of men who like to be seen."

I cut the flame and began the slow ballet of making clarity physical. I don't talk when the lines are being drawn. I count and I listen. Counting reminds me I'm alive. Listening reminds me why.

On the office whiteboard I kept a column I don't let anybody else fill. WHAT I KNOW / WHAT I CAN PROVE. The first line had two plates and a time. The second said: path salted, window closed. Under that I wrote in small letters: who knew the phrasing. I didn't write a name. I don't put the words I'm not ready to kill next to the words I am.

Amanda's smelled like onions and fryer heat and patience. Pudge slid me a Pepsi and leaned his forearms into the counter the way men do when what they want to say can't afford a seat.

"You hear about AB?" he asked.

"I hear everything," I said. "What did I hear this time?"

"Just mouth. Small mouth. Wrong mouth."

"Whose ears?"

"Two kids from Laurel. One of 'em thought he was getting scouted. AB knows how to say nothing like it's an opportunity."

"He repeat anything I never said?"

Pudge hesitated a beat—that half second where loyalty takes inventory and chooses. "He mentioned a Thursday night window," he said. "Said it like a man who forgot smart people listen."

I sipped and let the bubbles remind my tongue about consequence. I'd told exactly two different men two different lies about the bridge and the tunnel. MMC had the Sunday before noon story. Someone else had the Thursday after nine. AB didn't carry either detail legitimately. Which meant he was picking crumbs off a plate he wasn't invited to sit at.

"What did the kids do?" I asked.

"Smiled and nodded," Pudge said. "Which is how boys die trying to be noticed."

"Tell them to look the other way," I said. "Not because I'm God. Because I own the storm that's coming, and I don't like writing names on things I can avoid destroying."

I smiled without teeth. "Copy," he said. "You want me to say anything to AB?"

"No," I said. "Let him feel handsome."

I didn't plan to give AB a stage. I planned to give him silence wide enough to hear his own footsteps echo wrong.

Cal walked in while I was still deciding how to sit in my chair. He didn't ask for an invitation. He never has. He carries keys like a man who thinks doors belong to him. It's part of why I kept him close this long.

"We good?" he asked, tone casual like men who rehearse lines and then try to throw them away at the last minute.

"We breathing," I said.

He leaned a shoulder into the doorway and let the frame hold him up. "Heard your canary sang."

"Bird hit the note," I said. "Kelly sketched the music."

"You burn the singer?"

"I never kill the song to spite the choir," I said.

I nodded. "You want me to talk to Laurel?" he asked. "Quiet talk. Not the kind with applause."

"Not yet," I said. "Let them assume we're arguing about gasoline while we learn where they buy matches."

"You still doing Thursdays?" he asked, eyes neutral, voice careful.

"Thursdays are for men who think the weekend forgives," I said. "I like Sundays. God pays attention to the wrong things."

He smirked. He thinks that line is a joke. It isn't.

Ie started to leave and then turned with that half-memory look, like he needed to file one more detail under "I asked permission." "You want me in the room for the next Josh run?"

"No," I said. "If you're in the room, the room is no longer mine."

He nodded and disappeared down the hall with the stride of a man who had somewhere else to be before he remembered where he actually belonged.

That night I boxed the city with my headlights and let the map crawl into my hands. I made a slow loop past Lincoln Arms because ghosts appreciate a nod, then crossed to Country Circle to watch the way porch lights flick when the house breathes wrong. Laurel got a glance and a prayer. Cross Street got a promise. The triangle got nothing. I only visit a trap once when it works.

MMC called at midnight and a half. His voice had that iron-on-canvas rasp the county gives men who think sound survives cinder block.

"I heard a lie," he said.

"You'll hear more," I said. "I'm learning which ones belong to me."

"Window?"

I told him the opposite of the thing I'd told the other man. I laughed in that way that isn't laughter. "You ever get tired of knowing the future?"

"I don't know the future," I said. "I know how people fail. That's enough to build a calendar."

I kept the call short. Tin in the throat doesn't help you sleep.

Christa texted after one. "Inspector's meeting got pulled up to Wednesday," she wrote. "If you know a prayer, say it. If you know a contractor, send him."

"I know both," I typed. "Prayers are cheap. Good contractors smell like scarcity."

"Then send scarcity," she replied.

"Consider it hauled," I said.

I didn't sleep. I sat at the kitchen table with a pen I don't use and a notebook I don't write in. I let the hours stack and did math in my head, the kind that steals your pulse and hands it back stronger. Somewhere near dawn I shaved with the same razor I've used since before I learned longevity is a weapon.

Morning, Josh, process, cadence, silence. It all repeats when you design your day on purpose. Repetition is the only prayer I believe in.

By afternoon, Kelly sent a single line: "Pipe salted. DA route rerouted. Paralegal reassigned to paper that never leaves the building." Mercy, earned at interest.

I took a drive to the waterfront and let the gulls audition for a choir I'll never join. A man can sit near water and pretend he's forgiving himself. I don't forgive. I redistribute weight.

I didn't plan to see AB. I forced myself into the day. That's the thing about men who need notice—they're allergic to being ignored.

I stood in the back lot of a sneaker boutique two doors down from Amanda's, telling a story with his hands. Two young faces tilted toward him like plants that never learned the sun moves. I stopped in the shadow of the delivery bay and listened to a sentence I didn't say get repeated with the confidence of a man who'd found a coin on the ground and told everyone he minted it.

"Thursday nights after nine," he said. "If you know you know."

I stepped forward. I didn't see me until the boys were already offering their nods to a future that wouldn't recognize them.

"You like Thursdays?" I asked, voice level, eyes on the boys so they could see what weight does when it walks in.

AB's smile died on the vine. The boys evaporated like steam.

"I was just—"

"You were just selling proximity," I said. "A cheap cut of it."

"You know me. I make sure the city knows we still—"

"Stop," I said. "If you need the room to know your name, you don't deserve the room."

He looked down. "My bad," he said.

"I don't want your apology," I said. "I want your silence."

I nodded, swallowed, nodded again. I left him with his breath and his habit. Habit is the only enemy I don't know how to outshoot.

After sunset I met Divine and Big Abe above a mechanic's garage that does its best work when nobody's car is on the lift. We sat on milk crates and shared a Pepsi because men like us know how to make one cold thing feel like a plan.

"Laurel's whispering again," Divine said. "Not loud. Just… waiting."

"Let it wait," I said. "I don't answer knocks I didn't order."

"You still want Ock to sit on his hands?" Abe asked. Idle offends his physics.

"Tell him to sharpen, not swing."

"He's not built that way."

"He can learn," I said. "Or he can watch."

Divine smiled at nothing. "You make patience sound like violence."

"It is," I said. "Ask anyone who ever wanted to be seen."

We folded the map twice and then twice again, until the night could carry it without tearing.

On my way back I drove past Cross Street and parked without turning the engine off. The front window was taped in a grid that promised more than paint. There's something about seeing a future before the drywall believes it that makes lungs remember to expand.

My phone lit up. Not a number—just a single initial. K.

Kelly knows when to be a letter. "FYI," she wrote. "Affidavit drafts reference a 'Sunday corridor with light traffic between 11:45 and 12:15.' That phrasing is not ours."

I stared at the text until it lost its shape and became a door.

Only three men had that phrasing. One was on a county phone that still smelled like jail. One was me. One walked through my doors without asking who was on the other side.

I didn't write a name. I added a line to the whiteboard in my head: PROOF IN DRAFTS / PHRASE MIRRORS MINE. Then I let the night pretend I was tired.

The next day I made errands a religion. I moved slow through hardware, slower through paper goods, slowest through the kind of store that sells towels to men who forgot what comfort is for. Small chores remind me I am not obligated to live only in rooms where gunshots make sense.

Christa's inspector drop-in landed when she said it would. I stood outside with a coffee I didn't drink while a man with a clipboard looked for reasons to deny a future he didn't have to pay for. I found none. The expediter did exactly what the envelope had promised.

When the inspector left, Christa pressed both hands flat against the wall and exhaled like she'd been underwater for a year.

"You prayed?" she asked.

"I scheduled," I said.

"Same thing," she said, smiling without apology.

"Have dinner with me," she said. "Not a date. Food. Forks. People talking like they have somewhere to be tomorrow."

"Tomorrow is a moving target," I said.

"Then we'll eat close to it."

"Tonight," I said. "If the weather cooperates."

"It never does," she said. "Come anyway."

I left and drove to the warehouse. Josh had the room singing again. I walked the aisle and counted packages like rosary beads. Each one meant a man wouldn't have to steal to make his rent this month. Each one meant a different kind of risk we were deciding to carry on purpose. I sealed three, tagged two, set one aside for a purpose that didn't involve scales.

In the office I put four lines on the real whiteboard and then erased three. I kept one. WHAT I KNOW: PHRASE IN STATE PAPER MATCHES PHRASE I SAID IN A ROOM THAT TELLS THE TRUTH. I underlined it once and capped the marker like a man sheathing a blade he isn't ready to show yet.

AB sent a peace offering—two pairs of sneakers he thought would remind me I used to care what my feet wore. I sent them back with a note that said: WALK RIGHT. I didn't respond. Good. I wasn't teaching a call-and-response. I was building a silence.

Evening stretched itself across the block and pretended to be soft. I know better. Soft is just hard without an audience.

Dinner at Christa's was everything you think it is when you believe the world still rewards honest work. A small table, clean plates, food that was cooked to be eaten not photographed. She talked about kids and calendars and a father who believed you could turn a dream into a job if you wrote the schedule in ink. I talked about paint colors like I knew something about them. Maybe I do. Gray that isn't sad. White that doesn't try to be pure. Blue that reminds the room that sky exists somewhere people can't afford yet.

She reached for my hand once and then didn't take it. I thanked her for the food and for the hour. She thanked me for showing up. The door closed without the latch clicking like a promise. Better than a promise. A choice we could make again.

On the way back, my phone hummed. Ock. I took it.

"C," he said. "They said your name on Laurel three times in a row like it was a spell."

"You count?"

"I don't have to," he said. "I hear tone."

"Don't move," I said. "I want their mouths empty when we walk in. Not full of explanation."

"You always want to eat after saying grace," he said.

"You always want to flip the table," I said.

I laughed quietly. "Tell me when."

"I'll tell you when. And it won't be today."

I parked behind Amanda's and stood in the alley long enough to feel the brick pull the heat out of my spine. The kitchen was quiet. The office was quieter. I sat with my back to the wall so the wall could say what it needed to. It said: you already know. It said: don't write it down until you're ready to carry the weight of being right.

I slept for an hour on a couch that had learned the shape of a man who doesn't trust pillows. When I woke up the room hadn't changed. That's the point of having rooms like that. They don't judge you for needing to be still.

Morning again. Work again. Discipline again. I put one foot in front of the other and didn't pretend movement equals progress. Progress is where you end up after you out-wait the things that want you to rush.

Kelly sent a final note on the pipe: "Roommate cleaned, paralegal boxed, courier route rekeyed." Translation: the institutional leak would have to learn a new language if it wanted to speak about me. I sent her a single dot back. Full stop.

Then the draft. It came through a friend-of-a-friend channel the way all dangerous gifts arrive—wrapped in the wrong paper. I read it three times before I admitted words had chosen their side. "Sunday corridor 11:45 to 12:15." Phrasing doesn't lie when it's repeated with your commas.

I thought of Cal's shoulder in my doorway and his question about Thursdays. I thought of his casual smirk when I said a thing true enough to be mistaken for a lie. I didn't let the thought become a sentence. I don't accuse until the proof asks me to pull the trigger.

I drove. Not to cool down. To heat up correctly. There's a difference. One makes you sloppy. The other makes you clean.

Laurel had a new mural of a boy who hadn't earned one. I nodded to it anyway. Respect is free. Worship costs everything you have and then asks for more.

I parked, stepped out, and let the street breathe me in. Two kids playing dice on a milk crate stopped mid-throw. A woman with a bag of groceries tucked her chin like my name was weather. A runner across the way checked his pockets too often. Anxiety always counts its own change.

I didn't talk. I didn't need to. The quiet moved ahead of me and rearranged furniture. People make space when they remember what you did with rooms before.

Back at the warehouse I erased the line on the board and wrote it again. Sometimes you have to see the words arrive twice to admit they plan to stay.

Pudge came by with a stack of invoices thicker than the patience of a man who thinks he deserves applause for breathing. We went through them line by line. Food trucks. Barbershops. Nail salons that don't paint nails at night. Boring money. Holy money. Money that never wears a chain.

"You ever miss the noise?" he asked.

"I never left it," I said. "I just made it sing at a volume that doesn't call the cops."

I grinned and signed the last page with a flourish that said he still enjoys ink. I do too. I just don't need it to see me.

At dusk I stood on the roof of a building that kept us dry when storms couldn't find a church to drown. I looked toward the triangle and didn't think of birds. I looked toward Cross Street and thought of tape and calendars and a woman teaching me the difference between hope and scheduling. I looked toward the part of town where the DA keeps its paper and thought about how words become affidavits when men who don't know you choose a comma for you.

My phone buzzed. AB again. I let it ring out. I texted a photo of shoes and a caption trying to sound like humility. I put the phone back in my pocket. Mercy has a schedule. I wasn't on it.

Night wore the street the way a suit wears a man who's better without it. I went home, put the gun where it belongs, and lay on my back with my hands folded like a man who knows funerals are rehearsals for decisions. I thought about Grim and how grief is a ledger that never goes to zero. I thought about James and how some debts get paid in languages nobody can prove. I thought about Cal and said nothing to the ceiling.

Silence isn't empty. It's the sound of everything deciding what it wants to be when the lights come back on.

Tomorrow would ask for proof again. I would show it without speeches. I always do.

Chapter 22

Proof is a map, not a verdict.

I woke before the sun and let the house stay dark on purpose. The quiet held shape like a cup in my hands. I stood at the kitchen counter with a pen I never use and a notebook I never write in and recited the columns out loud in a whisper only I could hear.

What I know. What I can prove.

The phrase was still there, heavier than ink: Sunday corridor 11:45 to 12:15. Not a rumor. Not a guess. The same commas I use when I speak about clocks. That wasn't coincidence. That was handwriting without a pen.

I didn't circle a name. I drew a door.

The city was cold when I stepped outside. I walked instead of drove. My feet needed to count the cracks in the sidewalk like rosary beads. Every morning has a number. I don't move to the next one until I've prayed the last one clean.

By the time I reached Amanda's, the fryer smell had already started to argue with the morning. Pudge slid a Pepsi toward me without words. I didn't crack it. I just tapped the cap twice.

"I need a chalkboard," I said.

I nodded toward the back. I took the small one we use for specials and wiped it with the sleeve of a hoodie that has survived more storms than headlines. I wrote two words:

WATERMARKS. PHRASES.

Kelly understood before I finished the text. She always does.

"Parlor?" she replied.

"Not today," I wrote back. "Parking deck. Third level. East corner. Wind at our backs."

The deck was a wall of cold light and concrete. Kelly arrived with a knit cap pulled low and a calm that wouldn't shatter if the world did. I set the chalkboard on the hood of a car and wrote three sentences, each identical but for a single word.

a) Sunday corridor 11:45–12:15, church let-out window.

b) Sunday corridor 11:45–12:15, choir-break window.

c) Sunday corridor 11:45–12:15, vestibule window.

She read them once and then looked at me.

"Three suspects," she said.

"Three possibilities," I said. "Only one is a suspect. Two are witnesses I trust with my life. They won't repeat it. That's the point."

"You sure you want to put even a shadow on the other two?"

"I want a mirror," I said. "People reveal themselves when they think they're helping."

She exhaled steam. "You'll need eyes on internal paper again."

"You'll need a way to pretend you're not reading them," I said.

Kelly smiled without moving her mouth. "I'll be stupid in the right direction," she said. "Who gets which hymn?"

I wiped the board and wrote the assignments on my own palm like a man who loves secrets more than comfort.

"You'll hate me if you're wrong," she said.

"I'll hate the mirror," I said. "Not the woman who held it."

I left her with the chalk dust and the cold and walked to the block where Christa's tape grid had begun to look like a calendar. The electrician's van was out front. Inside, wires were neatly curled like sentences waiting for verbs. Christa stood near the back wall, arms crossed, chin lifted in that posture hope uses when it is learning patience.

"How many outlets does a dream need?" she asked.

"As many as it takes to keep it from borrowing power," I said.

She laughed softly. "You always talk like that?"

"I always think like that," I said. "Talking is optional."

She pointed at a spot near the door. "Deadbolt here. Not because I expect danger. Because I reward trust."

"I'll bring a locksmith who knows how to be quiet," I said.

She leaned back against the wall. "You ever consider that you already are one?"

"I make rooms safe," I said. "Locks are for people who haven't learned how yet."

She tilted her head. "Dinner again tonight?"

"If the weather cooperates," I said.

"It never does," she said.

"Then we'll eat close to it."

I left before the moment asked for more than it needed to carry the day. The warehouse door rolled up and Josh nodded me in like a foreman who treats discipline like communion. I watched the cook-up without touching the process, counted the beats without counting the money, and let the quiet of precision remind my lungs how to breathe.

After noon, I called Divine. We met in the mechanic's room above the lifts again. The smell of oil and tired rubber and work made the room honest.

"I'm going to say a sentence to you," I said. "You are going to nod and then forget it."

"I can forget on command," he said.

"Sunday corridor 11:45–12:15," I said. "Vestibule window."

He nodded once. "What now?"

"Now nothing," I said. "Now you forget."

He smiled. "You mean remember not to remember."

"Exactly."

From there I drove to Big Abe's spot. He was at the pool table, a cue across his palms like a weightlifter resting between sets.

"Same drill," I said. "Different word. Choir-break."

I nodded. "You want me to say it out loud back to you?"

"I want you to never say it again," I said.

I looked him in the eye until the room held its breath. "Copy."

Cal got the last one. I waited until the day had worn thin. Amanda's back hallway was lit like a prayer candle. Cal leaned into the frame the way men lean into doors they think belong to them.

"You good?" he asked.

"We're always good," I said. "Sunday corridor 11:45–12:15. Church let-out window."

He smiled like someone had let him in on a secret the room didn't deserve. "We back to cadence?"

"We never left," I said.

"You want me to sit on it?"

"I want you to forget you heard it," I said.

He chuckled. "You always liked magic tricks."

"I like mirrors," I said.

We left it there. The chalkboard in my head had one more line. Not yet. Patience is the only weapon that never jams.

Evening brought the kind of cold that peels lies from faces. I drove to the waterfront and listened to gulls pick through what the river throws away. A message from Kelly came while I watched the water pretend to be innocent.

"Draft language moving," it read. "Your word appears once. Not in the body. In a margin."

"What word?" I wrote back, although I knew.

"Let-out," she replied. "Spelled exactly the way you say it."

I put the phone down and looked at the water until it became something else. Anger is a river that wants to be an ocean. I don't let it. Oceans drown men who think they can swim through anything.

I didn't call Cal. I didn't call anyone. I drove to the laundromat on 13th and sat in the dark lot where the timer bulb clicks every six seconds like a heartbeat that refuses to panic. The sixth click brought a car. A sedan I recognized from county errands. Not the same driver. A cousin. Or a courier with a cousin's face. The man got out, dropped a letter in the blue box that no one uses anymore, and left. The letter didn't move. It just sat. The next click, a Civic with a campus sticker rolled past without stopping. Curiosity is lazier than fear. I wrote that on the inside of my skull and walked away.

Ock called after midnight. The street behind him sounded like men inventing reasons to be loud. "Laurel's mouths are practicing your name," he said.

"Let them rehearse," I said. "I want the performance to feel familiar when I interrupt it."

"You want me to put a hand on someone's shoulder?"

"I want you to polish your shoes," I said. "Clean violence is patient."

"You always did like a sermon," he said, then hung up before the street could make our words do something they weren't built for.

I slept in a chair that has learned the shape of my backbone. Dawn found me with my eyes open. Boredom was the soundtrack again. Josh. Cadence. Counting. Christa's call about the locksmith. A quick stop to buy a deadbolt from a man who still says "thank you" with both hands.

At noon, the message came. Not from Kelly. From a mouth that didn't know it was a messenger.

AB sent a photo of a flyer for a dice game off Clinton with the caption: "Pull up after church." I stared at the words until the punctuation told on the author. The phrase had been living in his ear. It had guests.

"Meet me," I wrote back.

We met in the alley behind Neesha's Custom Kicks. AB came with apology already rehearsed. I let him say it and then let the wind take it. Apology without discipline is noise.

"I'm not going to repeat myself," I said. "You can wear our name or you can wear yours. Not both."

"I'll wear silence," he said.

"Good," I said. "Treat it like a suit."

I left with his head down. I let him go without salt. I wasn't the river. I was a puddle. Boots get wet. Boots dry. The ground remembers the print and then forgets.

I spent the afternoon on the roof above the warehouse, watching cranes lift steel for a building that would become another excuse for rich men to buy views of people they don't want to meet. The wind felt clean. My head didn't. I called Divine.

"Do nothing," I said. "It's the loudest move we have."

"I can shout with my hands behind my back," he said. "Copy."

By dusk, the city had dressed itself for trouble and then decided it could wait. I drove to a smoothie shop we own on paper through a cousin who doesn't even like fruit. Johnny Ross had been sniffing around it for weeks. Pretty boy with light eyes and a father who liked shaking hands more than washing them. Not a threat. A mildew. Annoying. Persistent. Ugly only if you ignore it.

He arrived late with a borrowed smile and a jacket he didn't deserve. He leaned across the counter and tried to sell protection like a man tries to sell used charm.

"Couple of my folks could make sure nobody bothers this place," he said to the cousin who was playing register. "We keep it real safe for a small love offering."

I stepped from the back room before the cousin answered. Johnny turned and brightened like I had just turned into his plan.

"CJ, my guy," he said. "Was just telling family—"

I held up a hand. "Don't call me your guy."

His mouth clicked shut and then opened wrong. "We all on the same side."

"There are no sides in math," I said. "There is an answer and a lie."

He tried a laugh. "You always been poetic."

"I've always been literal," I said. "You're asking to tax a room that pays its rent on time. That isn't business. That's laziness."

He spread his hands. "C'mon, champ. It's love. We put your name on the receipt."

I looked at the cousin and nodded toward the door. "Take a walk."

When we were alone, I leaned on the counter and spoke quietly enough to make him lean forward.

"You're not worth murder," I said. "You're not even worth a conversation. I'm only here because mildew turns to mold if you let it stay comfortable."

He tried to square his shoulders. "You think you can just—"

I pulled the pistol and shot him through the calf. One clean pop. No flourish. No sermon. I screamed the way men scream when they meet consequence for the first time as adults. I put a towel on the wound and pushed him into a chair.

"Breathe," I said. "That's a gift. Use it."

I stared up at me with eyes that finally looked honest. "Why—"

"Because you're not worth murder," I repeated. "And because the hospital is open late."

I wrote a word on a receipt and tucked it into his jacket pocket: WALK.

Then I carried him to the back exit, put him in the passenger seat of his own car, and set the GPS for the emergency room. I would make it. I would limp for months. Every step would remind him I chose mercy out of contempt, not kindness.

Back inside, I sprayed the floor with bleach and called the cousin back in. "You didn't hear a gunshot," I said. "You heard a blender."

"Say less," the cousin said, eyes wide and grateful and scared in the correct proportions.

The phone buzzed while I was throwing the towel into a trash bag. Kelly.

"One more margin," she wrote. "Same word. New hand."

"Copy," I texted back. "Stand down. We know enough."

I didn't rush to Cal. I don't sprint to fire when I already know the shape of the ash. I drove instead to Christa's and installed the deadbolt myself because the locksmith finished early and left the hardware. The night smelled like sawdust and victory. Christa watched me work without talking. When the bolt slid home and the door clicked with honest weight, she smiled the way windows smile when the morning finally arrives on time.

"You stay for tea?" she asked.

"I stay for ten minutes," I said.

We sat at the small table that will one day hold children's drawings and principals' letters and a ledger full of honest debts paid on time. She poured, I listened, we didn't lie to each other by pretending we wanted the night to be longer. I left before the tea cooled.

The warehouse was quiet when I came back. Josh had shut down the lab like a man folds a flag. I walked to the office and drew the door again in my head. The column on the whiteboard was no longer symmetrical. What I know was taller than what I can prove, but now both had the same word written in ink I couldn't pretend I hadn't seen.

I took the marker and wrote one line across the bottom.

WHEN THE TIME COMES, SPEAK TO THE MAN BEFORE YOU SPEAK TO THE GUN.

I capped the marker. I locked the door. I went home and slept a kind sleep that felt like concrete curing—hardening with purpose, not malice.

Morning found me outside Amanda's again, because the fryer smell has become a meditation I can't cheat. Pudge slid the Pepsi across the counter. I cracked it this time. I took one sip and closed my eyes. The day would ask for more than yesterday. I was ready.

Cal walked in later than usual. He carried the room like a man who wants the furniture to thank him. I let him do it. He leaned into the doorway and waited for me to nod. I didn't. He spoke anyway.

"You heard?" he asked.

"I hear everything," I said. "What did I hear this time?"

"Johnny," he said. "Limping out of St. Mike's like he just learned to pray."

"Miracles still happen," I said.

Cal smiled. "You always had a soft spot for mercy."

"I have a hard spot for order," I said.

I nodded at the chalkboard on my office wall. I couldn't read it from where he stood. I tried anyway. Then he looked back at me.

"You need anything?" he asked. "Want me to sit a church lot with a coffee and a clean conscience?"

"I need you to forget the times I don't say out loud," I said.

He laughed softly. "You always did love a mirror."

"I love the truth it shows," I said.

He let the silence hang between us like a jacket you only wear when the weather lies. Then he walked away without looking back. The doorframe remembered his shoulder.

Kelly's message came before noon. "Pipeline quiet," it read. "Margin notes dried. Your word had one carrier."

"Good," I wrote back. "Let it rest."

"Until when?" she asked.

"Until the ground stops pretending to be a floor," I wrote.

The rest of the day moved like a metronome. Josh. Inventory. Pudge with invoices. Ock with a text that only said "polished." Divine with a nod I could hear over the phone. Big Abe with a single question mark that I answered by not answering.

At dusk, I walked to the roof again. The sky over Fourth and Monmouth was the color of a bruise trying to heal. Cars moved like they were practicing for a parade no one would attend. Somewhere in the distance a siren tried to make itself important.

I thought about Grim and the way grief reroutes blood. I thought about James and the way justice writes in invisible ink until the paper learns how to show it. I thought about Christa and a deadbolt that clicked without apology. I thought about Cal and a margin note that spelled my sentence the way I spell it.

I don't build toward rage. I build toward decisions.

The phone vibrated in my palm. Logan's initial flashed and vanished. I let it go. That boy wasn't a leak. He was a lesson. I had already learned it.

I put the phone away and spoke to the night the way men speak to God when I'm not sure if I want an answer.

"Proof is a map," I said. "I know where it leads."

The wind didn't argue. It just moved the cold from one cheek to the other and gave me the kind of quiet that feels like a room making space.

Tomorrow will be louder. I will not be. I never have been. I never will be.

I went home instead of to war. The board was already set. Anger only knocks pieces over.

I pulled the travel chess set from the drawer and laid the pieces out on the coffee table the way Grim used to—kings last, queens quiet, pawns steady like prayer. I played both sides until the board stopped being about wood and started being about rooms I had walked through. Knights only jump when there is cover. Rooks don't travel far without partners. Queens do the most with the least noise. Kings move one square at a time and somehow still get blamed for everything that happens two blocks away.

I ran a line I learned from him back when sneakers squeaked on a floor our mother had just mopped. Line up your shot and shut up. In chess, it translates. Finish the calculation. Then move. No speeches.

The phone buzzed. County number. MMC.

"Date got pushed," he said. "Public defender caught the flu. God bless germs."

"You good?" I asked.

"I'm alive," he said. "Tell the street to keep my name off dice."

"I can tell the street whatever I want," I said. "It listens to hunger."

He chuckled. "You always was a poet in a bad suit."

"I'm a thesis in a fitted," I said. "Sit tight. Eat the chow. Write the letters you won't send."

"Copy," he said, and hung up before the county could turn our line into a rope.

I stared at the board until the black squares looked like holes and the white squares looked like lies, then reset the pieces and put the king down last. Grim used to make me kiss the top of the king like it was holy. I never believed in the ritual. I believe in the reminder. The man with the smallest step still controls the math if the rest of the room respects gravity.

I drove one more loop before bed. Not to look intimidating. To be reminded. Fourth and Monmouth was quiet enough to lie to a man who wanted to hear a promise. Country Circle breathed like an old boxer who still knows how to move his feet. Lincoln Arms kept its lights on like a lighthouse for people who never learned to swim. Laurel Ave whispered. It always does. The wind carries that block's voice farther than mouths do.

Logan texted a single sentence while I was parked in the cut behind the post office: "I was stupid." There are grown men out here who will write page-long explanations and never say that. The sentence bought a meeting in a coffee shop where no one knew either of us. He walked in with campus shoulders and the kind of fear that can learn if you let it.

"I was stupid," he said again, before I could sit.

"Curiosity wants to be a career when it grows up," I said. "Don't feed it."

"Am I in trouble?"

"You are in a classroom," I said. "The lesson is silence. You pass or you repeat."

He nodded into his cup. "Thank you."

"Don't thank me," I said. "Be boring."

On my way out I watched a father show a girl how to tie her shoe with a patience that would fix half of this city if you could put it in the water. I let that picture tuck itself into a pocket of my mind that violence never finds.

Back home, I stood in the doorway and listened to the house breathe. The refrigerator hummed the A note it prefers. The hallway settled one board at a time. Somewhere outside a cat negotiated with the darkness and won. I put the pistol on the table and let it face away from me like a dog that doesn't need to be told to stay.

Proof is a map. I had one. Tomorrow I would follow it. Not because hurry makes men brave, but because patience makes men inevitable.

Chapter 23

Maps don't accuse. They predict.

I woke before the alarm and refused to turn on a light. The dark keeps its own order if you let it. I stood at the kitchen counter with my palms flat and breathed until the house stopped trying to choose a mood for me. The list was already written on the back of my eyes.

What I know.

What I can prove.

What I'm willing to carry.

Proof had drawn a faint line across the map and spelled my phrase with my commas. Sunday corridor. 11:45 to 12:15. Let-out. I didn't learn anything new from reading it again. I learned something about weight. Knowledge without action collects dust. Action without knowledge collects bodies. I wasn't in the business of collecting either.

I didn't make coffee. I like the day plain when it's going to ask for discipline. I put on the navy sweatsuit that fits like a plan and walked out into air that smelled like a sermon without an amen.

Amanda's had the lights half up and the fryer pretending it could hold back the cold. Pudge slid a Pepsi across the counter and didn't speak. Good men know when silence is the tool you came for.

"Chalkboard," I said.

Ie jerked his chin toward the back. I took the small board we don't use for specials anymore and wiped it until the ghost of yesterday's handwriting disappeared. I drew three boxes, evenly spaced, the way Grim taught me to set feet before you throw a punch you want your body to remember.

WINDOW / WORD / WITNESS.

I wrote "Benediction" in the second box and let it dry there. A new watermark. A new hymn only one man would hear.

Kelly replied to the text before I could hit send. "Deck. Wind at our backs. I'll bring the stupid."

We met on the third level again, early enough for the city to pretend it was honest. Kelly had a knit cap and that straight-back posture she uses when the problem is institutional. I set the chalkboard on the hood of a sedan that would never belong to either of us and wrote the sentence slow enough to feel like a nail being driven into clean wood.

Sunday corridor 11:45–12:15, benediction window.

She read it once and didn't make a face. "Same watchers?" she asked.

"Different roofs," I said. "I want them to wonder if the sky moved."

"Internal pipe?"

"Salt stays," I said. "You did what I asked. Now we let the paper think it won. People who think they won get lazy."

She nodded at the word "benediction." "You're sure?"

"I'm not sure of anything," I said. "I'm tired of pretending I need to be."

She smiled with only one side of her mouth. "Your not-sure is cleaner than most people's certainty."

"That's because I clean it," I said. "Every day."

We didn't hug. We don't. We left the deck with the chalk dust still hanging the way breath hangs on a cold morning after a run that proves you are still alive.

Christa's van was outside the space on Cross Street, the electrician's ladder leaning like a promise. Inside, the grid of tape had grown corners and confidence. The inspector's sign-off sat on a clipboard with a paper clip like a small crown refusing to be gaudy.

"You came early," she said, wiping her hands on a rag with paint on it that wasn't hers yet.

"The morning is when rooms tell the truth," I said.

She laughed. "And afternoons are for lies?"

"Afternoons are for optimism," I said. "Lies wear perfume. Optimism smells like sweat."

She handed me a pencil. "Walk the room with me," she said. "Tell me where the children will trip. Tell me where the parents will stand when they want to look like they aren't watching."

We mapped it the way we did the first time—drop zone, promise wall, calendar shelf, quiet corner for the kid who learns by listening and the girl who doesn't need to be taught how to lead. She pointed at the door. "You bring the deadbolt?"

"In my trunk," I said. "I'll put it on before I leave."

"You're becoming my locksmith."

"I'm becoming a man who wants doors to feel like decisions," I said.

She leaned against the frame and looked at me the way sunlight looks through a clean window. "Dinner tonight?"

"If the weather cooperates."

"It never does," she said.

"Then we'll eat close to it," I said. The repetition wasn't lazy. It was a small oath we could carry without hurting our backs.

The warehouse door took both hands to roll up. Josh nodded once and kept his eyes on the flame. He doesn't talk in the first hour of a cook. Neither do I. The room smelled like chemistry and math and patience—the only trinity I ask for help.

"Cadence?" he asked when the steam subsided.

"Same song," I said. "Different chorus." I tapped the whiteboard in the office as I passed: WHAT I KNOW / WHAT I CAN PROVE. Under it, one line in fresh ink: "When the time comes, speak to the man before you speak to the gun." I wrote it for myself and for the part of me that thinks it knows better.

Divine's mechanic loft felt right for the morning's second conversation. Oil, rubber, tools that don't lie. He was already there, legs dangling off a workbench, a socket wrench in his hand like punctuation.

"Laurel?" he asked.

"Waiting," I said. "Let it."

"You look like you're ready to cut someone loose."

"I'm ready to cut the word 'maybe' out of a man's mouth," I said.

I chuckled. "You want me to make a call?"

"I want you to not make three," I said. "We're going to test gravity. If the apple doesn't fall, we make jam. If it falls, we don't celebrate. We sweep."

He set the wrench down and came off the bench. "Just say the hymn."

"Benediction," I said. "Sunday corridor."

He nodded and let the word float out of his mind like a balloon a kid chose to release on purpose. Divine knows how to forget. It's part of why he's still breathing.

Big Abe had a pool cue across his palms and the look of a man who is trying to be polite to a game that keeps pretending it needs him. I told him nothing. Not because I don't trust him, but because muscles talk sometimes when silence would have been better. I asked him about his mother's knees instead. He smiled and said the cortisone took, and for a minute we were two boys in older bodies remembering what it felt like to care about things that weren't trying to kill us.

Ock texted, polished. That was all it said. I sent back a dot. Full stop.

Fly and Mani were already on the roof of a laundromat that pays its bills with quarters and gossip. I met them there with a pair of binoculars I didn't plan to use. Fresh eyes see more without glass.

"You brought us to church," Mani said, nodding at the steeple two blocks over.

"I brought you to a clock," I said. "The building is an accent."

"What we watching?" Fly asked.

"Nothing," I said. "And then we'll watch who arrives to look at nothing."

They grinned like boys getting permission to be patient. That makes them dangerous in a world that rewards sprinting until your lungs forget their job.

I left them with a thermos and a warning. "Do not move even if the street decides to perform. A man who can't hold his seat doesn't deserve a ticket." They nodded, serious now. I walked away before I tempted myself to say more.

Amanda's was the staging area and the church basement for men who think strategy is a sacrament. Cal walked in with his shoulder in the doorframe the way men do when they believe the wood owes them gratitude. I let him stand there. He likes thresholds. He likes choosing when to cross.

"You eat?" he asked.

"I count," I said.

He glanced at the chalkboard I'd cleaned and reset. He couldn't know what had been on it earlier, but he tried to read anyway. Cal has always been smart enough to look and confident enough to assume he's seen.

"We good?" he asked, casual. Casual is a costume honest men should never want to wear.

"We're breathing," I said.

I smiled the way a man smiles when he thinks the test is multiple choice. "You want me on Laurel or in the corridor?"

"Neither," I said. "You're going to sit in a room where nothing happens and remember what patience tastes like."

He grinned. "You always did love a sermon."

"I love the choir," I said. "It teaches the words without letting you pretend they aren't heavy."

He dipped his chin like a bow that doesn't want to look like one and walked back out into the day that was already pretending to be evening.

By the time the church bells started practicing, I had the triangle set. Two cars that looked like they didn't belong to anyone. A van that belonged to half the city. One box in a trunk that didn't have a bottom. One compartment under a seat that didn't exist. The map didn't need lines. It needed breath.

I sat two streets out and let the engine idle at the same rhythm hearts pretend to keep when their owners are lying. The air had that cold edge it gets when a winter afternoon tries to convince you it's later than it is. I checked the clock without looking at it. Some clocks live inside your neck.

At 11:41 a county sedan drifted past the first corner and did the kind of slow that looks like math. I watched its hesitation. Men who know where they're going don't hesitate. Men who are looking for an excuse to be where they are do.

At 11:48 a campus Civic with a new bumper and an old sticker took the long way around the block and never looked at the church. That's how you know he was told to. Civilians look at buildings that stop noise. Professionals look at corners that start it.

At 11:52 the triangular hum began. No sirens. No radios. Just the sound a city makes when it pretends it isn't arranging itself. A van blocked the line of sight from the east road to the west and a sedan no one owned pretended to be a friend. Fly texted a single period. Mani texted nothing. Good. They were seeing instead of narrating.

At 11:57 a tan SUV with a missing hubcap parked in a place people don't unless they were told to. A man in a black coat who wanted to look like a father in a hurry watched the door of a car that didn't contain anything. He watched it so hard he made it important.

At 12:04 the DA's courier cousin did the one thing paperwork never admits to—got out, opened a mailbox, put a letter in, and then remembered nobody uses those anymore. He got back in the sedan and drove off with the relaxed shoulders of a man who accomplished a task without knowing what it meant.

At 12:09 two unmarked cars rolled past each other like cousins at a reunion after a bad funeral. They didn't stop. They didn't touch. They just exchanged momentum. That's how institutions kiss when they don't want anybody to see.

At 12:12 the church released its first breath. The door opened and a child ran down the steps in shoes that needed to be replaced. His mother's hand came late and caught him without lifting him off the ground. That's what good hands do. Heads turned. Voices changed keys. The corridor opened. The window arrived.

Nobody opened my empty compartment. Nobody opened the seat that didn't exist. The triangle had been tuned to test a man's certainty, not the police's appetite. I had seen enough. The people who needed to be on the street were on it. The people who needed to be recorded in the corners of my mind had written their initials in the air without knowing it.

I texted Fly: "Walk." He replied with a dot. Full stop.

I drove a loop that wouldn't look like a loop to anyone who wasn't drawing it. The city was full of cars trying to not be noticed and doing a bad job of it. I let them sit in their own performance and went to eat a piece of fish I didn't taste.

Cal texted: "You want me to pivot?" I wrote back: "No." He replied with a thumbs up that made the muscles in my jaw move. Men who send symbols forget words weigh more than pictures.

After the window, after the echo, after the van forgot it had a job, I met Do Dirty and Divine in the back of the barber shop that holds more truth than a courtroom on a slow Tuesday. We didn't sit. We stood the way men stand when they know chairs won't help.

"You see enough?" Do Dirty asked.

"I saw people learning to enjoy the idea they're smarter than me," I said.

"You want me to disappoint them?" he said, smiling without warmth.

"Not yet," I said. "This isn't the lesson. This is attendance."

Divine rubbed his knuckles and nodded like a man nods when he hears the beat he expected. "And Cal?"

"He's getting benediction," I said. "We gave him a hymn nobody else sang. The margin wrote the chorus back to us before noon."

Divine didn't flinch. "You talking to the man or the gun?"

"Man," I said. "First and last."

Do Dirty leaned on the wall and watched the ceiling like it might write his future. "You want company?"

"No," I said. "If I bring company, I bring a verdict."

They didn't argue. They've seen me choose my tools. They know the difference between a conversation and a sentence.

I went to Christa's instead of going to war. That was on purpose. You don't put your feet in blood when you need your head to remember how to be precise. I installed the deadbolt in fifteen quiet minutes and let the click at the end settle into my chest like a new rule.

She made tea without asking. I sat without pretending I planned to stay.

"You look like a city map," she said. "Lines and corners."

"I'm trying to be a calendar," I said. "Boxes and days."

"You can be both," she said. "So long as you don't let other people draw on you."

We didn't touch. We didn't make promises. We just let the steam do what steam does—rise and disappear and still leave warmth behind.

On my way out she touched the new lock like it was a jaw she was proud of. "Thank you," she said.

"For what?" I asked.

"For not erasing what I'm building," she said.

"That's new for me," I said.

"Keep it," she said.

The warehouse was closed and clean when I walked through. Josh had shut off the flame like a priest covers a chalice. I left him a note he didn't need: "Cadence holds." He would smile when he found it and then go back to treating chemistry like worship.

I stood in the office and looked at the sentence I wrote yesterday about speaking to the man first. I put a finger on the period and pressed like I was testing a bruise to see if it still hurt. It did. Good. Pain is a teacher if you don't give it a microphone.

Amanda's back hallway was the right place for what came next. The light is always crooked there. Walls hear and don't repeat. I sent a short text: "Walk in." Cal did.

I leaned in the doorway because he doesn't know another way to enter a room. I let him take the posture. I think doors make him taller. Doors make men honest.

"You called," he said.

"I did."

"We good?" he asked, rehearsed casual.

"We're breathing," I said. "Sit."

I didn't sit. I didn't ask again. I took the chair and angled it so the wall was at my back and the light cut his face in two pieces the way a good story does when it wants you to choose.

"I'm going to say a thing," I said. "You're going to hear it. You're going to decide what kind of man you are. Then I'm going to be done deciding."

He didn't blink. "Alright."

"Benediction," I said.

He frowned for a quarter second and then smoothed it over with a smile he couldn't afford. "Pretty word," he said.

"It showed up today," I said. "In a margin that thinks it's private. Your shoulder has been heavy on my doorframes. Your mouth has been light in rooms with new paint."

"CJ—"

"Don't call me that right now," I said, calm. "Call me the man who gave you everything you needed to be safe enough to be ungrateful."

I swallowed. "You questioning my loyalty?"

"I'm questioning your hunger," I said. "I'm questioning whether you ever learned the difference between partner and owner, between worker and weight. I'm questioning whether you know that every time I didn't say your name out loud, it wasn't because you were small. It was because other people's mouths aren't holy enough to carry you."

I stared at me and let the silence stand there like a third man. Then he stepped closer. "I've been with you since we claimed a corner with nothing but shoes that weren't paid off," he said. "I stood there when the wind blew the wrong way and the cops learned our names before our mothers did. I've been with you when you were wrong and when you were right and when you were quiet for too long. And you know what I got?"

"Everything," I said.

I laughed once. "A salary," he said. "An allowance dressed up like respect. I get to talk when you want a mirror. I get to sit when you want a shadow. I get to be your mouth when your mouth needs an echo. You built the kingdom and forgot kings can't move more than one square without someone watching the angles."

I let him finish. I didn't let him be finished. "Everything that was mine was yours," I said. "You never had to ask because I thought you knew I already gave it. I don't write the ledger on walls. I write it in how I feed a man's mother without putting my name on the envelope. I write it in how your nephews didn't have to sell lemonades to leave town for a weekend. I write it in how I never let your mistakes make your face public."

I took a breath like the air owed him money. "And how much of the vote do I get?" he asked, softer. "How much of the name? How many rooms do I walk into where people don't look past me to see if you're standing there, and if you aren't, they tell me we'll talk later?"

"You get all of it," I said. "You just didn't pick it up. Respect is heavy. It doesn't come in a bag. It comes in silence you have to be brave enough to wear."

I stared. Something in his jaw moved like a man trying to chew through a memory. "So that's it?" he said. "I'm ungrateful and you're misunderstood."

"That's not it," I said. "What's it is: you knew a word only you knew. You let a room that doesn't love you write it down. And you watched them aim at a window that had nothing in it because you wanted to be the man who delivered the angle. You didn't deliver anything. You signed your name in a margin."

He shook his head slow. "You always think you smarter than everyone."

"I always think gravity wins," I said. "You can throw whatever you want in the air. It's coming back. The question is whether you catch it or let it break on your own floor."

I looked past me like the wall might tell him a different ending. It didn't. I stood. I didn't step back. I didn't, either.

"Listen to me," I said. "I spoke to the man. Do not make me speak to the gun."

My eyes flashed, that old stubborn we both earned in the same wind. "What if I already did?"

I nodded once. "Then you understand where the map ends."

I left him with the crooked light and the smell of fryer oil that never quits and the awareness that there are some doors you can't lean on anymore because your shoulder's memory is no longer welcome there.

I didn't go home. I went to James.

Not to the man, to the perimeter around the man—quiet coffee, quiet room, quiet hour. He came in without a jacket because winters don't recognize him the way they do the rest of us.

"You look like someone who finished an equation," he said, sliding into the booth.

"I look like someone who stopped pretending a number will change if I stare at it longer," I said.

He smiled. "You want a solution or a solvent?"

"Neither," I said. "I want a buffer. Institutional attention needs a sandwich. Feed it somewhere else for a week."

He nodded like meetings had already been set. "Done," he said. "And CJ?"

"What."

"Don't put this in the paper for them," he said. "Whatever you do, do not make it easy to write down. Make it a rumor."

"Rumors last longer," I said.

"Rumors can be denied," he said. "Denial is a tool. Use every tool."

I studied his face for the boy I used to run with and the general the world thinks he became overnight. Both were there. I squeezed my forearm and left first. I let him pay without letting the bill be a favor.

On my way out, Logan texted another apology he didn't owe me. "I stayed away today," he wrote. "I understand." I typed back two words: "Be boring." He sent a prayer hands emoji because he's young. I let it be what it was and didn't teach him the older word.

Night carried itself like a man who knows he's being watched and doesn't care. I drove to the smoothie shop Johnny Ross tried to tax and stood in the back with the lights off, watching the door through a gap that wasn't a gap to anyone who didn't know to look for it. The cousin on paper ran the register for an hour without looking up at nothing. That's how you stay alive. The receipt with the word WALK was gone. Good. He had learned.

I stopped at the laundromat lot where the bulb clicks every six seconds like a pacemaker in a man who tells his doctor he's fine. The sixth click brought two things: a black coat that had been on a county corner earlier, and a different driver in the same sedan. They didn't do anything. They did enough.

I sent Ock a single word: "Polished?" He sent back: "Shining." I smiled for the first time all day because some men tell the truth without needing to prove it on a body.

Back home, I sat at the table and put the pistol in front of me and turned it so it faced away like a dog that's learned the command. I pulled out the travel chess set and let the pieces warm my fingers. Kings last. Queens quiet. Rooks straight. Knights only jump when there's cover. Pawns steady like prayer. I played both sides until the board stopped being wood and started being a mirror. My face didn't change. Good. I was the same man who walked into the day. I was the same man who would walk into the next one.

Before I slept, I wrote one sentence on a note I folded and slid into the drawer with the spare keys and the little scraps of paper Grim once used to write plays we ran on cracked asphalt: "Respect is heavy. Pick it up."

Morning is always honest. It found me tired and clean. Amanda's fryer sang its low hymn. Pudge gave me the nod that says the ledger balanced when nobody was looking. I cracked a Pepsi and let the first sip remind my mouth that some rituals still matter.

Cal didn't come in. That told me more than any margin ever will. I did not chase him. I don't chase men who want to be caught. I stack my steps and wait at the place the map says they will trip. That's not arrogance. That's math. And math doesn't care about your feelings.

Christa texted a photo of a child's drawing she found under the space's old baseboards. Crayon house. Blue sky. Two stick people holding hands with a dog that looked like a cloud. "Found a future in the floor," she wrote.

I stared at it longer than I meant to. "Frame it," I wrote back. "Hang it where the light hits first."

"On it," she wrote.

Kelly sent a single line: "Pipe quiet. Margin quiet. Your word went out. Your word came back."

"Good," I sent. "Let it rest."

She replied with a dot. Full stop.

By noon, I had touched every room that needed to know I was still breathing. Josh. Divine. Do Dirty. Ock. Fly and Mani, who came down from a roof with the posture of men who had graduated from a school that doesn't hand out diplomas. We stood in the alley behind Amanda's and didn't talk about anything that would ruin the afternoon.

"Chess tonight?" Mani asked.

"Always," I said.

The day ended without drama. That's how day twenty-three needed to end. Not with a gun. Not with a speech. With the kind of quiet that tells you the floor you're standing on isn't a trapdoor. Not today. Maybe tomorrow. I can live with that. I have.

Maps don't accuse. They predict. Awards ain't given for reading them. Only for walking them right.

Chapter 24

Verdicts are loud. Proof isn't.

I woke before the heat clicked and let the house stay cool on purpose. Cold air is honest. It makes breath visible. It makes lies stiff. I stood at the kitchen counter with my palms flat and let the morning ask me what I planned to do with the truth I already had.

The line I drew yesterday didn't change overnight. It just darkened. "Benediction" returned to me in a margin written by a hand that doesn't know where its words come from. That was enough to end it. But endings are easy. Precision costs more and buys you silence in the places that matter.

I poured tap water into a glass and drank it like I was on a witness stand and oath was the only thing I still respected. Then I took the small chalkboard from beside the fridge—the one I stole from Amanda's and never returned—and wrote three words:

BLUE TAG PERMIT.

Not a church window. Not a Sunday corridor. A contractor's phrase. The kind of small detail bureaucracy uses to decide whether to look at your door or pretend it doesn't exist. I underlined TAG until the chalk almost split. Then I wiped it with my thumb and left the ghost of it there on purpose. Ghosts make men confess.

Amanda's smelled like oil and onions when I walked in. Pudge slid me a Pepsi and two invoices. I tapped the cap, left it closed, and looked out the back window at an alley that has heard more truth than any courtroom I've ever seen.

"Need the board?" he asked.

"Not today," I said. "I brought my own."

Kelly answered my text before I finished typing it. "Deck?" she sent.

"Too windy," I wrote. "Meet me where the parking meters lie— block where two say No Standing and one says your mother's name."

She knew it. We met there five minutes later. Her knit cap was pulled low, and her eyes were steady the way you want a surgeon's to be steady when the room is quiet enough to hear the machine decide whether to beep. I showed her the chalkboard.

"BLUE TAG PERMIT."

She raised one eyebrow. "We're leaving the church."

"We're leaving hymns for forms," I said. "If a word repeats itself in the wrong mouth, I want it written in filing cabinets I don't own."

"You want me to plant it?" she asked.

"I want you to forget it in a room where forgetting is a crime," I said.

She smiled without her mouth moving. "You always want me to be stupid in the right direction."

"It's a talent," I said. "Use it sparingly."

"Who gets the phrase?"

"One man," I said. "And I'm already late."

Christa was drawing a grid on the floor with blue tape when I walked in. The tape matched the chalk word on my board. Signs happen when you're paying attention. She looked up, breathless with work in a way that never looks like exhaustion because purpose knows how to keep its mascara from running.

"Walk me again," she said, handing me the roll. "Drop zone. Promise wall. Quiet corner."

We paced it like we'd built rooms our whole lives. The electrician had finished. The inspector had signed off. The deadbolt I installed yesterday clicked like a sentence that knows where to end.

She pointed at the corner near the window. "I found this under the baseboard." She held up a crayon drawing. House, sky, a dog that looked like a cloud. Two stick people held hands in the middle. It could have been anyone. It was all of us.

"Frame it," I said. "Hang it where the light hits first."

"Done," she said. "Dinner?"

"If the weather cooperates," I said.

"It never does," she said.

"Then we'll eat close to it," I said. The repetition settled into the room like furniture that refuses to wobble.

I left her with the tape and the drawing and drove to Josh. The warehouse rolled its door up like an eyelid that trusts the room it's waking to. Josh nodded once and kept his eyes on the flame. I don't talk in the first hour of a cook. Neither does he. There are sermons that don't need priests.

When the steam thinned and patience had done its work, he spoke without looking at me. "Cadence?"

"Hold," I said. "Two days of low tide."

He nodded. Josh understands that sometimes the best proof of strength is restraint you can't brag about.

Divine's mechanic loft smelled like rubber and forgiveness. He sat on a bench with a socket wrench in his hand like a punctuation mark. "Laurel?" he asked.

"Let it hum," I said. "A voice that loud eventually teaches on itself."

"You want me to move any pieces?"

"Not on the board," I said. "On paper. I'm giving a phrase to one man. If it echoes in a room it doesn't belong in, I need you to hear it without being seen."

He tipped the wrench once. "Copy."

Big Abe was at the pool table, rolling chalk onto the tip of a cue the way old men roll worry onto rosaries. I didn't bring him a problem. I brought him a story about his mother's knees. He smiled. The cortisone had taken. Good. The world finds too many knees to punish. We need some that still bend without screaming.

Ock's text came in while I was leaving—"polished." I sent back a dot. We understand each other with punctuation.

I saved Cal for last. Amanda's back hallway was lit like a prayer candle again. He leaned into the doorway like a man who believes frames are furniture. I let him.

"You good?" he asked.

"We're breathing," I said. "Say it back."

He smirked. "We're breathing."

I held his eyes and handed him the sentence. "Blue tag permit." I let the words sit between us long enough to turn the air into a decision. "Electrical follow-up, ten-day window. Only needs a glance if the tag's the wrong color."

I nodded, a little too fast. "Copy. You want me to babysit the clipboard?"

"I want you to forget the sentence," I said. "And remember the silence you owe me more than you owe yourself."

He grinned, that soft kind men wear when they need teeth to look like trust. "You always did like magic tricks."

"I like mirrors," I said. "Keep them clean."

He dipped his chin and vanished down the hallway like a magician who forgot the audience was smarter than his sleeve.

At noon I moved money that didn't look like money. Trucks that sell fish become confessionals if you know what you're doing with numbers. The food truck near the bus terminal needed new tires and a lending hand. That lending hand was a ledger. We made it look like neighborhood love. Sometimes it is. Sometimes you get to call it both.

The afternoon brought habit. Walks past Fourth and Monmouth. A nod at the Elks. Two kids arguing over a ball that should have been replaced last winter. I told them to be nice to the net or the net would be mean back. They laughed. They will learn.

At three, Kelly's text arrived. "Pipe moved," it said. "A margin note asked about blue tag status."

I stared at the words until the period flickered. "From where?" I wrote back.

"County," she sent. "Not DA. Cousin to the cousin. The one that mails letters no one reads."

"That mailbox," I wrote. "The one that doesn't have a job."

"Same," she said.

"Stand down," I sent. "No more salt."

"Copy," she replied. "You sure you don't want me stupid one more time?"

"I want you brilliant and safe," I wrote. "Stupid gets flowers. Brilliant gets old."

She sent a heart I pretended not to see.

By four, the test was ready. No compartments. No bricks. No drops. Just a van with nothing in it and a route I wrote with my feet. I told one man where it would idle. Nobody else. I pulled into the lot behind the laundromat where the timer bulb clicks every six seconds like a pacemaker that refuses to learn a new song and let the engine idle the way hearts pretend to when their owners lie to them.

At 4:17, a county sedan made a circle that didn't look like a circle unless you were counting on your fingers. At 4:19, the DA's cousin-courier drove past and checked a mailbox that has never contained anything anyone should mail. At 4:21, a Civic with a university sticker took the long way around the lot and never looked at me.

Then at 4:23, two unmarked cars performed a dance I wouldn't have noticed a year ago. One paused long enough to decide whether pausing was suspicious. The other turned slowly enough to pretend turning was its idea all along.

Nobody approached the van. Nobody needed to. The city had arranged itself for a play that never started.

I put the van in drive and rolled out slow, not because I was being dramatic but because I wanted them to see what restraint looks like when it decides not to embarrass you.

I parked three blocks away, locked the doors, and walked. I always walk when the answer arrives. Cars tempt men to speed past their own decisions.

Do Dirty met me behind the laundromat on 13th where the bulb clicks and the concrete remembers every fight. He didn't ask what the test showed. He read it on my face.

"You want company?" he asked.

"No," I said. "Not yet."

"You going to speak to the man?"

"I already did," I said. "He chose a margin."

I nodded, jaw tight. "You want me to stage a coincidence? The kind that reminds a man the city can touch his shoulder without asking permission?"

"Tomorrow," I said. "Tonight I want the room to tell him he is still invited."

"Kindness as a weapon," he said, smiling without humor. "You always liked scalpels more than hammers."

"Hammers break floors," I said. "We built ours."

We walked to Elliott's and stood by the pool table without playing. Some rooms know you're working even when the cue never touches chalk. Big Abe rolled in and leaned a shoulder against a pillar. Divine nodded once. Ock texted a single word—"ready." I didn't reply. Readiness doesn't need applause.

I didn't go hunting for Cal. I made it easy for him to find me. I sat in Amanda's back booth with a Pepsi sweating onto a napkin, invoices fanned the way prayer hands look when a man is trying to look humble in public. He showed up with his shoulders already in the room. I let him have the posture. I let him keep his smile. Men confess faster when you give them the costume they believe in.

"You hear about the blue tags?" he asked. The sentence came out too casual, the kind of casual a man rehearses in a mirror.

"What about them?" I asked.

"Inspector said they switching colors next quarter," he said. "Citywide update. Ain't going to be blue anymore. Just a sticker with a code."

I sipped and put the cup down without breaking eye contact. "City don't change its mind until a committee does," I said. "Committees don't change until the minute after the last man decides he thought of it first."

He laughed. "You always got poetry for bureaucracy."

"I got discipline for gossip," I said. "Let it die."

He nodded. "Copy."

I didn't press. I didn't have to. The sentence had already traveled. The mailbox had already been fed. The van had already been encircled by cars pretending they were on their way to better things. All that was left was a choice.

I left him there and walked to Christa's. The night had put on its coat. The air bit the way honesty bites when it's tired of being polite. She opened the door before I knocked. The deadbolt clicked like a bow at the end of a recital.

"You look like judgment," she said.

"I feel like math," I said.

"Tea?"

"Ten minutes," I said.

We sat at the small table that will one day hold permission slips and science projects and birthday cupcakes contraband to a school nurse with too much time. She poured, I watched steam, we let quiet be company.

"You ever think of leaving?" she asked suddenly.

"Rooms or cities?" I asked.

"Both," she said.

"Every morning," I said. "And then the day starts."

She nodded, eyes on the steam. "I don't want you to die," she said, simple as a grocery list.

"I don't want me to die either," I said.

"Can you not?"

"I can try to be patient until patience is a lie," I said. "After that, I'll still try."

She didn't say that was enough. It wasn't. She reached across the table and touched the back of my hand with two fingers. That was enough.

I left before the tea cooled. Some good things need to stay warm on their own.

James was waiting at a coffee shop that doesn't belong to either of us. He doesn't wear winter like the rest of us do. Money is a coat if you know how to cut it. He slid into the booth and looked at my face the way men look at maps when they are deciding whether to take the highway or the road with the good views.

"You done with the equation?" he asked.

"I'm done pretending there's an extra variable," I said.

"You want buffer?"

"Enough to make a headline in another borough more interesting than a whisper here," I said.

He nodded. "Done," he said. "And CJ?"

"What."

"Do not let this become a story they can explain," he said. "You give them rumor. You take the rest."

"Rumors live longer," I said.

"Rumors can be denied," he said. "Denial is a tool. Use every one."

We paid without letting the bill become a favor and walked out separate doors. Men who have survived the same storm don't need to hug every time it rains.

Logan texted while I was waiting at a red light I didn't need to obey. "I stayed away again," he wrote. "Thank you for not making me important."

"Be boring," I sent. I replied with the prayer hands because he's young and still thinks emojis can carry weight. Maybe for me they can. I didn't punish him for hope.

Back at the warehouse, I walked the fence line alone. Steel links told the story of hands that had climbed them in other years for other reasons. I wasn't twelve anymore. I kept my feet on the ground. Proof doesn't climb when the gate is open.

The night ended the way good nights end—quiet, tense, honest. I put the pistol on the table and turned it away from me like a dog that knows how to stay. I set the travel chess set down and lined the pieces up the way Grim taught me—kings last, queens quiet, rooks straight, knights only jump when there's cover, pawns steady like prayer. I played both sides until the board stopped being wood and started being a mirror. My face didn't change. Good. I was still the man who would walk into the morning.

Morning does what it does. It told the truth even when I wanted to negotiate. Amanda's fryer sang its hymn. Pudge slid the Pepsi and didn't ask me whether the night had done its math. He knows better than to make me put numbers into sentences before I'm ready.

Cal didn't come in.

Absence is a sentence when a man has trained a room to expect his shoulder in the doorway. I didn't chase him. I don't chase men who want to be caught. I went to the roof above the old record store instead and watched the street learn how to keep its balance without help.

Divine joined me, hands in his coat pockets, breath steady. "You want me to pull him into a room?" he asked.

"No," I said. "He needs to decide what kind of man he is without anyone else's eyes on him."

"You got a date for that decision?"

"Soon," I said. "Soon is a room. I'll know when the door opens."

Fly and Mani texted nothing. That's how I knew they were watching. Silence from watchers is applause if you know how to hear it.

By noon, the phone calls started sliding in from corners that pretend they don't know my number. Questions wrapped in compliments. Invitations wrapped in concern. I accepted none. When you are finally at the part of the equation where subtraction is the only operation left, addition becomes begging in a different shirt.

I ate at Amanda's like a man who has time. Catfish, cornbread, mac, collards. Salt on the tongue, sugar on the memory. I let the plate empty itself in front of me and didn't look at the door until it opened because if you look too early you start trying to wish men into rooms they aren't ready to enter.

When I finally looked, it wasn't Cal. It was a paper bag with a receipt stapled to it. Pudge dropped it on the table and nodded at it without words. I opened the bag and read the first four words of the receipt.

BLUE TAG PERMIT—QUESTION.

No signature. No logo. Just the handwriting of a man who learned to disguise his letters in middle school and never stopped.

I folded the paper and slid it into my pocket. I finished my plate. I wiped my hands. I stood up.

The day didn't get louder. It got clearer.

I texted one sentence to one man. "Meet me where we first believed the block belonged to us."

Fourth and Monmouth at dusk looks like a memory even when you are standing in it. The light cuts everything in half and asks you which side you plan to keep. I leaned on a pole with my hands in my coat pockets and let the wind decide whether it was going to be kind.

Cal arrived five minutes late and pretended it was on purpose. He didn't lean on anything. Not at first. He stood in the open like a man ready to swear under oath.

"You called," he said.

"I did," I said. "I'm going to talk. You're going to listen. Then you're going to show me what kind of man you are."

He smirked. "You already decided."

"I decided to end pretending," I said. "Not to end you."

He spread his hands. "Say your poem."

I looked past him for a second and saw Grim teaching a boy to shoot on a crate and a broomstick. I heard James laugh at a joke he wouldn't repeat in front of our mother. I felt the wind the day we first looked at this corner and realized it could be ours if we could stand it.

"Blue tag permit," I said. "Benediction window. Church let-out. Choir-break. Vestibule. I handed you every mirror I own. You chose a margin. You let a room I don't recognize write down something it didn't deserve to hear."

He shook his head slow. "You always think you the only one drawing the map."

"I built the table," I said. "If you wanted a map, you ask for one. If you wanted a crown, you never understood what I gave you."

I took a step closer. "You gave me a salary," he said. "You gave me respect in rooms that still waited to see if you were going to walk in before they shook my hand. You gave me first bite and last checkin. You didn't give me a name."

"Everything that was mine was yours," I said. "I never wrote it on a wall because other people's mouths aren't holy enough to carry you. I fed your mother without receipts. I put your nephews on planes they didn't have to brag about. I kept your mistakes inside my ribs."

I laughed once, ugly. "And still you expect me to say thank you."

"I expect you to not sell me to a mailbox," I said quietly. "I expect you to know the difference between being treated like a worker and being trusted like a partner. A partner gets silence and weight. You wanted applause."

I stared, eyes bright with a heat pride always mistakes for righteousness. "Maybe I wanted what you never gave me," he said.

"What's that?" I asked.

"Credit," he said.

The word tasted like a coin when he said it. Small. Dirty. Necessary for men who don't know how to count.

"You got credit," I said. "You just didn't have the balance for the interest."

I clenched his jaw and looked over my shoulder at a street that used to be kinder. "So this is it?" he said. "You going to say I betrayed you and expect me to fall on a sword you forged?"

"No," I said. "I'm going to say I love you. I'm going to say I built this with you. I'm going to say I never needed to write your name on a flyer because every room I walk into was built on a floor you helped pour. I'm going to say you chose a margin over a man. And then I'm going to ask you to come back to the center."

I blinked like the wind got in his eyes. Or guilt. Or the thought that maybe I wasn't lying.

"And if I don't?" he asked, voice low.

"Then I'll speak to the gun," I said. "But not tonight."

I nodded once, tight. "You won't have to," he said, and walked away with a stiffness I had never seen on his back before.

I didn't watch him go. I watched the corner instead. It still belonged to us. Or to me. Or to the boys we used to be when the only thing a map promised was a way to get home.

Night put its arm around the block. I let it. I went home. I put the pistol on the table and turned it away from me again. I took out the chalkboard and wiped BLUE TAG PERMIT until only the ghost of it remained. Ghosts do good work when you let them.

Sleep came like a verdict I didn't have to listen to out loud.

Morning will be louder.

I won't be.

Chapter 25

Maps don't save you. They just keep you from lying about where you are when the ending shows up. I woke before the thermostat clicked and let the house stay cold on purpose. Cold air is honest; it makes breath visible, makes excuses sound like frost breaking under a boot. I stood with my palms flat on the counter and let morning ask the only question that matters now: What will you do with proof?

I didn't make coffee. I wanted the day plain. I wanted to feel the grain of the wood under my fingertips and the weight of what I already knew. "Benediction" had come back to me in the DA's margin. "Blue tag permit" had surfaced through the county cousin who mails letters no one reads. The triangle formed without a siren. The van with nothing inside had attracted cars pretending to be on their way to better things. That was enough for a verdict.

I wrote three lines on the small chalkboard I stole from Amanda's and never gave back.

WHAT I KNOW.
WHAT I CAN PROVE.
WHAT I'M WILLING TO CARRY.

Under that, I added a fourth.

WHO I'LL LET LIVE WITH IT.

The house breathed. The refrigerator hummed the A note it prefers. A cat outside negotiated with the dark and won. I cracked a Pepsi and let the first swallow tell my mouth there were still rituals in the world that didn't lie.

Christa texted a photo of the crayon drawing. She'd found a cheap white frame and hung it where the light hits first. "We're open in a month," she wrote. "Hold me to it."

"I will," I sent back. "Doors as decisions."

"Locks as boundaries," she wrote. "Come by and put the last one on when it arrives."

"Text me an hour before you need it," I sent. "If I don't answer, call Kelly."

"Is that a plan or a warning?"

"Both," I typed. "Keep the kids close to the light."

Kelly's message came a beat later. "Pipe is quiet. Cousin's cousin took a personal day. Your echo stopped."

"Good," I wrote. "Let it rest."

She replied with a single dot. Full stop. The language we built for moments when more words only tempt people into lies.

I pulled the travel chess set from the drawer and laid the pieces on the coffee table the way Grim taught me when sneakers squeaked on a floor our mother had just mopped. Kings last. Queens quiet. Rooks straight. Knights only jump when there's cover. Pawns steady like prayer. I played both sides until the board stopped being wood and started being a mirror. My reflection didn't change. Good. I was the same man who walked into yesterday, and I would be the same man who walked into what was coming.

I called no one. I sent no flare texts. Divine didn't need direction to hear a rumor without being seen. Ock didn't need a reminder to stay polished. Big Abe knew to keep Fly and Mani where fresh eyes could do what old eyes forget. Do Dirty knew the difference between ready and visible. James—James was the weather. He shifts clouds without telling you the name of the storm.

I put on the navy sweatsuit that fits like a plan and drove the rectangle slow, letting the city rehearse the parts it didn't know I had already heard. Fourth and Monmouth watched me back. The Elks breathed seasoned air and quiet pride. Country Circle practiced being harmless and failed like always. The old record store still wore its boarded windows like scars a man decided not to cover because truth looks better unpainted.

When the loop was done, I parked two streets from Amanda's and walked the rest. Pudge had the back door propped with a crate of onions. He nodded at me without words. Good men know when silence is the tool you came for. I took the last booth, the one with the view of the alley and the crooked light that always cuts a man's face into before and after.

I texted a sentence to a number I know better than my own. Where we first believed the block belonged to us. "Two hours. Come alone."

Cal responded with a thumbs-up I pretended not to see. Men who send symbols forget that words weigh more than pictures. I put the phone face down and let time do what it does to men who need it to pass before they can act brave.

I ate like a man who had time—catfish, collards, mac, cornbread. I tasted salt and memory and let the plate empty itself. Every bite was a sermon about patience: eat slow when everyone else wants you to rush.

Before I left, I wrote two notes. One I slid into the drawer with the spare keys and the little scraps of paper Grim used for plays we ran on cracked asphalt. RESPECT IS HEAVY. PICK IT UP. The other I folded into my wallet behind James's old library card from a summer we thought reading would be enough to save us. SPEAK TO THE MAN BEFORE YOU SPEAK TO THE GUN.

Dusk reached for the block with both hands. I let it. Fourth and Monmouth always looks like a memory at that hour, even to people who weren't born when the corner learned its first lesson. I leaned against the pole with my hands in my coat pockets and let the wind decide whether it was going to be kind.

Cal arrived five minutes late and pretended it was on purpose. He didn't lean on anything at first. He stood in the open, shoulders squared, like a man ready to swear under oath about things he wasn't sure happened the way he remembers.

"You called," he said.

"I did," I said. "I'm going to talk. You're going to listen. Then you're going to show me what kind of man you are."

He smirked. "You already decided."

"I decided to stop pretending," I said. "Not to end you."

"Say your poem."

"Benediction," I said. "Blue tag permit. Choir-break. Vestibule. Sunday corridor. I gave you mirrors. You chose a margin. You let a room that doesn't love you write down something it didn't deserve to hear."

He shook his head slow. "You always think you the only one drawing the map."

"I built the table," I said. "If you wanted a map, you ask for one. If you wanted a crown, you never understood what I gave you."

"You gave me a salary," he said. "You gave me a seat when you wanted an echo. You gave me first bite and last checkin. You didn't give me a name."

"Everything that was mine was yours," I said. "I never wrote it on a wall because other people's mouths aren't holy enough to carry you. I fed your mother without putting my name on the envelope. I put your nephews on planes they didn't have to brag about. I kept your mistakes inside my ribs."

"And you expect a thank you."

"I expect you not to sell me to a mailbox," I said quietly. "I expect you to know the difference between being treated like a worker and being trusted like a partner. A partner gets silence and weight. You wanted applause."

I looked past me at the street like it might offer him a better argument. It didn't. Wind touched his cheek and didn't ask permission. I took a breath like the air owed him money.

"Maybe I wanted what you never gave me," he said.

"What's that?"

"Credit."

"You got credit," I said. "You just didn't have the balance for the interest."

"You talk like a preacher when you're about to pass a sentence."

"I talk like a man who still prefers a conversation," I said. "If you come back to the center, we don't have to finish this the way everyone expects we will."

"You would still stand next to me?"

"I never moved," I said.

For a second something in his eyes softened, the way ice pretends it might become water again if you tell the truth quick enough. Then the look changed. Pride put its hand on his shoulder and squeezed.

"Since when are you the one who forgives?" he asked. "You built a world on consequence."

"I built it on gravity," I said. "Throw whatever you want in the air. It's coming back. The question is whether you catch it or let it break on your own floor."

"What if I let it break?"

"Then I sweep," I said.

We held each other's eyes until the light finished choosing sides. I stepped forward and put a hand on his shoulder, not to move him but to remind myself I still knew the angle of a brother's bone. "I love you," I said. I didn't say it like a threat or an excuse. I said it the way men say it when they put it off too long.

"You got a funny way of showing it."

"Come inside," I said. "One last time. No crowd, no choir. Just walls that remember."

I followed him without asking where. The second-floor office above the old pool hall on Bangs had a door that sticks unless you know where to press. I knew. The room smelled like chalk and old tobacco and victories no one bragged about because bragging invites theft.

"You always did like rooms like this," he said. "Dead air. Slow clock."

"Dead air keeps you from lying," I said. "Slow clocks don't forgive, but they don't rush the truth either."

I wandered to the window and looked down at the street. Amanda's sign glowed two blocks away. The crooked bulb over the laundromat clicked its same six-second heartbeat. I stood with my back to the wall and my hands empty on purpose.

"Say what you couldn't say at Fourth and Monmouth," I said. "Say it without thinking you have to win."

"You're the one who always has to win," he said. "That's what this is about. You stand in a room and the air decides to behave. People start adjusting their posture. I talk and they look past my shoulder to see if you walked in. I bled like you bled. I earned like you earned. But when it comes time for names, mine comes second. Or not at all."

"I never needed the room to clap," I said. "I needed it to hold. You were part of the holding. You always were."

"Then why didn't you ever say it?"

"I thought you knew," I said.

"Men die behind what they think the other man knows."

"And men live behind what they finally say."

He turned from the window and put his shoulders square. "You took Barry's head off," he said. "You put Rell down like a dog."

"Barry removed my name from his mouth," I said. "Rell put his hands on a part of my life he didn't earn. Neither of them were you."

"But you brought me in this room anyway."

"I brought you here because you are," I said. "Because you have been since the first day the wind forced us to learn each other's breathing."

"You ain't God."

"I'm gravity."

"You meet me in a room with no windows worth jumping from and say it isn't personal."

"It's precise."

I looked toward the door with a softness I recognized from men waiting on an arrival that will do their talking for them.

"You invited company," I said.

My eyes came back to mine and didn't apologize. "I invited insurance," he said.

Footsteps on the stairs. Not fast—heavy, organized, confident. The kind that doesn't worry about being heard because it expects cooperation.

"I didn't wear a wire," he said, like a favor. "But I gave them a time and a place."

"Why?" I asked, not angry—curious the way you have to be one last time if you're going to shoot clean.

"Because I'm tired of being a shadow. Because you won't ever step aside if I ask. Because if you get removed, the city will finally look me in the face and see something other than your echo."

Three knocks.

Boom. Boom. Boom.

I already knew what it was before the third knock hit.

Cal's mouth opened—maybe for sorry, maybe for air. I didn't wait. The room had run out of time.

I drew and fired once. In his face without a flinch. Surgical. A shot a city can feel.

Brain matter sprayed like art. His body laid open like a confession. Still twitching. But dead.

Silence.

Boom.

The door flew open. Police stormed in—boots heavy, guns drawn —but none of them fired. They weren't looking at a criminal. They were staring at a ghost with a pulse.

Gun in my hand. Blood on the wall. Cal at my feet.

"Hands where I can see them," one said.

I set the gun down like a glass I owned and raised both hands. Slow. Deliberate. No apology.

They circled, eyes trying to reconcile the story they were trained to serve with the silence standing in front of them. One younger cop blinked like a childhood myth had just chosen a face.

"You got the right to remain silent," another said.

I smirked.

Then you already know who the fuck I am.

They moved. I didn't. Cold metal on the wrist. Weight on the shoulder. The hallway took us like a throat swallowing something it didn't want but knew it couldn't refuse. Down the stairs. Out into the air that still smelled like Amanda's fryer and old chalk from the pool hall.

Fourth and Monmouth watched, the way a block watches when it understands that endings are just beginnings with less noise. No one fired. No one shouted. The city listened.

The back seat plastic translated the night into simpler grammar. I sat in the center, back straight, eyes forward. We rolled past the boarded record store that wears its scars like truth, past the Elks that keeps history in wood, past streetlights that work half the time and are still better than none.

At the station, chairs pretended to be comfortable. Lights pretended to be neutral. Fingerprints. A photo of a face people will argue about for reasons that bore me. A room with a table that has heard more lies than any church pew.

I said nothing. That's home for me.

A door opened. Not a detective—air, then a lawyer I didn't call. James doesn't knock when the rain he sent was mine to stand under.

"Silent?" he asked.

"Is there another way to be?" I said.

He nodded. "Do not make this a story they can explain. Leave them rumors, not headlines."

"Paper burns faster," I said.

"Rumor floats longer," he said. I set a folded something on the table and didn't push it toward me. "From Kelly."

I didn't touch it. "Valves?"

He half-smiled. "Closed."

Processing. A cell. Cinderblock squares that refuse to become anything but what they are. Somewhere a radio talked too much. Somewhere a door argued with its hinges. Somewhere a cop told a story with his name in it.

I laid back and let the ceiling become a map that doesn't promise an exit.

Here is what remains, with no poetry: I spoke to the man. I spoke to the gun. I'll speak to neither again about this.

The silence ain't empty.

It's a ledger. And I'm still standing.

For permissions, contact:
Crown Cipher Publishing
crowncipherpublishing.com

ISBN (Paperback): 979-8-9994700-4-1
ISBN (Ebook): 979-8-9994700-3-4

First Edition: 2025

Cover design by Crown Cipher Publishing
Interior design by Crown Cipher Publishing

A Crown Cipher Publishing Release
We Protect This F**king House

www.ingramcontent.com/pod-product-compliance
Lightning Source LLC
Chambersburg PA
CBHW030241030726
47493CB00023B/368